6/12

EVERY LAST
SECRET

EVERY LAST SECRET

A MYSTERY

Linda Rodriguez

THOMAS DUNNE BOOKS / MINOTAUR BOOKS ☏ NEW YORK

This is a work of fiction. All of the characters, organizations, and events portrayed in this novel are either products of the author's imagination or are used fictitiously.

THOMAS DUNNE BOOKS.
An imprint of St. Martin's Press.

www.thomasdunnebooks.com
www.minotaurbooks.com

ISBN 978-1-250-00545-8

First Edition: April 2012

10 9 8 7 6 5 4 3 2 1

To Joseph Rodriguez, youngest son and first reader

ACKNOWLEDGMENTS

A book is written by a writer sitting alone in a room, but many other people contribute to its existence.

First, for valuable technical assistance, I would like to thank Harry Hylander, retired after many years with the campus police force of the University of Missouri-Kansas City, and Chato Villalobos of the Kansas City, Missouri, Police Department. I picked their brains and asked many questions. What I have right is their doing. What mistakes I have are my own.

Next are my writing groups. The Latino Writers Collective is my writing familia and always next to my heart. Jacqueline Guidry, Deborah Shouse, and Jane Woods, the Novel Group, have read and reread much of this book, and their comments have made it stronger.

The Alliance of American Artists and the Joyce Foundation made possible a residency at Ragdale during which this book was extensively revised. I am grateful to have had that time and space and the dedicated care of the wonderful Ragdale staff.

Malice Domestic has been offering an incredible conference

for writers and readers of mysteries for over two decades. They also provide judges who give their time and attention to the task of reading manuscripts by unpublished writers in competition for the Malice Domestic First Novel Competition in conjunction with St. Martin's Press. I would like to thank all of the volunteers for Malice Domestic, especially the judges. Luci Zahray, I will always be grateful to you.

I have been blessed to have the help of two marvelous professionals in the publishing business, my editor Toni Plummer and my agent Ellen Geiger. I am immensely grateful for both of them.

Finally, my family has supported my writing career, even when it has taken my attention away from them. Heartfelt thanks go to my husband, Ben Furnish, and to Crystal Christian, Niles Rodriguez, Joseph Rodriguez, Gustavo Adolfo Aybar, Erika Noguera, and Becky Ross.

EVERY LAST
SECRET

CHAPTER 1

I look back and second-guess myself about Andrew McAfee, imagine I could have seen further into the cloud of dangerous secrets that surrounded him. But I know nothing that happened can be changed, no dead brought back to life. I had no way of recognizing the tangled webs all around me at the very time I thought I had found sanctuary.

A middle-of-the-night call used to mean a dead body. All that changed when I moved twelve miles out of Kansas City to this little college town. Not only did I trade the war zone of inner-city policing for a peaceful college campus, but I owned a house, a dog, and plants that were actually alive. Now, my collie, Lady, was barking at the ringing phone, unaccustomed to disturbances at two in the morning.

I jerked awake in practiced reflex. My first thought was of murder, but my new reality came back to me. Couldn't be Homicide. Was it my ex-husband to tell me my dad had wrecked his car while driving drunk?

I grabbed the phone from the bedside table. "Bannion here."

"Chief! It's Dave Parker. I found a body!"

On automatic pilot, I swung out of bed, wondering how the hell that brand-new hire for the campus police had managed to find a corpse on Chouteau University's pristine campus. Wilma Mankiller, the survivor cat I'd brought from the city, jumped from her side of the bed and hid. She knew the phone ringing in the middle of the night meant I'd be storming around with no patience for pets.

"Where? Report, Dave." I pulled underwear and a sweater from drawers.

"Sorry. I just never . . ."

I seized one of my old black Homicide pantsuits from the closet and started to dress. "Slow down and breathe, Dave." I heard him take several uneven breaths. "Now, report."

"Sorry, Chief. I was making rounds, going past the *News* offices like you wanted."

I had asked the whole department to keep a special eye on the *Chouteau University News* editor in chief, Andrew McAfee, after breaking up a fight between him and his news editor and hearing from the faculty adviser about sexual assault and theft claims against him. My second-in-command belittled me in front of night and morning shifts for using woman's intuition. Frank Booth thought I stole the chief's job from him—though they'd never have hired him since he lacked investigative experience. I retaliated by claiming I was using detective's instinct. Then, I insisted everyone keep watch for trouble from McAfee.

"A light was on in the inner office so I opened the door," Dave continued. "To make sure it wasn't someone it wasn't supposed to be. It was McAfee. I thought he'd just fallen asleep till I got close enough to see the blood. God!"

Blood. Damn! I fastened my belt and put on my shoulder

harness. "Manner of death, Dave?" Pulling open the drawer in my night table, I checked my gun before holstering it.

He took a long, deep, steadying breath. "Back of his head's smashed in."

"Did you touch anything?" My voice jerked as I ran down the stairs to the front door.

"Just the door. When I went in. Once I saw him, I backed out quick into the hall and . . . I guess I panicked. I haven't called it in to Dispatch yet or anything. I called you because it was like you knew. Having us keep an extra eye on him and all."

That extra cop-sense at the back of my skull had niggled at me ever since my run-in with Andrew McAfee. I'd lived down the street from him, his wife, and his stepson, who walked my dog and mowed my lawn, but I'd never really met Andrew until breaking up that fight and learning he was probably stealing money from his student reporters.

"Your first time finding a body is hard, Dave. You've done fine. Kept the scene intact." I reached my car and unlocked it. "Call Dispatch and have them contact Gil and the coroner and the county evidence techs. Tell Dispatch not to send anyone else over there. I'm on my way to you. I don't want anyone messing up the scene. Keep everyone out till I get there or Gil does."

"Okay, Chief." His voice sounded less strained.

"And, Dave," I added, as I started the car and peeled away from my peaceful house into the night, "you did fine."

My name's Marquitta Bannion, but everyone calls me Skeet. Don't ask. My mom is Cherokee and nutty. They're not necessarily connected, but I'm not responsible for what she decided to name me. I left the Kansas City Police Department six months ago after becoming their highest-ranking female officer, and I'm now chief of the campus police force of Chouteau University in nearby Brewster, Missouri. Some, like my ex-husband, might see it as a comedown. My best friend and surrogate mother, Karen Wise, tells me not to worry about what they think, but she's the one who talked me into coming here in the first place. I wanted to get away from the city and the job that ate my life—and, most of all, my dad and the Internal Affairs investigation that led to his retirement. Between Big Charlie and me, the name Bannion used to mean a lot in the KCPD. I didn't like seeing that change, so I left—force, father, and ex-husband. It was an easy decision.

My Cherokee grandmother always said, "If you're waiting for things to be perfect in life, young lady, you'll be waiting a long time." Though I've always ignored what my mother told me and finally learned to ignore Big Charlie, I listen to Gran. I've learned not to wait.

I made that short drive back to campus in record time and parked illegally in front of Moller Hall. Using my master key to let myself in, I paced through the dark, echoing building, carrying my crime scene kit from the trunk of my car.

The shadows moved with me as I headed to the offices of the university's student-run newspaper. At the end of the hallway, Dave Parker stood nervous watch in the gloom surrounding the pool of light that poured through the office door. With his young face, he could have been one of our students, if not for the uniform.

"How are you doing?" I asked.

Beads of sweat stood out on his ashen face despite the chill of the hallway. Dave had recently graduated from the regional police academy and joined our department just two days earlier. Night patrol had seemed a safe, innocuous place for him to start.

"Are you going to be okay here? Or should I ask Bill to trade with you? He's seen dead bodies before."

Dave shook his head resolutely. "I'm okay. You don't have to drag the sergeant out. It was just a shock at first."

I nodded and smiled to reassure him. "What have you done, and what have you touched?"

"I left the lights on," he said. His hand twitched in the direction of the light twice before he got it under control. "I turned on these in the newsroom as I went through to the office where I saw lights already on. When I came out, I left them on." He grimaced. "I didn't think to turn them off at first. I just wanted to get out and call you. Then I figured it's best if I don't add any more fingerprints."

"That's fine. No sign of anyone?" I set my kit on the floor and opened it.

He shook his head vigorously. "I checked pretty good."

He probably had, dismayed at standing watch alone in a place that might be hiding a murderer. I squatted on the cold tile floor and dug through my bag to pull out surgical gloves. "So you just touched that light switch and the door to the office?"

"And the body. I checked for a pulse. That's what we're supposed to do, right?" He looked at me, frowning and biting his lip.

"You handled this like an old pro." I stood and slipped on the gloves.

His face relaxed and regained some color. "I sure didn't want to mess up something this major."

I smiled at him. He was going to be worth bringing along. "Was the exterior door to Moller locked when you entered?"

Dave nodded. "Had to use my master to open it."

I frowned. Either the killer had an office in Moller or access to a Moller key or master.

Closing my kit, I picked it up. "Is Gil on his way? And the coroner?"

Dave nodded. "Dispatch said she'd send them out and notify the sheriff's office for techs."

"You keep watch here. Only those people get in. Call Bill to cover the front in case the media show up. He can keep them out."

As Dave nodded and pulled out his radio, I headed into the newsroom of The *Chouteau University News,* eyes scanning the room. To my left, a bulletin board fluttered with flyers, a large poster from the movie *Front Page* beside it. On the next wall, another bulletin board held the last issue of the *News,* comments in ink scribbled all over the pages. The work of the faculty adviser, I assumed. Six desks crowded the room. The staff would tell us if anything was out of place.

I took a deep breath before moving through the door opposite the hall. No matter how many I've seen—a lot—I never get completely used to corpses. I'd never have made an undertaker.

Facing me in the shallower room inside was a beat-up wooden desk. The body sat behind it, bloodied head resting on the desk surface. Moving into the room and to the side, I smelled the coppery blood scent and the odor of feces and urine, an inevitability of death. Another reason for the deep breath before entering. Death stinks.

I could see the face of the dead man, Andrew McAfee. Since the blows damaging the skull had come from behind, his face was basically undamaged. Andrew didn't look surprised or in pain. He looked unconscious, with the faded waxiness of death and mottling where blood had settled in the cheek on the desk.

He wore jeans and a striped sweater. The blood on the back of his head had darkened in the thick hair, so he hadn't just been killed.

I remembered two days earlier when I'd had to break up a fight between him and his news editor, Scott Lampkin, Scott furious and accusatory, Andrew mouthy and profane. He'd been so angry, so irritating, and so very alive. Andrew had obviously been headed for trouble, but I hadn't expected it to catch up with him quite so soon or so violently. I hoped Scott Lampkin had a good alibi. I liked that kid, but he'd had a real mad-on for Andrew.

Hearing voices in the hall, I whirled to see Gil Mendez pulling on gloves as he spoke to Dave. I moved around the room, checking for signs of violence other than the dead man at the desk. A large hole in the plaster wall next to the door caught my eye, and I walked over to it as Gil entered the newsroom.

"Come on back. Found something here."

Gil crossed the threshold next to me as I measured the hole in the wall. His eyes were fixed on Andrew's bloody head, and his face looked pale but determined. "First dead body?" I'd forgotten that when it came to violent death, most of my force was going to be as inexperienced as young Dave.

Gil turned to face me. "No, but my first murder victim." He looked a little shaken, but his voice was steady.

I smiled at him. "Probably not a lot of that here."

I indicated the hole in the wall with a jerk of my head and silently cursed myself for not pointing. I couldn't break that habit, formed so young because my mother and Gran would never point a finger. Gran always said a pointed finger carried power, and it was rude to inflict your power on others. I don't buy all that, of course, but I still have to make a conscious effort to point like normal people do. "This looks recent," I said quickly, hoping Gil hadn't noticed.

I knelt where flakes of plaster lay crushed against the flat-pile carpet. "Not scuffed into the carpet yet. Still right on top of the fibers."

As I stood again, Gil examined the smashed-in wall. "Looks like something heavy did this. Same kind of thing that would do that to a man's head."

I nodded. "That's what I thought. I've looked around. Don't see anything that'd do either. At least not in this room."

Gil nodded. "You think he took it away with him."

"He may have brought it with him and taken it away again." I shrugged. "We won't know about that until we find out what was usually in here."

On the desk sat a phone and a folding double frame with pictures of Tina and Brian Jamison, my neighbors, Andrew's wife smiling, his stepson looking very serious. I would have to tell them both that murder had invaded their lives.

"Wonder if the techs will be able to pull anything from those?" Gil asked, pointing to a stained copy of the *News* and other documents on which Andrew's bloody head lay.

"You'd be surprised what they can find." I looked around the room for anything else that might have done this job on Andrew's head.

A waist-high bookcase ran the length of the wall to the left of us. On top of it were several piles of books and papers and a cardboard box. I walked over to check inside the box. An eight-inch-tall trophy lay on shiny conference programs and brochures.

"Did you know the *News* won a trophy for best reporting?" I asked after reading the engraving and tilting the box to better read the program cover. "At a regional conference of campus newspapers. I wonder why the trophy wasn't out on display in the newsroom?"

"Think it could be our weapon?" Gil asked from across the room near a pair of french doors.

"Not the right size or shape, I'd think, and it looks clean, but Sid'll know for sure."

He turned back to the doors, examining the catch. "Skeet, these have been opened."

I left the box undisturbed and hurried over. All the old french doors in the building had had deadlocks installed. Keys were kept in the campus locksmith's storeroom; those to any student office would never have been handed out. Security policy.

This one had been unlocked and opened from the inside, however. Whoever exited through it had pushed it closed but not quite all the way. I inspected it closely. Old and stiff. It had been locked so long that it wouldn't quite swing shut. From the outside, it might well have looked as if it were, though. Someone thought he'd been slick.

Voices in the hall pulled my attention away. "The county guys. Why don't you bring them up-to-date?"

He nodded and headed away from the murder victim with relief on his face. I knelt to check the low sill for any visible footprints. Nothing certain. A smudge. Maybe the evidence techs could get something from it, though. And they could check outside once the latch was dusted. If the murder had been committed after the evening's storm, there should be footprints.

"Look at this. Got the heap big chief out in the middle of the night." The sneering voice came from behind me. I turned to face the skinny form of Dud Bechter, my least-favorite tech from the Deacon County Sheriff's Office.

Like the town police force, the campus police didn't have evidence technicians on staff or a lab, even a less-sophisticated one like the county's, to process crime scene findings. So, in any major crime investigation, we relied on Sheriff Dick Wold's techs and lab.

The sheriff was a crony of my resentful second-in-command, Captain Frank Booth. Wold also didn't approve of women officers, let alone chiefs, and he'd made this quite clear when we first met. I'd made it equally clear that I expected professional cooperation, or I'd just turn to KCPD and tell the media and voters why in his next election. Since then, I'd had no problems getting the help I needed, but from the attitude of some county officers, I could tell the sheriff was still seething.

"Whatcha got?" Dud set down his kit on the edge of the bookcase. "Must be somebody important to bring the chief out at this hour."

I gestured his partner, Cal, over to me. "We've got a possible footprint here. I don't know if it's enough to get anything, but—"

"But we'll try," answered Cal with an easygoing smile. I never understood how he could bear to work with Dud. He headed over to the corpse with a camera to take photographs.

Gil returned to the room with Sid Ambrose, the county coroner. Sid had an ambulance team with him, which surprised me. Since the county ambulance service had been put under the sheriff's supervision, it had deteriorated to the point that everyone expected to wait thirty minutes or more when one was needed. As usual, Sid looked half asleep, clothes wrinkled and hanging awry, but he could describe most of the room if I quizzed him. I'd come to have great respect for the sloppy old man when he was with the medical examiner's office in Kansas City before he retired to be Deacon County's part-time coroner, a less stressful job that added to his pension and left him with time to fish.

I acknowledged his languid wave as he trudged over to the body.

"Who do we have here, Skeet? Do we know?" His voice rumbled like a truck on the highway through town.

"Student employee. Editor of the campus newspaper. Andrew McAfee."

"Does the young man have any family here in town?" Sid drew on gloves and flicked on a small penlight. He leaned forward to shine the light into the bloody mess that was the back of Andrew's skull, whistling under his breath.

"Yes. A very nice wife and stepson."

"You haven't sent anyone to notify them already, have you?" Sid hated it when hysterical survivors showed up at his scenes.

"No. I'll do that myself when I'm done here. They're neighbors."

"So you knew this guy? Should we take your prints, too, Chief?" Dud snickered.

"Sorry to disappoint you. The wife and kid are the ones I know."

"How well do you know them?" Sid asked in his usual death-scene growl. "I suppose the wife will want to come down and make the official identification? And fall apart in my morgue?"

"They can't help it if they start to cry when they see their loved ones all cold and dead."

Sid harrumphed and went on examining the death wound. "Don't see why she couldn't let you ID. Save herself the trip down."

"Because they never do. People always have to see for themselves before they can believe in death. It's human nature, Sid."

He snapped off his penlight and straightened up with a groan. "Animals are smarter."

"Look at this and tell me if you think it could have been done by whatever did the damage to the vic." I made myself point to the hole in the wall with a deliberate effort.

Sid walked over, carefully avoiding the pile of plaster at the base of the wall. "Yes. The same object could have hit this wall. Have you found anything? It would be damn bloody. Something heavy and rounded but rough or carved on at least one side. Not a smooth surface."

"Could it have been this?" I indicated the trophy.

"No. You'd need something more rounded and much heavier. A rock or paperweight." He looked into the distance for a moment. "Or the weighted handle of something carved or rough surfaced."

"Chief, do you see the problem I do?" Gil looked from the body to the hole in the wall.

I nodded. "If whoever did this threw whatever it was into the wall first, why on earth did Andrew let him come up behind him with it in his hand? And if he did it afterward, why aren't there any traces of blood on the plaster?"

Sid led the ambulance team over to the body. "Are you ready for us to take him away?"

I nodded, and the team began to maneuver the corpse into a body bag for the trip to the morgue.

"Have you got a time of death for me, Sid?" I asked.

Still whistling, he peeled off his gloves with a snap. "Ten P.M. to one A.M. That's it for now. I may be able to narrow it down some with the autopsy. Then again, I might not. You know how these things go."

I nodded. "At least that gives us a time frame. I'll send Gil over to witness the autopsy."

"Breaking in the boy the hard way?" Sid grinned.

I gave him a rueful smile. "He's all I've got. It's a far cry from KCPD Homicide here. He'll do fine."

I looked around the room. Gil sorted through papers on the desk. Dud fingerprinted the french door. Cal had finished with the plaster and was measuring the hole in the wall and photographing it.

I walked over to Gil. "Stay and see the rest through."

"You going to break the news?" he asked.

I nodded. "I'll head for home after I get the wife settled and someone to stay with her. God knows how long that'll take, and I have to be up early to meet with the chancellor. If you need me for anything, just call."

Gil looked at me quizzically. "Sure you want to leave me in charge when you know I've never done a murder?"

"You're a good investigator. Look at that vandalism-and-theft case you just closed. The only way you'll ever get experience of a murder is to handle one."

I smiled to encourage him. Gil was my only investigator and had two left feet, falling all over himself from nervousness. When he was investigating a case for the department, however, he was a different man, logical, rock solid. He was the most valuable member of my team.

"I'm not leaving you holding the bag. We'll both be investigating this baby. But you're capable of handling crime scene ops. You've done it before. It's pretty much the same thing, now that they're carting off the body. Just make sure they look for footprints outside the windows. That ground's wet. It should hold some."

Gil smiled broadly. "Thanks for the vote of confidence."

I turned to stare at the body bag being lifted to the gurney, then back at Gil. Gil looked as grim as I felt. "I never thought I'd see something like this in Brewster."

"It's happened here now. Our job is to catch the guy who did this and make sure he can't do it again." I looked back at the medics strapping down the body bag. Turning back to Gil, I patted him on the shoulder. "I'll have a sunrise meeting with the chancellor. Get some rest once you're done. I want you to witness the autopsy, and you don't want to do that when you're exhausted. Trust me. We'll be working irregular hours. Rest and eat whenever you can."

I headed out through the echoing halls into the night to call on Tina and Brian. I hated the idea of bringing such terrible news to two people I liked.

Violence always threw the world out of balance. I knew this from Gran's earliest teachings. The Cherokee are big on balance. They think imbalance allows dangerous forces into the world. I had to agree. My job was to bring this small world back into balance again, and tonight I had a long way to go.

CHAPTER 2

I parked in front of Tina Jamison's bungalow, two doors down from my own, and knocked on the front door, dreading the moment it opened. Most cops hate giving news of death, especially violent death, to next of kin, but it seemed ridiculous to send Gil when they lived so close to me. I knocked again, and a tousled Tina opened the door. "Skeet? What on earth?"

"May I come in?" I moved through the door Tina held open wordlessly. She gestured to a chair in the small living room, running her hand over her ash-blond hair to smooth it.

"What's wrong?" She took the couch herself. "Did you lock yourself out of the house? I can get Brian's key for you." I had given fourteen-year-old Brian a key so he could take care of my pets when I worked late or had to travel.

I sat on the very edge of the chair. "Tina, it's Andrew."

"Oh my God, he's been in an accident," Tina cried. "Is he hurt bad? Is he at the hospital?"

She stood as if to run to her missing husband. I moved over to the couch, taking Tina's hand and pulling her back down beside me. I held her small hands in my own. "I'm afraid he's dead, Tina."

"No!" The one screamed word hung wavering in the atmosphere of the night-quiet house. Tina's face turned as ashen as her hair, and she stared at me, eyes blank and unseeing. She began to rock back and forth silently. A low moaning escaped her lips.

"I'm so sorry." I slid my arm around her thin, bony shoulders. "I hate to bring you such awful news."

Tina shook her head in violent negation. "No. It can't be."

Brian appeared on the stairs. "Mom? Skeet? What's wrong?"

"I've seen the body myself." I gestured to Brian to join us. He got along with his stepfather, but I didn't think he'd had a strong emotional attachment.

"Where . . . ? How . . . ?" Tina began to shake with violent sobs, and tears poured down her face.

Brian ran down the stairs to sit on the other side of his mother, throwing his arms around her. "What is it?" he asked.

I sucked in a deep breath. "Andrew's been killed."

Brian's mouth dropped open and his eyes widened.

"In his campus office. Someone hit him over the head."

Tina looked up in shock. "It wasn't an accident?"

"It doesn't look like any kind of accident."

Tina's entire face seemed to slide downward as if it might run right off her chin and drip to the ground. In the past few minutes she had turned old, her skin losing all color and tone, features fading into a background of wrinkled parchment.

"Who killed him?" Brian asked in a tight, breathless voice.

"Who? Who?" Tina echoed him like a small bird. Her tears had never ceased flowing down her face. Brian held her and rubbed her shoulder.

I turned to Brian. "We just don't know yet."

Brian's jaw set hard and stubborn. "You'll find him, won't you, Skeet?"

I nodded, knowing my own jaw must be a twin to his. "We'll find him. I promise you both."

Tina shook her head and abandoned herself to shaking sobs. "He's gone. He's gone."

Brian and I comforted her until her sobs quieted.

"Tina, do you or Brian know what Andrew was doing at the paper or in his schoolwork? Can you think of anyone he'd made angry?" I pulled my notebook out. "I know this is a bad time for you, but the sooner we start our investigation, the better our chance of finding who did this."

Tina lifted her teary face and hiccupped slightly. She sat up straighter and wiped her eyes. "I don't really know a lot about what he was doing," she said in a husk of her normal voice. Her smile threatened to turn to tears. "He said I worked so hard it wouldn't be fair for me to have to listen to his troubles. He always wanted to hear about my day, not tell me about his." She took a shaky breath. "He was different from most men that way. Sympathetic and caring."

She gave in once more to tears. I thought that if Tina was right, Andrew had indeed been a rare man. I suspected he hadn't wanted to tell her what he was doing because so much of it wouldn't bear scrutiny.

"He used to work for Professor Oldrick as well as the paper," Brian said finally while doing his best to console his mother. "Research assistant. There was something funny about the research. I remember he made a joke about it when he first started. I didn't understand, but he said it was just as well I didn't. He told me to stay away from Oldrick if he wasn't around."

I scribbled in my notebook. "Can you remember why?"

Tina raised her head from Brian's arms. "He was a wonderful stepfather to Brian. Very protective. If he thought something was wrong, he'd have been determined to protect Brian."

"Did he ever say anything to you about this research, Tina?"

Tina started to shake her head, stopping midmotion. "He did when he first got the job. He started working for Oldrick before he got the job at the paper, and we really needed the money." She stared at something much further off than the cream living-room walls. "He said if we didn't need the money he wouldn't help the bastard. That was his word."

"You don't know what the research was about? Not anything?" I pushed at her memory.

Tina shook her head in frustration. "He said something about Oldrick stepping over the line. Maybe something about criminals." She shook small fists at the room. "I can't remember. It disgusted him, though, and Andrew was a very tolerant man."

I found it hard to put the man Tina and Brian were describing together with the foulmouthed troublemaker I'd encountered just yesterday. It was called compartmentalization. Men did it all the time, but guys like Andrew, who straddled the line of the law, were extremely good at it.

"Brian, can you remember what Andrew said to you about his work with Oldrick?" I asked.

He stared at me with distress in his eyes. "It was something about kids . . ." He shook his head in frustration. "I'm sorry. It was last spring. I just can't remember. It wasn't a big deal at the time. Except for telling me to stay away from Oldrick. He was real serious about that. And Andrew wasn't real serious about much. At least not with me."

I looked up from making notes. "When did either of you last see Andrew?"

"This morning," Brian said. "He was just getting up when Mom and I left."

"He worked so late on the paper," Tina added defensively. "He had to put in a lot of late hours there so he didn't usually get up as early as we did."

"Did you see him after that, Tina?"

"No. He'd planned on an evening at home with us. But his news editor just quit, and he was going to have to work instead." Tina's face started to crumple again.

The doorbell rang, startling all of us. Tina clutched Brian, as if afraid whoever it was had come to take him from her, as well. I rose as it pealed again. Had Gil found something I needed to know immediately? "Let me get it."

Opening the door, I looked down into the narrow face of Carl Haskins, reporter for the *Brewster Mercury* and stringer for the *Kansas City Star*. Carl wore his dark hair Julius Caesar–style, including the growing baldness, and his head came only to my shoulders. "Notifying the next of kin, are you?" Carl made a note in his slender notebook and tried to step inside.

I blocked his move, stretching my arms across the doorway. "Get out of here, Carl."

"Hey. Freedom of the press. First Amendment." His features were too large for his face and appeared scrunched into a permanent scowl. His bulbous nose twitched, and the nostrils flared, as if he could scent the tragedy inside.

"Wrong. The First Amendment doesn't guarantee the right to invade a grieving family's privacy. Leave."

He ducked his head under my outstretched arm. "Hey, Mrs. McAfee. Who do you think killed your husband?"

Once more, Tina dissolved into sobs and a moaning wail. She fell into Brian's arms, and her wailing grew louder and higher, becoming an eerie keening. Brian looked shaken, trying to comfort and calm her.

He shouldn't have to do that, I thought. It looked like he'd had to do too much taking care of his mother. He shouldn't have to handle her grief.

"Haskins, you're leaving now." I stepped forward, forcing him backward, so I could step out the door and close it.

"Hey. No need for police brutality. Public has a right to know. Give me a break. This could get me a byline in the *KC Star* and out of this one-horse town. Any idea who killed him?" Carl prepared to write in his notebook, as if he thought I would actually answer him.

"I'm having Joe Louzon post an officer here to keep anyone from bothering the family. You'd better stay away." I turned and reentered the house, closing the door on his cries of, "Hey. Hey!"

Tina had broken down completely. Brian tried to comfort her. Joe, chief of police for Brewster's small force, probably couldn't afford to keep a man outside Tina's house for long, but he might manage the rest of the night and part of the day.

When I asked Brian whom to call to sit with them, he shrugged, continuing to comfort his mother. It seemed they had no relatives in town, except Tina's ex-husband. I didn't think calling in biz-school dean Tom Jamison would be a good idea right now. The man had dumped Tina and Brian for a student two years earlier. I called Tina's boss, Annette Stanek, dean of the art school and a good friend of mine, and stayed with the two of them until Annette came to the door.

Annette instantly gathered up the smaller woman and took her up the stairs. "Come on, Tina. We'll get you a bath and some tea."

Brian, looking older than his fourteen years, saw me out. "Is my mother in danger?"

"We have no reason to believe that. It looks as if he may

have been killed because of some things he was doing on campus. I'd be surprised if you or your mother were in danger just because I doubt you knew any of the stuff he was doing."

Brian looked puzzled. "We didn't know he was doing anything except going to school and running the paper."

"That's what I mean." I patted his shoulder. "I'm going to ask Joe Louzon to add your house to one of his men's regular patrols, just in case."

"Thanks, Skeet." His mouth smiled, but the smile never made it to his eyes.

"Bri, I'm really sorry this had to happen. I saw you and your mom eating supper at Pyewacket's earlier tonight. Can you tell me what you did after that?"

"Are we suspects, Skeet?" Brian looked wary.

"Technically, everyone who knew Andrew's a suspect right now." I smiled, trying to set him at ease. I didn't want to think this kid had anything to do with his stepfather's death. "It lets me check you guys off if I can verify where you were."

Brian nodded thoughtfully. "We came home after eating. Probably about seven thirty. Mom did laundry. I did homework. Then I played a video game for a while and read this book I got from the library. I kind of do both at once." This smile was closer to the one I was used to.

"Mom worked at the dining-room table on a project from work. Ten thirty's my regular bedtime. Mom was still working, but I heard her run water and take a bath around eleven." He grinned sheepishly. "I don't usually go right to sleep. I read for a while."

"Did you hear her go to bed?" I noted down times.

"About eleven forty-five. She always checks doors and windows to make sure they're locked. She makes sure I finally go to sleep by turning out the light. She was in her nightgown and went on to her room."

I nodded. "I didn't want to bother your mom with this tonight." Inside, I grimaced. No real alibi for either of them. "There will probably be unpleasant information coming out about Andrew as we go through this case. Be prepared."

He nodded abruptly. "I always figured he was slick, but he made Mom happy after she was so miserable." He ruffled his thick, blond hair and dropped his hands to his side. "You're going to be busy with this, aren't you?"

I nodded without paying much attention. I was trying to imagine Tina or Brian traveling to campus at midnight and killing Andrew. I couldn't see it.

"Don't worry," he said. "I'll watch out for Lady."

"You don't have to mess with that. Not now, with all this." That was so like the kid——to worry about my dog when his own family was being torn apart.

"I want to." His voice was fierce. "School will be crap. Everybody staring and whispering. Mom will be a basket case. It'll be one normal thing for me."

After a moment of inner debate, I nodded. "Okay. If it gets too intense, you're welcome to let yourself in and chill out. Lady and Wilma'll love it. Just be sure you let your mom know."

"Sure. Thanks, Skeet."

I watched him close the door and turn out the lights downstairs. My teeth were clenched, my jaw stiff. I'd felt the fury building as I sat with them.

Some bastard came to my peaceful town, *my* campus, and killed a student, leaving Tina in shreds, Brian worrying about her safety, and both under suspicion. I stalked down the block to my house. The quiet little street had lost some of the charm it had always held for me.

I would track this animal down and bring him to trial. Andrew McAfee may have been a petty crook, but he had been under my protection. Someone had snuffed out his life, and I would see whoever it was behind bars.

I suddenly realized I could run away to this peaceful place to hide from who I was, but I couldn't turn away from it now. My old boss from Homicide had been right when he said it was something inborn. I had to unravel this nasty tangle and see this killer face justice.

Now, I realized as I reached my door, I had to call the interim chancellor and tell the man who feared all bad publicity what had happened on his campus tonight.

My collie, Lady, waited at the door with tail wagging and eager whines. Rubbing her ears, I dropped my things on the table and stepped out of my shoes. Lady sniffed them as I padded into the kitchen.

My mind kept flashing pictures of Tina Jamison and Brian at dinner earlier that evening in Pyewacket's Café and Andrew McAfee bellowing curses at his news editor on campus. When I headed down the hall to my bedroom to change clothes, with Lady in tow, Wilma Mankiller appeared from the bedroom to say hello, then turned around to lead the way back.

As I undressed, I thought about McAfee trying to assault a female student and skimming money from his student writers. Had one of these infractions caused his death? Or were they just the visible tip of Andrew's troublemaking?

Didn't bode well for Tina. From the sounds of it, she and the kid had already had a bad time. I only knew the outlines from Karen and Annette. After Tom Jamison left Tina and the boy in bad financial shape, Annette hired Tina as her assistant and swore she was the best she'd ever had. But Tina disappeared from everyone else's radar.

Academia has a stricter hierarchy than even the police force. When Tina Jamison stepped out of the world of faculty and their spouses, though her position was a high-level professional one, she was suddenly dismissed as beneath notice. Pretty crappy. I liked Tina, largely because she seemed never to let that attitude get to her.

Jamison's second wife left him almost immediately for a wealthy developer. Meanwhile, Tina married a nontraditional student her own age. This marriage to McAfee had apparently shocked the university community much more than Jamison's had.

"Separate rules for girls and boys," I told the pets, "from preschool to death."

I took off my shoulder rig, removing my gun from its holster and storing it in the drawer of my bedside table. I undressed and slipped into pajamas, but was too wired to sleep. I thought I'd put on Eric Marienthal. The Rippingtons. Take a minute to prepare myself before I had to deal with the chancellor. Let the man sleep a little longer. He probably wouldn't get any more after my call. Besides, he would try to hamper my investigation or hide news of the crime. That was a chronic problem with universities, so Congress passed a law to force them to make crime on campus public. I would put off that battle a bit longer.

I stacked CDs on my stereo in the living room, Lady at my side like a gold-and-cream ghost. Afterward, I turned back to the kitchen for hot chocolate, my late-night comfort crutch. Hot chocolate with plenty of whipped cream on top. All the necessary food groups right there.

Waiting for the kettle to boil, I picked up the handpainted yarn I'd bought earlier that evening and smoothed it against my cheek. It would make soft, springy socks. A bit of rainbow on my feet. The Homicide guys always made a game of getting me to raise my pant leg so they could see my bright, handknit socks. "Strictly nonregulation," Hoag Masters would say in his deep voice. "You better watch out you don't flash some bigwig one of these days."

Hoag and Dan always laughed about my knitting, but I swore it was better stress relief than getting drunk and helped me concentrate when I was figuring out complicated cases. Dan threatened to make me teach Hoag how to knit after that.

The kettle whistled, and I came back to this night. After mixing chocolate in the cup, I spooned a dollop of whipped cream on top, sticking my tongue out at the thought of fat or calories. I really missed the Homicide guys. I missed calling them up and tossing around ideas on cases, since I'd moved up to a desk job at my dad's urging almost two years earlier.

I carried a lacquer tray with cup, spoon, and yarn out to the living room, depositing it on a table. Lady curled on the couch beside me. I petted her absently as Andrew McAfee's angry face flashed in my mind again. I've learned to pay attention to these memory tricks trying to get me to see some pattern or warning.

I pulled a set of double-pointed bamboo knitting needles from my knitting basket. As the music shed its spell over the lamp-lit room, I cast on stitches and began a sock, knitting from one needle to the next in a ring. Needles clicking softly, I replayed the whole fight scene with McAfee and his news editor, as well as my confrontation with Frank Booth about the complaint of sexual assault against McAfee.

I'd checked the files and learned that Chouteau was way under the average for sexual-harassment and sexual-assault reports. When I asked Frank if his laxness was the reason why, he'd come back with "boys will be boys," and I'd hit him with "good cops protect all the people, and that includes the female kind." I'd told him I would document him from now on, and he'd walked out of my office, angry but shaken, protesting he was a good cop. Now, I was going to have to rely on him while working this case.

We underestimated how much trouble McAfee was going to be. Everything, except the possible assault, seemed minor, but when put together, you got a picture of someone working in a disturbing number of ways to create problems for himself and others. Angry, aggressive, and dishonest. But was any of that reason for someone to bash his head in?

What if he'd been up to more than I knew? Of course he had. If there was one thing experience had taught me, it was that criminals are always into more than you know.

I set down the needles and stirred the whipped cream into my chocolate slightly. I had to call the chancellor. His reprieve— and mine—was over.

CHAPTER 3

Morning came without much sleep. I skipped my usual run and headed over to the Herbal Coffee Shop for breakfast and my first hit of caffeine before facing the chancellor, who'd been speechless at first when I called last night. He'd regained verbal powers all too soon, of course. We set an early appointment, and I knew that once I hung up, he would dial his pal, the mayor, and his senior vice chancellor, Jeremy Coulter.

That brightened things a little. Jeremy was vice chancellor for community development, the fancy academic name for fundraising, and he was the only one of the vice chancellors I had any respect for. Smart and supportive of me from my first day, he was also skilled at handling our volatile interim chancellor, appointed after the death of the man who'd hired me. I hoped Jeremy would also be at the morning meeting.

On my way to the coffee shop, I passed Tina's house, still closed up tightly. A train whistled, lost and lonely, in the distance. I could only shake my head. Like too many women, Tina was a poor judge of men. Two for two. It was enough to turn you lesbian or celibate.

I parked in the quiet, empty town square as the early-morning light increased. The train rattled through the heart of town, blowing its whistle loud and close now. That regular noise of trains right through town had bothered me when I first moved to Brewster. Now it was a sign that life outside the circle affected by murder was normal.

As the first customer in the Herbal, I relished the quiet, ordering scrambled eggs, biscuits, and bacon with my coffee. Dolores Ramirez, the owner, was busy getting ready for the morning rush, and that was fine with me. I usually enjoyed conversations with Dolores, but I wanted time to think. I had to take time to sit back and look for the thread end in this tangled mess.

While drinking my coffee, I went over everything Gil and I had found at the crime scene. Put together with what I'd learned about Andrew before his death and what Tina and Brian had told me, it added up to just so many holes. The knowledge necessary to figure out who and why was missing. That's what a homicide case often was at the beginning—multiple big and small mysteries. You solved them bit by bit and found your answers.

I began a list in my notebook to clarify my thoughts. I function by intuition as much as logical deduction, but Dan always told me intuition worked only for a prepared mind.

Why did Andrew or someone else steal Scott Lampkin's article and notes? I needed to find out what that article was about.

What was Andrew working on with Alec Oldrick that bothered him so? Why did he warn Brian to stay away from Oldrick?

Who were the student writers Andrew ripped off? I'd check with Mike Berman, the faculty adviser, and find out from Alice

Fremantle whether the vice chancellor of student affairs would have reimbursed them or expected Andrew to do it. And how many of the student writers knew or suspected?

Had any neighbors noticed Tina's car leaving the house after they came home last night? Had any of them noticed the car coming home from Pyewacket's? I made a note to have Gil check that.

Did Tina know that Andrew had possibly been unfaithful? I thought about the alleged assault on the student Janice Carmo. Were there other instances? Did Tina know about them?

What had been used as the murder weapon, and where was it now? Gil could check with the *News* staff to see if anything fitting Sid's description of the weapon was missing from Andrew's office or the newsroom. Had the murderer brought it with him?

How had the hole in the wall happened? And why had Andrew still let the killer sneak up behind him with the weapon?

Questions and more questions. Who did we have as possible suspects? Scott Lampkin, Janice Carmo, Janice's boyfriend if she had one, all the unknown student writers, Tina Jamison, Brian Jamison. And maybe this Alec Oldrick?

I looked over my list, breathing a sigh of frustration. A case was in trouble whenever there were more questions than suspects. I'd start at the top and come up with answers.

I pondered Scott Lampkin's missing research, wondering where it belonged in the final picture, when Mike Berman walked through the door straight to my table, as if my thoughts had summoned him. He was talking before he reached me. "I saw your car so I thought I'd ask you about a weird thing that happened."

"What's that?"

"Remember that fight between the guys from the *News*? I gave the evidence of Andrew's theft from the writers to Alice Fremantle in Scheuer's office. She said they'd come down hard. Late yesterday when I checked with her, she told me they're not prosecuting Andrew. Said Eugene was pursuing a nonpunitive solution." His voice rose in outrage.

I stared at him, running new equations in my head. "That's strange. Did Alice know what changed things?"

He sat down, looking puzzled. "That's the weirdest part. She didn't know any more than I did. Eugene Scheuer won't make a decision that doesn't run through her, so what's going on?"

Scheuer was vice chancellor for student affairs. His executive assistant, Alice, ran the show. If you wanted something done, you went straight to Alice Fremantle. Eugene wasn't good at decisions (or much else his job required). Alice made them for him.

"That's not the weirdest thing. Andrew McAfee died in the middle of the night. Right here on campus. Someone pursued a very punitive solution."

Mike stared, openmouthed. "You're not serious."

I took another drink of coffee. No one believed violent death could come to anyone they knew. That was true only for the middle class, though. On city streets, I'd tell someone that a person he knew had died, only to get a nod of the head as if to say, *What did you expect?*

"What happened? He was getting in trouble, but not the kind that gets you killed."

Dolores came up with a coffeepot to refill my cup with strong black Colombian, my drug of choice, then set it down to take Mike's order.

He looked bewildered for a second. "Muffin and juice. Did you hear a student was killed last night?"

Dolores looked up sharply. "So that's why Skeet's getting a real breakfast instead of just a muffin. That'll stir up the locals plenty." She turned back to Mike. "What kind of muffin? What kind of juice?"

He looked at her blankly, startled by her matter-of-fact acceptance of Andrew's death. "Both orange, I guess."

The bell over the door rang as Stuart Morley, the university's director of research and grants programs, entered. It had started raining again, and he brought a gust of wet wind through the door as he shook off his umbrella with a quick snap of his wrist. Stuart had made a point of telling me when I first arrived that he was a retired army major. He did everything as if he were still in the military, though he must have been a civilian for a number of years now.

Dolores picked up the coffeepot. "Your food'll be out in a minute, Skeet." She headed over to seat Stuart.

"It didn't faze her," Mike said with some petulance.

I sipped my coffee. "It's not as big a deal to her. She's used to it." Like me, Dolores had moved to Brewster from Kansas City. "Kansas City's always in contention with Detroit and Newark for the title of Murder City, USA. Also, she doesn't know the guy."

I could tell Mike was disturbed, so I changed the subject. "I'd like copies of the evidence you turned over to Alice. Can you get it?"

He blinked. "Get it back from Alice?"

"No. Get it the way you did the first time."

He nodded hesitantly. "But why not get it from the vice chancellor's office?"

"Because the prosecution was called off." He gave me a puzzled look. "It may no longer be the same."

He licked his lips nervously. "I see. Something funny's going on, you mean. Is Eugene or Alice involved?"

"I don't know. I just want the same papers you turned over to Alice. Andrew had plenty of funny stuff going on. From what we already know. I suspect that's not half of it. We need to find it all and sort through it." I gave him my reassuring smile. "Everyone involved in his funny business didn't kill him, but we have to find them all to question and check leads."

Mike ran his hand over his face. "This could get tricky if it runs into a VC's office. You don't know academic politics. You could lose your job if you step on the wrong toes."

I stared at Mike. "I don't give a damn about academic politics. Someone smashed in the skull of one of my students. I intend to bring him to justice. If that means stepping on some high-level toes, so be it."

Mike held up his hands. "Okay by me. I'm all in favor of not having a killer running loose on my campus."

Dolores brought our orders, and I asked for more coffee. When I'm working a case, I practically live on it. I worried that it was Big Charlie Bannion's addictive personality coming out in me, just the way his temper does. Time and again I've sworn I'd cut down on caffeine, but I'd wind up mainlining coffee to keep going through investigations. I'd thought I'd left all that behind, but here I was again. I'd only been fooling myself.

The Herbal had been filling up as we spoke, and Dolores moved quietly and swiftly around the room, taking and delivering orders. She had a good thing going in the coffee shop and herb store she'd set up here, away from her more traditional family in Kansas City.

I turned back to Mike to ask him for more information about Andrew, as Dolores showed up to refill my almost-empty coffee cup. I was desperate for any information he might have on my victim. We had nothing but questions on this guy. The bell over the shop door rang as it had again and again for the last fifteen minutes.

"Who's that?" Mike asked with a full mouth.

I glanced over to see a tall man in a worn brown leather jacket, jeans, and boots just inside the door: my ex-husband. I swallowed my mouthful of hot coffee too quickly, coughed and sputtered. My ex shook his head to dry his mop of blond hair and lifted his face. Dolores whipped out a towel and wiped up the coffee I had spit onto the table. I felt the sense of control I'd built with my list evaporate as Sam made his way over to our table. A piece of that darker life I'd left behind was catching up with me.

"Skeet," he said with a nod. "Sorry to disturb you. I tried your house, but you were gone. So I looked for the closest coffee shop between there and the college."

"I always said you could make detective if you put your mind to it." Ouch! Shouldn't have said that. All those fights. I didn't want to remember them myself—when I'd made detective, and he'd stopped trying.

"And I always said I'd rather stay where I was." His smile was stiff and awkward.

"Mike, Dolores, this is Sam Musco, my ex-husband. Sam, this is Mike Berman, faculty at Chouteau, and Dolores Ramirez, who owns this place."

Sam gave Dolores the glowing smile I remembered from the days before we married each other and stopped smiling. He ignored Mike.

"What are you doing here?" I asked in a deliberately mild tone.

He pointed to the other side of the room. "I need to talk to you. Won't take long, but it's important. Folks, my apologies for interrupting."

I shrugged and reluctantly followed him. I resented his arrival. I hadn't realized how much I didn't want anything negative from my past to contaminate my new life. Maybe when I was more settled, but not now. And today, of all days, with this murder hanging over me.

"I haven't got long, Sam. I've got an early appointment with the chancellor. What's the mystery? You must have headed out straight after work to get here this early. Unless you've moved from the night shift."

Sam shrugged. "I didn't want to bother you at work or before a date, so first thing in the morning was the only choice."

"I'm not dating right now. Thought I'd get settled first." I caught myself. Why explain? Sam had that effect on me, making me justify my decisions.

"Listen to you." He frowned. "You're shutting everyone and everything out of your life." He looked around the coffee shop. "Why'd you run away from a promising career to hide yourself in a backwater? You haven't even talked to Charlie in all this time."

I felt the old surge of hurt and anger. "Is that what this is about? Did he send you?"

He cut a big hand through the air, as if to destroy my words. "No. It was my idea to come reason with you. Charlie just misses you."

"Like hell he does. He's only ever wanted one thing from me—to be the boy he always wanted. And for years he's let me

34

know I never measured up." I spoke in a harsh whisper, working to keep my voice down and any hint of hurt out of it.

"This is old stuff."

"Oh, yeah, it's gotten real old." The fierce anger I always depended on to save me kicked in finally. "All that time he was pushing me, he stayed on the streets. Comfortable. While I killed myself trying to win his approval, good old Charlie took bribes. Why should I ever go see him?"

"You don't turn your back on your own father. No matter what people say he did." Sam's voice rose in volume.

I could read the signs. We were heading into another fight like we'd had in the bad old days. I was so mad I couldn't care. "Is this more of the unwritten cop code? He was one of the guys, the way I never could be. So what if he's a little crooked?" I shook my head slowly.

Why couldn't Sam see what a difference it had made in my life? When my father retired rather than fight charges of corruption, I'd been forced to take a look at my life and found it no kind of life at all. Just the job. The job I'd always wanted because of my father, Big Charlie Bannion, supercop. That had been the moment I'd made the decision to change everything.

"Go away, Sam," I said softly.

"Dammit! Look what you're doing to yourself!" He was shouting now. "You had the brightest future in the department. No one cares what your old man was accused of doing. It was never proved."

"Because he took retirement when Internal Affairs started investigating." I tried to bring my breathing under control.

He pushed his face too close, invading my space, but I wouldn't pull back. "You don't have to bury yourself like this. Chief of a campus police force! That's worse than being police chief for this rinky-dink town. It's like being chief of a security-guard service."

I felt my face turn red with anger. "That's bull. We're all duly commissioned officers. Every one of my guys has gone through the same academy we did. If you'd ever worked the Metro division with UMKC and Rockhurst, you'd know it. We respected those guys."

"Give this up and come back where you belong. Charlie needs you."

"I think you'd better calm down, pal, and take it easy." I jerked my attention from Sam's face at the sound of Joe Louzon's deep, calm voice. Joe had positioned himself right behind Sam. Though he stood a couple of inches shorter than Sam, he looked as strong and more determined. Joe's frown turned into a reassuring smile when he looked my way, however. "You okay, Skeet?"

I nodded, too embarrassed to speak.

His warm, sympathetic smile looked at home on his face. Joe had befriended me when I moved to Brewster. He'd made it clear for some time that he'd like to move beyond friendship. I hated for him to see Sam and me squabbling like angry children.

Sam twisted around to glare at him. "Who are you to butt in on a private conversation?" He turned back to me. "I thought you said you weren't dating?" I detested that belligerent tone.

"She's not." Joe's voice was cool. "I happen to be the police chief of this rinky-dink town, as you so kindly put it. I don't allow large men to verbally harass women. Or anyone else." He gestured to the door. "Why don't you take a walk outside and cool down?"

I pulled my anger under control and tried to quiet Sam's.

People were darting glances in our direction. "You're disturbing people."

"I'm disturbing people? I wonder how disturbed they'd be to know you haven't seen your old man in six months?" He deliberately projected his big voice, and I saw faces that had been avoiding the argument turn in curiosity.

"Okay, buddy," Joe said calmly. "You can leave peacefully or you can go in cuffs, but you're leaving right now."

"Go away, Sam." I kept my voice quiet but put iron in it, remembering again how I'd been forced to find the strength to leave him and why. I turned back toward the table where Mike was trying hard not to stare. Before I could take my first step, Sam's hand touched my shoulder.

"Skeet—" His voice was softer.

"Don't touch me." I didn't turn around. "Don't come back."

I wished the day were over so I could go home and hide instead of facing people as word of this made it around the town. One of the disadvantages of moving to a small town was loss of anonymity. Why now? Didn't I have enough on my plate already?

Sam's hand loosened. I heard the bell as he left, and I walked away through snatches of murmured conversations, holding myself erect against the stares of the other customers.

". . . Strange job for a woman . . . wonder who . . . first woman they've had . . . yelling . . . Kansas City people . . ."

I sat back down at my table. Nervous around me now, Mike wolfed down his food and left. His obvious discomfort reminded me how I'd lost friends before through Sam's jealousy and anger. We had gone through that period, I thought. Why would he come up here and start a fight with me now?

It hit me. *Charlie needs you.* Something was wrong with my

dad, and Sam wanted me to know without telling me. Charlie'd probably sworn him to silence.

I checked the time on my cell phone. I punched in Big Charlie Bannion's number, too harried to feel any anxiety about talking to my old man again. My personal life had turned into just another task to be rescheduled in the overshadowing priority of murder.

"Charlie, I want to come over this evening. Pay a visit. Will you be home?"

"Where else would I be?"

A bar, I thought. *Your home away from home.*

He coughed roughly into the receiver. "I'll be home. Wouldn't want to miss my first visit in six months. That's a long time to go without talking to your old man."

"I've been busy." My voice was flat. "I'll be there at six or six thirty."

"Hell, I'm not going nowhere. I'll be here whenever."

"Okay. I'll see you then."

His voice turned tentative. "That's . . . good, Skeet. I'll be real glad. To see you, I mean."

I hung up wondering about his tone of voice but set aside thoughts of Charlie and Sam until later. Finishing breakfast, I mulled over the little I knew about Andrew McAfee. Once again, my thoughts were interrupted—this time by Stuart Morley, who picked up his coffee and came to stand in front of me.

"Do you mind if I sit with you, Skeet?" he asked with a slight hill-country twang behind his carefully enunciated words, pulling out a chair and sitting before I had a chance to answer. Once, when I mentioned my childhood in northeast Oklahoma, he'd told me he grew up in the Missouri Ozarks. He seemed to think our background in the Ozarks tied us together.

Despite that, I'd never paid a lot of attention to Stuart until yesterday's chancellor's cabinet meeting, when he walked up as I was getting coffee and asked me to have dinner with him. I managed not to spill coffee on myself in surprise and explained that I wasn't dating until I'd finished settling into my new life in Brewster. Actually, I'd never date him. He was too tightly wound. I kept expecting him to start barking parade-ground orders. I felt especially awkward sitting at the table with him this morning.

"I saw you with Louzon last night," he said without preamble. I reminded myself that just because Stuart was short on social graces, it didn't mean he wasn't a good person. "I thought you said you weren't dating."

I took a deep breath and replied to the hurt I thought was there, rather than to the confrontational tone. "I was waiting in a long line at Pyewacket's for a table, and Joe's little girl offered to share theirs with me. That's all. She does that with people all the time."

Stuart smiled slightly. "I see." His smile never reached his eyes. "Have you given any more thought to my request to have dinner with me?"

"I've been too busy with work, Stuart. I don't foresee any time to have dinner with anyone. Right now, I'm going to be lucky to get any facsimile of regular meals."

I gathered my things and stacked plates on the table for Dolores. I hoped he'd take the hint. He didn't, just kept staring at me with his gray owl eyes.

"I have to leave now, Stuart. I have a meeting with the chancellor." I nodded to his unresponsive face and headed for the door with a sigh of relief. Something about Stuart wasn't quite right.

On my way out, I ran into Miryam Rainbow. Miryam was one of the women friends Karen Wise had given me when she talked me into taking the job at Chouteau University. They were all older than I was, but not as much as Karen. It was easy to forget that I was the young one among them all, though. Especially with Miryam. She was co-owner of Mother Earth Books, a former model of regional fame and current new-age kook.

"I didn't expect to see you today. Isn't it one of your running days?" After taking off her pastel-striped cape, Miryam twirled to show off a flared top and skirt made of multiple layers of sheer pastels. "Don't you think this just has the essence of springtime? Light, floaty, flower colored. It's the soul of spring innocence."

Miryam beamed happily, and I couldn't resist smiling back at her. In some ways, Miryam was still an innocent—after four husbands and a career in the most cynical business around.

"It's early," she said, pulling me back into the interior. "Annette's meeting me. Stay and have coffee with us. She'll be here anytime."

"I don't think Annette will be meeting you. She probably forgot to call." I gently detached her arm. "I had her come over to stay with Tina Jamison in the middle of the night. We found Tina's husband dead on the campus."

Miryam gasped. "What happened? Was there some accident? Andrew was a nice guy."

"Did you know him?" I asked.

Miryam gave a dainty shrug. "Not really, but he came over to the store to talk to me a couple of times about what photographers I knew in KC and some stuff like that."

"Was Andrew looking at a modeling career?" My voice

sounded skeptical. The angry, spiteful man I'd seen alive two days earlier had not been at all attractive.

Miryam's laugh was artificial and musical, as if practiced assiduously. "If he was, he sure wasn't going anywhere." She paused, her face twisted in perplexity. "Maybe that was his real reason for talking to me. He said it was for a research project, but I always thought that was a lame excuse." Her perfect features smoothed again. "That'd explain why the photogs he named were such losers. The ones I knew. Some of them I didn't even know, and, honey, I *know* Kansas City photographers."

"Photographers? What was wrong with them?"

Miryam shrugged. "Bottom-rung guys, mostly. Just barely making it. They even do stuff for cheap magazines for horny men. Nobody anyone any good would work for or use."

I pulled out my notebook and made a note. "Miryam, could we talk later today? You could give me the names of these photographers and tell me anything else Andrew said."

"Sure thing. Am I going to be able to help you solve a murder?" Her eyes sparkled with excitement.

"You could be a real help by steering us in the right direction."

"You're looking at the right girl for that. I know the photographers of KC and the whole modeling scene. When?"

"Ten o'clock."

"I'll be waiting." Miryam bounced enthusiastically on the balls of her feet. "This is so exciting!"

I left with ecstatic squeals sounding behind me. At least one person was happy this bleak morning.

•   •   •

"This is unbelievable! Just when we've started up the capital campaign again." Interim Chancellor Martin Willett glared at me as if I'd smashed in Andrew's head myself. "Didn't you hear Jeremy when he stressed the need to avoid scandal?"

"Yes," agreed Harvey Roberts, president of the board of trustees and mayor of Brewster.

He, the chancellor, and Jeremy Coulter sat around the conference table in Willett's office. I stood in front of them, looking out the window at the view of the campus they were ignoring, biting my lip, trying to control my temper.

Before I could reply, Jeremy Coulter spoke up in my defense. "Now, Martin," he said in a soothing voice. "Marquitta's not responsible for this. Like us, she's anxious to end it."

I nodded my tight-lipped thanks. Although two empty chairs sat at the table, Willett kept me standing as though I were a servant being called on the carpet.

"Well, it's done," said Willett in a bitter voice. "What are you doing about it, Chief?"

Restraining my temper, I stood ramrod straight. "Lieutenant Gilbert Mendez and I have been working the case since the body was found. The county coroner is performing an autopsy this morning. Lieutenant Mendez will attend. I called in the county evidence techs last night. Should have a report from them later today. I've questioned his family and co-workers. Already have leads to follow. I'll continue questioning—"

"Why the hell did you call in the sheriff's people?" Willett interrupted with a yelp of alarm. "We need to keep this quiet, entirely internal. No outsiders."

I pulled my gaze from the campus quad and stared at him. Of course. "This is a homicide. There's no keeping this quiet. I called in the evidence techs because we always use them. We don't have our own on staff. If something turns up requiring more-sophisticated analysis, I'll send it to the KCPD Regional Crime Lab in Kansas City."

Willett opened his mouth to respond, but I continued right over him. "You can't keep a murder quiet, Chancellor. So the best thing we can do is solve it as quickly as we can, using every resource at our disposal."

"Why can't we keep it quiet? It's an internal situation. It happened on our campus, for God's sake, not on some public street." Willett's face had turned as red as a turkey's.

I looked at the credenza behind his desk. It held a silver tray with a decanter of whiskey, an ice bucket, and a set of glasses. I wondered how often he sat up here and got snockered with his buddies, just an upscale Charlie with his drinking and bullying. "The Clery Act. It's federal law. Notice of all crimes committed on a campus must be made available to the press." I felt my anger gain sway. "This is a murder. You can't just sweep it under the rug. We've got a killer on our campus that we need to stop."

"Could there be lawsuits if we tried to hush this up, Marquitta?" Jeremy asked.

"Lawsuits, certainly. Quite possibly criminal charges against those issuing such orders."

"Now, we don't want that." The mayor pushed himself backward, holding his hands up in front of him as if to deny everything. "Martin, we obviously can't do that."

Willett glared at me. "I guess not. But there's got to be some way to keep this from exploding in our faces with the capital campaign going on."

"Perhaps Marquitta can tell us what to expect and what to

look out for," Jeremy suggested. "She's handled this kind of thing before."

I stared out the window at the peaceful green campus again, breathing deeply. I took another breath before speaking. "We'll pursue a number of leads. Most will turn out to be dead ends, but we don't know which they are until we've followed them. People who aren't involved with the murder will lie to us because they're ashamed of something totally unconnected to the murder."

I turned to stare challengingly at the chancellor. "The investigation will turn up dirty laundry here on campus. Some will turn out not to be involved with the killing, and some will. There's no way to keep that from happening. Right now, the Kansas City media are probably deluging the city police. We shouldn't be on their radar yet. I'll call Joe Louzon and ask him to stall them as long as he can. By the time they get here, I'll be out investigating, and Captain Frank Booth will handle them."

"My media-relations people can help with that," Jeremy said.

Willett frowned at me, then nodded abruptly. "All right, how do we control the damage?"

I breathed more easily and relaxed the ramrod-stiff pose I'd been holding. Maybe I'd get out of here without committing bodily assault, after all. "As we uncover things in our investigation, I'll let you know of anything that might come to the media's attention so you can plan a strategy for handling it." I hesitated for a second before continuing. "My recommendation is never try to stonewall the press or deny what they can find out sooner or later. That comes back to bite you. If it's a personnel issue, you can tell them it's under investigation. You've got legal grounds for not releasing that information. If it's some other kind of wrongdoing on campus, tell them such things aren't tolerated and you're taking steps to end it. Then do it. Obviously. Publicly."

Jeremy nodded. "So you'll keep us informed about what you're finding in the investigation? On a daily basis?"

Now they came to it. I'd have to tell them where this was taking me. "If something's about to come to media attention, I will inform you, but not otherwise." I turned to face Willett and prepared for the blast. "At least one current lead involves a vice chancellor's office. I'm sure you understand why the investigation must remain confidential under those circumstances."

Willett looked stunned by the revelation.

"Surely you're not suggesting that a vice chancellor on this campus is involved in a murder?" Jeremy asked with a strained laugh. "A murder of a student, I might add."

I stared at him. It would seem I'd lost my ally. "A student married to the ex-wife of a dean. An employee of the university. Involved in a professor's research. Our strongest leads are right here."

"All right," Willett said, startling me. "We have no choice. We'll do it your way. You've given good advice on handling the media."

I breathed a little easier. I wasn't going to have to fight my own people to do what I had to do.

"But I want this solved without delay and with a minimum of outside help. If you must use the Regional Crime Lab, I suppose that can't be helped. But no calling in of city or county officers. And no Metro Squad. We have our own police force. We've got a chief who was a decorated Homicide detective.

You handle it. Fast." The slight jowls on either side of his stern jaw quivered with the force of his words.

I shrugged. "You don't call the Metro Squad in for something like this. I intend to work this case, along with Lieutenant Mendez. It'll be slower if we don't ask for help from county investigators, but we'll have more control over the investigation and find it easier to keep it confidential."

"Good." Willet's nod was final, dismissing me. "Just find this killer quickly. Do your job."

I nodded and left the office with a sense of relief. The chancellor might still fire me, but at least he had enough sense to wait until after I'd caught the murderer.

I walked the steep downhill path to Old Central. Chouteau University centered around Old Central, that nineteenth-century castle built on a hill, the original home of Dolph Brewster, founder of the town that bore his name and of the college named after a French trader rumored to be, variously, his grandfather, his mentor, or the man from whom he stole the foundations of his fortune. A train whistled in the distance. The cloudy, threatening skies were slowly clearing above me. Streaks of sunlight pierced clouds and lit up elements of the campus, touching budding trees and early-growth lawn in the quad I was crossing. The campus carillon rang out from Old Central's tower in bright, clear tones.

One of the things that attracted me to this job was the environment. Instead of spending my days in cement-box buildings bounded by streets full of pimps, thieves, and homeless drunks, I worked in a historic mansion surrounded by trees, handsome buildings, and earnest college students. The job was the same, though. Change the surroundings. Lower the frequency of offenses. I was still dealing with the breakdown of civilized behavior.

I shrugged my shoulders against the chill wind that filled the morning air. It was always a mistake to assume winter was over and the bad weather past before May. I should have kept my coat on.

CHAPTER 4

I was chilled inside and out by the time I arrived at the squad room on Old Central's third floor. I keyed myself through the locked door next to the bulletproof window that was the department's public face. Along the outside wall of the sergeants' office in the long and wide squad room sat a heavy wooden table with a coffee machine, cups, napkins, and a box of doughnuts. Gathered around this table were officers from the night shift and the morning shift. Two days before, Frank and I had stood here and argued in front of these same officers about Andrew McAfee as a way of fighting for control of the department.

Now, both shifts stood around in front of the coffee without yesterday's laughter and joking. Everyone's eyes turned to me as I entered, rubbing my hands to get warm.

"Morning, Chief." Bill, my night sergeant, nodded from where he stood next to young Dave Parker.

Frank came out of his office, and my secretary, Mary, left her desk to join the gathering. I dropped the briefcase at my feet and moved past Bill to pour another cup of coffee. The expectant eyes all looked at me.

"Heard from Gil?" I asked Mary.

"He called to say Sid's doing the autopsy first thing this morning." Mary looked me over critically. "You don't look like you got much sleep last night."

"Not much." I turned to address everyone. "You've probably all heard what happened."

Bill nodded. "Dave and I filled them in."

"Heck of an initiation for Dave here, but he did a good job."

Dave shifted his feet in embarrassment, but smiled in appreciation of the praise. Bill slapped him on the back.

"How'd the chancellor take it?" Mary asked for all of them.

Frank gave a harsh laugh. "Bet he wanted you to make it all go away. They always do."

The whole group grew uneasily quiet. I looked at Frank and made myself smile as naturally as I could. "Got it in one." I slid one hip over the corner of the table and picked up my coffee to take a gulp. "You all know what we're looking at. Someone came into the *News* offices and bashed Andrew McAfee in the head. No weapon yet. I've explained to the chancellor that it won't just go away, so he's real anxious for us to solve it."

Stan Hovis snickered. "No kidding."

Bill frowned at him, but I just smiled. "Exactly. We've got crime scene stuff at county right now, and we'll use the Regional Crime Lab if we need to. I've explained that to the chancellor."

Frank burst into a loud guffaw. "I'd love to have been a fly on that wall."

Everyone grinned, and I felt my shoulders loosen slightly from their load of tension. Maybe we'd all be able to pull together in this. "Gil and I will be working it. That will put us out of commission for anything else until it's over. If something needing an investigator comes up, we'll have to put someone else on it." The officers gave me curious looks, wondering who would get the assignment.

"I'd been planning to send someone to KC to get investigative training pretty soon anyway. I'll use this case to prove that we need at least two investigators on staff. I want to send two of you for the training. If you're interested in trying for investigator, let Frank know. We'll discuss candidates later and assign one of you to anything lesser that comes up during this case." I smiled. "Give you a taste of what investigation feels like."

Bill tugged at his belt to pull his pants up. "What if we don't want to? I mean if we're a sergeant."

I laughed. "Then don't. I won't hold it against you. Investigation's not for everybody. Good sergeants are hard to find, too."

"Yeah, too bad you haven't found any yet," Stan said with a smirk. Everyone laughed.

Trish Cassell looked at me seriously. "Chief, do you think it was someone on campus who killed this guy? Not just someone who came on campus, but someone who works here or is a student?"

I could feel my expression sober. "It looks like that. So let's be extra observant and careful out there. It's early days yet. Lots of holes in the story to fill before we know the whole thing."

"Must seem like old times to you," Bill said.

"I have had a lot of experience with homicides," I said. "But one thing I've learned is that each one's different, even when you've seen dozens of the same kind. We've got a lot of work ahead of us. McAfee was a busy guy."

"You sure called it, Chief," said Milo with a sly glance at Frank. "Telling us to keep our eyes peeled because trouble was coming from McAfee or for him."

Frank's forehead creased in a fierce frown. I pretended not to see it.

"I'd rather not have been quite so dead-on." I grinned as everyone groaned. "Anyway, that's where we are. We'll need everyone's cooperation so we can solve this."

As Stan shouted, "Yeah," I picked up my briefcase and headed for my office. Mary grabbed my cup and followed, with Frank trailing cautiously behind. As I took my place behind my desk, Mary set my coffee down.

"Mary, I'll need to cancel meetings for the rest of the week, at least. And get me Joe Louzon, please?"

I gestured to Frank, who stood in the doorway, unsure of his welcome. "Come in. We've got to talk before I head out to interview people."

He moved into the office and took a chair in front of my desk. Mary hadn't moved. "Skeet, did you tell Tina?"

I nodded, trying not to think of Tina's crumpled face.

"How did she take it? And her son?" Mary looked distressed. "That poor woman has had such an awful time, and now this."

"It was hard," I said. "She's pretty torn up. I kept questions to the minimum. I'll do that later. When she's calmer. Brian's afraid for his mother."

Mary looked shocked. "What do you mean, questioning? Surely you don't suspect Tina Jamison of killing her husband. Or that sweet boy of hers. Doesn't he walk your dog for you?"

"They'd be my main suspects if he hadn't died on campus. They're still suspects." I felt my jaw firming up again. People never understood that my job wasn't to be nice.

"Surely you don't think . . . ? Brian . . ." I had apparently turned into someone she didn't recognize.

I sighed. "Listen, Mary. Most murders are committed by

the nearest and dearest. If Andrew had died at home, I'd never have left without grilling Tina and Brian last night. But since we already knew he was involved in trouble here on campus and he was killed on campus, they're not my number-one suspects."

My voice sounded stern. "But they're still suspects. I like Brian, but if he thought Andrew was hurting his mother, he might whack him. He's very protective. And what would Tina do if she caught Andrew cheating?"

"She didn't kill Tom when he did it, so why would you think she killed Andrew?" Mary said with some heat.

"The truth is that they'll be under suspicion until we find someone else did it." I pulled paperwork out of my briefcase and set it on the desk.

Mary stared at me for a second, then dropped her eyes and fled the office.

"She'll never understand," Frank said.

I shrugged, feeling helpless as I always did when up against civilian attitudes. People wanted you to solve crimes and keep them safe, but they never liked what that took.

"I'm sorry it bothers her. I'm not real thrilled about it, but there's no way to clear the two of them until we know for sure someone else did it. One of them could have come to the campus and bopped him on the head."

"You don't think so, though, do you?" he asked shrewdly.

"Not really. He had his fingers in a lot of dirty pies, and one of them led to his death. But they're still suspects." I looked him in the face.

He nodded. "Yeah. I think you're probably right. The answer's here, not there."

I tried to keep my surprise from showing. I would have expected Frank to push for their guilt once I said I doubted it.

"This thing about training a new investigator," he said, shifting in his seat awkwardly. "That's a good idea. Who'd you have in mind?" He looked at me suspiciously.

That surprised a laugh from me. Imagine Frank agreeing with me twice in a row. Maybe our relationship could be salvaged, after all. "Actually, I wanted your recommendations on who we should encourage to apply."

Frank looked surprised. He cleared his throat and leaned back, brow creased in thought. "I don't think any sergeants are going to be interested. Too old and set in their ways. They're not going to want to learn a whole new body of knowledge."

"That's what I figured. What do you think of Trish and Stan?"

He looked doubtful for a second, then nodded. "Stan's my first choice, but Trish has seniority." He paused and cleared his throat again, mouth working as if practicing words. "She's got good instincts. It wouldn't hurt to train them both. It'd give us backup when we need it."

I tried to keep my jaw from dropping. I'd thought I would have to order Frank to send any woman for investigator training. He wasn't thrilled, but at least he was trying. That deserved positive reinforcement.

"That kid, Dave Parker," I said with a big smile. "Good hire. His second night, and he handled it well."

He frowned. "Should have called Dispatch. He got rattled."

I nodded and flipped my hand outward to show it didn't matter. "I'd just mentioned keeping watch on Andrew so the call to me was reasonable. And otherwise, he was great."

"How'd he sound when he called?"

"Shook but professional."

He smiled with satisfaction. "That's good." He leaned

forward. "We need to expand the force. This is just an example. I've talked expansion for years and gotten nowhere."

"I agree with you there, Frank. They can't keep increasing the student body and faculty without corresponding growth here. Let's get this case cleared and then go to the chancellor, once we get a permanent one, with a documented case."

The need to enlarge the campus police department was the only issue Frank and I had agreed on in the months I'd been here.

He leaned back with a rueful smile. "I can write it up. I've been keeping track of the figures we'll need."

"That's great. Do that." I leaned forward and tapped my fingernail on the desk. "I'm shoving the media your way on this case. Jeremy's media-relations people are at your disposal. Use them."

His mouth fell open. "You want me to handle media? But what about . . . ?" He gestured back and forth between us with his hand.

I shrugged. "I need someone experienced, who knows police work, not just PR. And I need to investigate. Gil's never handled a homicide, and the chancellor doesn't want anyone else brought in." I looked him square in the eyes. "This is your chance to prove you're a good cop."

His jaw stiffened. He met my gaze for a few seconds, then nodded.

My phone rang. I punched the phone's speaker button. "Do you have Joe, Mary?"

Frank got up, but I gestured for him to sit down.

"How's your trouble?" Joe's voice came over the speaker.

"It's the pits. I've got you on speaker with Frank. Are the newshounds baying at your heels?"

"Local paper and TV and one KC station. I imagine the rest of the city stations will show up soon. Just been stonewalling. I left a man at Tina Jamison's like you asked, but I'm shorthanded. I'll have to pull him pretty soon."

"Thanks, Joe. I'm going to have Frank handle the press. Give him some time to get with our media-relations folks, okay? Then you can sic them on him."

"How long do you need?"

I looked at Frank questioningly.

"Can you give me an hour, Joe?"

"I'll try," Joe answered. "Anything else I can do, Skeet? I'm shorthanded with Mel on his honeymoon and Fargill busted up in that accident, but—"

"Thanks anyway. The chancellor doesn't want outsiders. So it's just Gil and me getting messy."

"Better you than me. I'll try to give you an hour's head start, Frank." We hung up.

"Go on over to media relations," I told Frank. "I'll check in with you as often as I can."

I pulled out my notebook and buzzed Mary as he left. "Get me contact info on Janice Carmo and Scott Lampkin, students, and Alec Oldrick, faculty. And an appointment with Eugene Scheuer. Tell Alice Fremantle I'll be dropping by to see her this afternoon. Also, when Gil comes in, tell him to interview the staff of the paper."

Frank turned in the doorway, his brows lifted. "Scheuer and his assistant? You got leads going that way?"

I smiled bleakly. "Lots of fun, huh?"

"Hell, Skeet. This is starting to sound nasty."

I laughed. "Frank, this is probably going to *get* nasty before it's over. Things have a way of doing that."

Janice Carmo was a tiny nineteen-year-old with enough wavy red hair for two women her size. It fell like a waterfall around her heart-shaped face, then down her back almost to her waist. Her major, according to Mary, was English, and she was on the dean's honor roll.

I caught her in her room in Herman-Kahn Residence Hall. Maintenance had turned up the heat too high in the building overnight, and sweat was trickling down my back under my suit jacket by the time I reached Janice's room. Her roommate slammed out the door with a loaded backpack, obviously late for class.

The room appeared too small to contain all their clothing, which was strewn over desks, chairs, and on the floor. The room smelled like a wild mixture of conflicting perfumes and bath powders with an undertone of dirty laundry.

"Is this about McAfee trying to assault me?" Janice asked after I introduced myself. She gathered pants and tops from a flimsy plastic chair for me to sit in. "Scott told me I'd be hearing from you about that. Finally." The girl's tone was bitter, and her mouth turned firmly downward, chin jutting forward.

She'd probably had to learn to stand up for herself as an undersized redhead when she was a kid. Tall and part Indian, I knew what that was like. "I intended to meet with you today to follow up on that. I'm sorry the officer on the scene didn't handle your complaint as he should have, and I've reprimanded him."

Janice made a fist with one hand before releasing it. "I'm glad someone's going to take this seriously." She looked around her. "Sorry for the mess. It's midterms." The tough chin softened with her apology.

"Things have taken a surprise turn. Andrew was killed last night. The sexual-assault complaint is moot, but I still need to ask some questions."

Janice's eyes grew round and huge at my words. "You don't think I killed him? I didn't. I was mad at him, but I wouldn't do that. I'm a dedicated pacifist, vice president of the Campus Greens. I don't believe in violence."

I shrugged. "No one's accusing you of anything. I'm trying to find out more about Andrew from people who knew him."

"He was a creep, always hitting on me. I just tried to ignore him." She looked up at me. "You know what I mean. You probably get a lot of that. The best thing is just to pretend it's not there."

I nodded. "That wasn't enough with Andrew?"

Janice shook her head, sending her hair flying. "He was too insistent. Too in-my-face. So I finally told him—'Listen, man, I'm not interested. And I've got a boyfriend.'"

"But that didn't stop it?"

"It seemed to at first. He was like—'That's cool. No hard feelings.' And he left me alone for a couple of weeks. Not like he was mad, but just like he'd gotten the message."

I nodded. "Then?"

Janice blew out an aggravated breath. "He called and said there were problems with my story. We were right on the deadline for the printer. He said I needed to come over and fix it quick. So I went to the newsroom."

"When was this?"

"A week ago. Sunday night really late. I'd already gone to bed. I needed to get up early to hit the library for a paper." She sighed, looking annoyed. "I can't believe I was so dumb. He'd

57

been okay all week. All I was thinking about was getting the story into the paper on time."

"What happened?"

"I got there and nothing was wrong with the story. By the time I figured that out, I was in his office with the door closed. He wouldn't let me go."

"Had he been drinking?"

"He was smashed. He kept grabbing me. I'd push him away and get loose, but he was in front of the door. He was stronger. I started to get scared. Finally, he grabbed my wrists, and I couldn't shake him off. The next day my wrists were all bruised. I've still got some."

She held out both wrists. The fading bruises circling them made me furious. "Did you show these to the officer you talked to?"

"No, I didn't think of it. He blew me off when Andrew said we were getting it on, but I changed my mind and . . ." Janice held her mouth closed tightly, but I could see the muscles in her jaw working. She sniffed. "I never led that creep on. I thought I'd never get free."

"How'd you manage it?" I asked in a gentle voice.

Janice gave me a bleak smile. "I kneed him in the balls and ran when he folded over."

Hiding my grin, I made more notes, then looked up. "You must have been frightened."

"Terrified." Janice raised her voice in emphasis.

"How'd your boyfriend take the news?"

"He was furious, wanted to hammer on Andrew, but I wouldn't let him." Janice's eyes grew round again. "He didn't do this. Duran might slug a creep like that, but he wouldn't kill anyone."

"We'll have to talk to him," I said. "We have to talk to everybody. What's his name?"

"Duran Hayward. Honestly, he's a nice guy. He wouldn't hurt anyone. Ever." Janice began to look frantic.

"No one said he did anything," I reminded her. "We just need to talk to him, along with lots of other people." I tried to smile reassuringly at the girl while my mind assessed the impact that one almost-raped girlfriend might have on a lovesick late adolescent, especially when the authorities had blown it off. "Tell me where you were last night and what you were doing between the hours of ten P.M. and one A.M., Janice."

"Is that when he died?" She nibbled on her thumbnail. "Well, Duran and I were partying with some friends. In Girlville until about one thirty. At least, that's when we left The Otter Slide."

I nodded and noted down the times and the names of Janice's friends. The Otter Slide was a college bar in Girlville, the commercial district right outside the college that catered to students. The name came from the days when Chouteau University had been a tony women's college. I made a note to have Gil check with the management of The Otter Slide and the friends about this alibi.

"Did you know anything about the research Andrew did for Alec Oldrick?"

"I did a story on it last year. I guess that was before you came. There was a big fuss about it. Oldrick's a psych professor, and last year he started studying guys who collect child pornography." Her lip twisted in a sneer. "Basically, why guys get off on pictures of little kids getting screwed. Pretty sick, I always thought."

"You seem to know something about his research." I scribbled hastily to get everything down. No wonder Andrew

59

had told Brian to stay away from Oldrick. Did reputable academics actually study things like this?

"I broke the story about it last year. I've listened to Oldrick get all pompous about how you can't help people change until you know what their psychological motives are and quoted him verbatim." Janice looked up at me in pride. "I won a reporting award for that story at the regional conference of university newspapers."

I remembered the trophy in the box in Andrew's office. "Can you think of anything else to tell me about Andrew?"

"He was a regular SOB, but I'm sorry someone killed him. I thought he should have been kicked out of school or arrested, but not killed. Lots of people really didn't like him, but I can't think of anyone who hated him enough to murder him. That's so cold. That takes a special kind of hate." Janice shuddered. "It's kind of scary, thinking there's someone that twisted running around campus."

As I left and walked down the hall past half-open doors with students clustered in groups and passing me on their own errands, I felt their vulnerability intensely. All these kids. Eight thousand of them. With someone willing to kill running loose among them. I felt a sudden chill despite the overheated air.

CHAPTER 5

Gil called as I left the dorm. His voice sounded drained. "Have you done many of these? Autopsies, I mean?"

"You do get used to it. To a certain extent. It's not ever something anyone enjoys doing."

"I'd hope not!"

I grinned to myself. "Did you throw up?"

There was a pause of several seconds. "Not until it was over, and I'd left the room. I barely made it to the men's room."

"That's actually pretty good, Gil. My first autopsy I had to run out right in the middle." I laughed ruefully at the memory. "What did Sid say?"

"No signs of drug use. He's sent for a tox screen. Death was due to that rough spherical whatever. No signs of a struggle on the body. It looks as if he just let someone walk up behind him holding this big thing that had just been banged into the wall and pound him with it. Slight traces of plaster in his wound. So the weapon was the same thing used on the wall first."

I whistled. "That tells us some interesting things."

"What have you found out?"

"A wild thread's come up about Andrew doing research for this professor who's into—get this—kid porn." I frowned, hating the twist this case was taking. It didn't bode well for my quiet little campus and town.

"Here in Brewster?" Gil sounded shocked.

"Probably not located here, though. Easier for the makers to stay anonymous in the city. Might have users here. I talked to the girl Andrew tried to rape. She's got bruises on her wrists."

We both fell silent for a moment.

"That could be a motive for murder," Gil finally said.

"Not only for her but also for her boyfriend. I'll find him and talk to him. She says they've got an alibi for the time of death. They were at The Otter Slide with other students. Check with them and The Otter management." I spelled out the names for him.

"I'm on it."

I hung up and headed for the town square and Mother Earth Books with a lighter heart. Maybe this murderer would turn out to be an outsider, after all. Someone from the underbelly of Kansas City. Consumers were everywhere, but child-porn producers tended to favor metropolitan areas with their greater anonymity. Maybe the chancellor would get his wish.

As I parked in the town square, the final wisps of cloud sailed east, and the full sun burst forth. It should start warming soon. Another train came rumbling and hooting through town, and the sound took on a more cheerful note. The day was looking up.

I entered the bookstore, accompanied by the jingle of a bell. The air smelled of sweet herbal incense. A bulky wooden counter with a cash register, vacant except for a massive long-haired cat with gray and white stripes, stood in the middle of the store.

Two women who looked more like housewives than college

students sat in armchairs in the front window nook, looking at books and talking in low tones. Barely visible through the rows of bookcases, a young male student sat on the floor in front of the back wall of shelves. Celtic music played over the sound system. Neither Miryam nor her co-owner, Carolyn, was visible.

I walked over and petted the cat. "Hey, Cernunnos, where's your mom?" He stretched his neck to put his head more fully within my caress. "She's supposed to be meeting me. Not to mention that anyone could rip off the whole store right now."

The cat was content to stay as we were forever. I, however, had moved into that state of restless energy that fed my investigations and kept me constantly on the move, trying to add to the pool of information until I could build a case. I gave Cernunnos one last pat, then headed for the back of the store.

Mother Earth Books was painted in warm, vibrant reds and golds to contrast with dark walnut shelves and counters. High walls above the shelving held richly colored ethnic wall hangings and rugs, courtesy of Carolyn's lifelong collection. Miryam's contribution to the decor lay in the large crystals— amethyst, malachite, rose quartz, I couldn't remember all the names—that sat on various tables and shelves.

When I'd first gone to the store, I'd told Miryam she was asking for theft by leaving the semiprecious gems lying around so freely. She'd replied confidently that her crystals would never allow themselves to be stolen. I thought she was nuts, but none of the stones ever turned up missing. I didn't really like to think about it.

People stood or sat as they browsed. I called out softly for Miryam, not wanting to disturb the readers. Just before I reached the back wall, a door opened and Miryam stepped out with an armload of books.

"Is it that late? Have you been waiting very long?"

"Not very, but people could have been stealing from you. You shouldn't leave things unsupervised."

Miryam laughed her musical, practiced laugh. "No one could steal from us. I've put strong mystical protections all around the store. We're absolutely safe."

I rolled my eyes. "I think an alarm system and an alert staff would be more secure."

"You are so tied to this material plane. When are you going to learn to let loose of that tight hold on physicality and let your spirit fly free?" Miryam set the books on the counter and picked up the cat. "Be like Cernunnos, absorbed in the sheer joy of being. He's a very metaphysical cat, aren't you, boy?"

I laughed. "He looks pretty absorbed in physicality to me. He must weigh twenty-five pounds. You need to put him on a diet."

She set him on the counter. "He spends most of his day meditating. He's really quite spiritual. Cats are very evolved beings, of course, but Cernunnos is especially highly developed."

"It's his appetite that's highly developed." I smoothed down the long hair on the cat's back. "Isn't that right, you pretty pig?"

"I think he eats so much in order to keep himself grounded while his soul is flying." Miryam was quite serious. "You're so tied to the physical realm that you can't see it."

I shook my head again. "It's that physical realm I've come to see you about."

Miryam beamed at me. I recalled a well-known commercial she'd filmed for a national restaurant chain. Miryam had probably been the most successful Kansas City model and commercial actress in years, and that wholehearted smile was part of the reason.

She gestured me to a couple of armchairs. "I've been thinking about the murder. Such a crime leaves a mystical residue. I'm sure we could use that to find your killer."

I tried not to laugh. "No, thanks. We'll fumble along with physical evidence. The courts would throw out the other."

"I suppose you're right." Miryam sighed. "They're so prejudiced. They're not ready yet."

And neither am I, I thought. "Tell me about your conversation with Andrew."

"I've worked with most of the photographers in Kansas City. Even after I went to California, I'd still come back here for photo shoots for some clients. And of course, I didn't stay that long in L.A., just three years, before I had my spiritual breakthrough and came back for good." She smiled with the confidence of one who knows she is superior to her listener.

Miryam had left great success in Kansas City, expecting even greater in Hollywood, only to find herself just another pretty woman in a city of pretty women. I often thought Miryam's spiritual awakening was a face-saving tactic to allow her return home without the stigma of failure.

"And Andrew came to you for information about a particular photographer?"

"Several. I'd never heard of one of them, but the other two weren't legit. They did some penny-ante stuff on the up-and-up, weddings, bar mitzvahs. But when it came to commercial shoots, they were strictly bottom feeders." She gave me a knowing look. It was similar to what I received from street people and hookers. For the moment, Miryam had abandoned her spiritual persona.

"Soft porn lingerie shots and nudes and sometimes worse. They talked young girls who wanted to be models into letting them shoot them to break into the modeling field, but they just exploited them. Work for them pretty much guaranteed you wouldn't get work with any real pros. No agency wants a model whose spread-eagle-nude photo is all over the place to embarrass their client."

I nodded, taking notes. "This makes sense to me now. Tell me, did you ever hear that any of these photographers were shooting child pornography? It would be a logical step from what they were already doing. Probably some of those young hopefuls were a little underage."

Miryam held her hands in front of her face as if to ward off an attack. She'd moved back into her priestess role. "I'm sure even lowlifes like these wouldn't stoop to that. Can you imagine the karma something like that would bring down? Destruction of innocence. Befouling of purity. It would bring the worst of rebounds. Threefold."

"I get it," I said, making a calming gesture. "Psychic bad news. Maybe these guys didn't care about their psyches. Maybe they just wanted the money they could make doing this."

Miryam nodded with a sad look on her face. "I guess it's possible. There are always people like that. I never heard of it, but no one I knew would know about that."

"Do you remember the names he mentioned?"

"Hugo Arkoff was one." Miryam stopped to think. "Virgil Gassner was the other. I can't remember the name of the other. Todd something. Mac something." She looked up at me apologetically. "I can't really remember that one."

I wrote down the names. "Will these two be listed in the phone directory?"

"Probably the Yellow Pages." She reached for a big amethyst and cuddled it to her breast. "Amethyst is a healing stone. It will heal the damage contemplation of such negativity did to my aura."

I tried to keep from rolling my eyes again. "I'd have to have one the size of Idaho."

Miryam looked at me quizzically. "That's funny. Andrew said something like that." She stopped and closed her eyes again. "No, he said he already had a great big one." She opened them again and looked at the shop blankly. She gave me a self-satisfied smile, pleased with herself for remembering, and held her hands apart about seven inches. "He had an amethyst geode that he said was this big. A gorgeous piece of rock, he called it. He didn't realize that crystals are intelligent with spiritual forces equal—"

"Did he say where he had this big rock?"

"He said he kept it on his desk at work," Miryam said with a careless smile. "I told him that was good because it could heal him from the negativity he said surrounded him each day."

I sprang to my feet. "You've been more helpful than I can say. I have to go now."

Miryam beamed at me. "I'm really enjoying this detecting."

I forced a smile at that and headed for my car. A rock that size—and jagged as a crystal would be—just might be my murder weapon. Of one thing I was sure: it hadn't been anywhere in Andrew's office last night.

Alec Oldrick's office was in Moller Hall on the floor above the *Chouteau News* offices but at the other end of the building. I took the stairs at a brisk clip, mulling over what I'd learned since morning.

I called Sid after leaving the bookstore and asked if a large crystal geode could have done the fatal damage, and he told me that if it was big enough and heavy enough, it could have. He also said he'd seen some at Indian Arts on the square and elsewhere that were more than big enough.

Where had the murderer disposed of it? If it was not the weapon, where had it gone and why had it been taken? Questions to add to my list.

I reached Oldrick's office in a cloud of unanswered questions. At my knock, a surprisingly rich baritone welcomed me. Inside, I found an extraordinarily tall, thin man twisted into an ordinary desk chair. He looked thirty-five, my own age, maybe a few years older. His lank, dark hair flopped around a melancholy face. When he stood to greet me, his entire body drooped from the stooped shoulders downward. I'd seen him when I attended a faculty senate meeting to answer questions about the new parking garage. I'd noticed him because he was younger and taller than most of the other senators, not realizing he was the infamous faculty rabblerouser Alec Oldrick.

I introduced myself and explained my reason for questioning him, carefully noting the bitterness that transformed his face when I mentioned Andrew. He showed no sign of regret and expressed no conventional sorrow at the news of Andrew's death. Instead, Oldrick moved directly into complaints about his own situation. His unusual reaction reminded me that the murderer had to have a key to get into Moller Hall that night, and Oldrick would have one.

"Those cretins took my research money away so I lost Andrew." He swung his hands as he spoke, not so much to emphasize his speech as to keep them moving. I found his rich voice at odds with the visual he presented.

"Said I endangered students. That idiot Stuart Morley." He glared at me as if I were the offending Stuart. "How could gathering my data endanger students when the subjects are sexually fixated on children? And Andrew, of all students. He's, uh, he was as old as I am."

I looked up, puzzled. "What does Stuart have to do with this?"

Oldrick waved his hands more frantically. "He's the head of bloody research and grants programs. Doles out the university's research moneys and administers all outside grants. And who gave that stupid little man any power at all over faculty, I can't begin to imagine."

"How were you endangering students?"

Oldrick cleared a pile of books and papers from an extra chair. "If you're going to listen to the full chronicle of absurdity, you need to sit down. You look like an intelligent woman. The shock could knock you to the floor."

I stifled a laugh. Oldrick folded his body back into his chair and began tapping his long fingers on the desktop.

"I was awarded a pittance out of the university research funds for student assistance with my project and photocopying. Morley and my chair have both always been jealous of me." He tossed his head in a defiant motion, sending his ear-length hair flying. "I need a real graduate research assistant, but those are saved for the bosses, of course."

I forced my mouth to hold back its smile and nodded.

"I needed someone to go with me into the city and interview subjects. I have a comprehensive questionnaire, but due to the intimate subject matter, the work absolutely must be done in person." He shot me a look, appealing to that intelligence he'd lauded earlier. "You understand."

I nodded. "Considering that child pornography is illegal, consumers might not want you to have their names and addresses to mail it to them."

"Exactly. The only way to reach this subject group is to go

to their venue and meet with them anonymously." His fingers tapped more rapidly on the desk.

"Professor Oldrick, could you tell me why on earth you chose this topic for research?"

He grew still for a moment as he assessed me. "Do you want the true reason or the usual bullshit?" he finally asked.

I laughed. "I prefer to avoid bullshit if I can, even though I know it's hard on a campus."

He laughed bitterly. "First off, I'm not a professor. I'm an assistant professor. Tenure track. Not tenured yet. They hire us and give us seven years. Then they either give us full tenure, meaning they can't fire us unless we kill someone, or they get rid of us. They'll tell you that they judge us on teaching, service, and research, but it's only research that matters. Research that's published."

I nodded. I'd heard about publish or perish.

Oldrick shot me a fierce look. "Do you have any idea how hard it is to get research published? Not only are you competing with all the other poor tenure-track slaves out there, but you've got the tenured bosses to contend with. Their raises are contingent on publishing, so they keep on with it."

"Do they all have to?" I asked.

"None of them have to," he bellowed. "They've got their permanent status. The ones who do are just greedy. Not all of them, of course, but enough to make it tough to get into any refereed journal." He noticed my mystification and added impatiently, "An academic journal that sends articles out to be vetted by experts in their fields."

"I see."

He shrugged his thin, droopy shoulders. "You can see it's extremely difficult to get into a good journal. You certainly can't do it with ordinary research. You have to find something cutting-edge."

"You decided child pornography would be cutting-edge?" I asked, unable to keep the skeptical tone from my voice.

"Alternate and transgressive sexualities are big right now in psych research," he replied angrily.

"Child porn is about as transgressive as you can get."

"Exactly." He nodded with great satisfaction.

"How do you go about finding these guys to interview?"

"There's a porn palace of sorts in the unincorporated area between Kansas City and Independence. They don't openly sell child porn, of course, but vendors show up and so do consumers. We go out there. I know some of the vendors by now. They introduce us to consumers, and we interview them in complete confidence."

I nodded. "Andrew used to do this with you?"

Oldrick beamed. "He was the one who actually found the porn place. He and his girlfriend did some research on photographers and found out about it from one of them."

"Have you met Andrew's girlfriend?"

Oldrick avoided my eyes. "I understand she's a redhead. I wonder if she's the girl who interviewed me for the paper last year?"

I had trouble reconciling this girlfriend who'd happily help Andrew find porn places with Janice Carmo. Still, this was something else to be checked. I wrote it in my notebook.

I looked at Oldrick. "I don't understand the problem with your funding. Didn't you have to tell them how you would spend the money when you applied?"

He dropped his glance farther, and his skin reddened. "In the original proposal, I intended to find subjects through the

Internet." He looked up, and his voice grew belligerent again. "I could never have gotten enough subjects that way. They were too leery of entrapment."

"They weren't when you showed up in their home territory?" I asked, incredulous.

His jaw stiffened, lower lip jutting out. "They spoke from behind the curtains in a viewing booth. I made an arrangement through one of the vendors to pay a token amount for their cooperation."

"Isn't that kind of taboo?"

"There are precedents." He drew himself up behind his desk and looked down at me from a great height. And I am tall for a woman.

"Andrew went on these expeditions with you until when?" I deliberately kept my gaze focused on my notebook.

"After Thanksgiving break, old Morley dropped the bomb on me." He looked disgusted. "Endangering students! Andrew found the place for me." He shook his head sadly. "He was a great research assistant. Probably because he was older. Not always reliable about showing up, but very helpful."

"Did Stuart say what prompted his decision?"

He shook his head until his hair flew. "Just that it had come to his attention that we were doing this, and he was pulling my money. Said it showed a lack of judgment on my part. That'll probably go on my promotion-and-tenure report."

"I'm sorry," I said, not even trying to sound like I meant it.

"That's all right. I'm the junior faculty rep to the senate, and I'm giving them hell over there. They'll never give me tenure anyway, so I'm making the last of my time here count. These morons will remember Alec Oldrick for a long time." His big voice boomed, but his face looked young and sad.

"It may be necessary for me to see your research interviews," I said.

"Absolutely not! Those are confidential materials. I can't violate the confidence of my subjects." Oldrick waved his hands dramatically.

"Child-pornography sellers and consumers, you mean." I stood and put away the notebook. "If I have to, I'll come with a subpoena for those interviews. Are you willing to go to jail to protect the confidence of your subjects?"

His face turned pale, and his eyes grew round. I left him sitting there.

I would never have believed that someone on this lovely campus was paying pedophiles to tell him their fantasies so he could get tenure. Somehow, the muggers and second-story men of the city seemed cleaner.

CHAPTER 6

"I didn't kill him," Scott Lampkin said bluntly. "Plenty of people hated him. He made a career out of pissing everyone off."

Later that afternoon, at Carney Residence Hall, I sat in the manager's office, interviewing the former news editor of the campus paper. He'd been upset to learn about Andrew's death, but it hadn't taken any of the bite off his anger.

Small, windowless, lined with floor-to-ceiling bookcases, the room held a desk in a corner, and I sat behind it while Scott sat in front of me. Behind his curly hair, I could see bookcases filled with massive notebooks and plastic file boxes. He slumped, showing a soft belly that wasn't apparent at his full height. His attractive features had an innocent, childish look, at odds with the man's body, and I wondered if he'd stopped growing yet.

"He did go out of his way to anger people," I agreed. "How did he manage to become the chief editor of the paper?"

Scott rolled his eyes. "He was a bullshit artist. He found out what people wanted to hear, and that's what he told them."

"Tell me about the article that disappeared. Why did you think Andrew took it? Was it about child pornography?"

He looked confused. "No, accounting mistakes. Here on campus."

"Accounting mistakes?" This was a new thread in the tangle.

He leaned forward. "I'm an English major, but I helped my mom with bookkeeping for Dad's business in high school. I know what bookkeeping ought to look like."

"You found something that looked wrong?"

He cut through the air with an excited hand. "At first, I thought I'd have a story of embezzlement." He laughed. "I pictured myself as the new Bob Woodward. I was researching for an editorial on the disproportionate percentage of the budget athletics gets." He grinned. "It's an old perennial for campus papers. Athletics programs rule when it comes to getting money. Campus newspapers write articles and editorials. No one pays any attention. The money to athletics keeps flowing year after year."

I nodded.

He ran a hand through unruly black curls. "I noticed an entry that shouldn't be there, then another. I got all excited, but the university's accounting structure is byzantine—nothing straightforward like my dad's books—so I realized there might be an explanation. I went to a friend in accounting. She checked into it and told me someone just made some dumb mistakes and Hamlisch—you know, he's the VC for admin—accounting and purchasing and all that's under him—"

I gave him an impatient nod. "Departments for running the university like groundskeeping and maintenance."

"And athletics. Oddly enough, that's under Hamlisch. Anyway, my friend said Hamlisch was pissed about the whole thing and heads were going to roll. It didn't turn out to be a great criminal exposé, but I got a nice story about accounting mistakes that would embarrass the administration a little." He flashed his bright grin again. "We live to embarrass the high bureaucrats. It's what gives meaning to our labor."

"Andrew didn't like the article?"

Scott's dark brows pulled together in a frown. "That's what's so odd. At first, he was all for it. Andrew loved to skewer the big guys. His wife had been married to one and got screwed big-time."

I pursed my lips, puzzled by this latest twist. "Do you mean Andrew actually approved the article?"

"He took it to double-check before publishing. A couple of days later, he tosses it on my desk in front of the whole newsroom and says it's a piece of shit and he wouldn't dream of publishing it." His voice grew dark with anger. "I figured he'd wimped out about tweaking the administration."

He looked up at me. "I was pissed at the way he did it, but I let it go. Until he stole everything connected with it. All my notes. Like he was scared I'd go publish it somewhere else."

I put down my pen and looked directly at him. "Why are you so sure it was Andrew who took it?"

"No one else knew about it. Everyone else works in the newsroom when others are around. Only Andrew stayed till all hours of the night. Alone."

"That's why it was so easy to kill him." I looked off into the distance as I thought about it. My glance caught one of the fattest of the notebooks in the shelves before me—STUDENT JU-DICIALS.

"Was it well known that he stayed alone in the office late at night?" I asked.

"Sure." He ran his hand through his hair again. "He could have done it without being seen. No one else could. They'd have to go to my file cabinet and through my desk to get the article and notes. People would wonder what they were doing. It had to be him." He tightened his lips. "It's the kind of chickenshit thing he'd do."

I flipped a page over in my notebook. "You didn't like him at all, did you?"

"I thought he was destroying the *News*. Morale's never been worse. He drove away our best writers. He always had some scam going. He didn't give a damn about the paper, except for how he could use it for his own benefit."

I raised my eyebrows in surprise at his vehemence. He dropped his glance and looked uncomfortable with the passion he had just displayed.

"Can you tell me where you were last night between ten P.M. and one A.M.?"

He looked up in shock. "I didn't kill him."

"We're accounting for the whereabouts of everyone who had a grudge against him." I gave him my best smile. "It's a big job."

Scott ran both hands through his hair. The curls sprang out wildly around his face. "I was in the library until it closed at eleven. Researching a paper for American lit. Then I came back here and worked before I crashed."

I wrote it all down. "Do you have a roommate?"

"He left school earlier this semester when his dad died. They haven't stuck anyone else in with me." He stared at me anxiously. "That means I don't really have an alibi after eleven o'clock, doesn't it?"

"It doesn't mean I'm putting the cuffs on you, so relax." I looked down at my notes for a second. Accounting errors. Serious enough that Wayne Hamlisch was going to fire someone over them. Apparently not embezzlement. In the back of my head, I felt a tiny click, a piece of the puzzle finally falling into place. But I still had to find out what it meant.

I looked up at him again. "Could you reassemble those article notes?"

"I don't know why not." He looked bewildered. "You want them?"

I nodded. "They might have a bearing on Andrew's death. I have to look at everything that doesn't figure. And these don't make sense. If he didn't steal them, he probably knew who did. If he did steal them . . . Either way, they must have more importance than you knew."

His face shone with suppressed excitement. "If I reconstruct them, they might give you a lead?"

"Yes, they might." I gave him a stern look. "You can't let anyone know you're doing this. If they have anything to do with his death, someone may not want them restored."

He nodded vigorously. "Got that. Don't want some badass smashing in my head."

"When you've got what you had before, bring it to my office. The third floor of Old Central."

"I'll do it."

"If I'm not there, leave them with my secretary."

"I'll get right on it." He gave me an excited smile.

I liked this smart kid with the little-boy face. I hoped I wouldn't have to arrest him for murder.

Since Duran Hayward also lived in Carney, I arranged for him to meet me in the manager's office after Scott. I had only a few minutes to struggle with the complicated knot that was Andrew's life before Duran arrived.

Tall, black, athletic-looking, he was Janice Carmo's opposite. But after a few minutes of conversation, I understood the attraction between them. Duran was as intelligent and committed to social causes as Janice was. She may have been vice president of the campus Greens, but he was the president of the campus Amnesty International and Habitat for Humanity.

"That must keep you busy," I said. "Along with your classes."

He shrugged it off. "It's a matter of priorities. Time management. I use the time most guys spend watching MTV or playing video games."

"You still find time to go to The Otter with friends," I pointed out, since he'd repeated that alibi.

"We're not boring. We do other things with our time and have fun."

"Janice writes for the *News,* in addition to all that. That must cut into your time together."

He grinned at me as if he'd caught me playing a prank. "I was fine with Jan's writing. We support each other totally. I just drew the line when that imitation of a man tried to rape her."

"Made you mad, did it?"

"In what world wouldn't it? I was furious with the guy. It was one of the few times in my life that I've been tempted to resort to violence." He dropped his eyes as if ashamed. "I gave serious thought to clobbering him. I probably would have, but Jan talked sense into me. She said it would violate everything I believe in and stand for, that it would mean he and all the oppressive forces would win."

"That kept you from pounding on the man who attacked your girl?" I asked, unable to keep the skepticism from my voice.

He gave a sheepish grin. "She promised we'd get a place together next fall. I've wanted to for a long time. She has, too, but she's been holding off because of her folks." He waved his hands as if to ward off my negative thoughts. "Not 'cause I'm black. They're okay with that, just don't want her living with anyone. She's their only kid."

He looked troubled and turned away to stare at the full bookcases as if they held answers. "I'm a committed pacifist, but I can't let anyone hurt Jan. If I had to resort to violence to protect her, I would. I'd use intimidation first. I'm a big guy. If that didn't work, I'd try to keep the violence to the lowest levels. But I will not let Jan be hurt. That's my bottom line. I hadn't realized it until this happened."

"Plays hell with your pacifism, doesn't it? I've always wanted to be peaceful, but too many rotten people do rotten things. I can't stand by and let them get away with it."

His face showed serious thought. "I truly believe the path of pacifism and nonviolence is the only sane way to live. At the same time, I can't let anyone hurt Jan." He turned back from the bookcases and looked directly at me. "I imagine I'll feel the same way about my kids when I have them. I don't know how to reconcile these beliefs, but I have to find a way. I don't want to be just confronting it when I'm old like . . ." He stopped speaking and looked wary. "Like some people."

"What does Jan think about your dilemma?"

He grinned again, his whole face lit with the pleasure of speaking of his girl. "She tells me to loosen up. Says my heart's in the right place, and I should stop being so serious. She's so good for me."

"So you can't tell me anything else about Andrew McAfee?"

He hesitated, reminding me that he'd started to refer to someone in a similar situation. Then, his jaw hardened. "All I really knew about the guy is what he did to Jan."

I wondered what he was hiding. People did that in murder

cases, lied about things that had nothing to do with the case. Covered them up because they were afraid. But Duran didn't strike me as someone who was afraid.

"I don't know what to tell you. I don't know why he did it." Alice Fremantle plucked a bright green candy from the glass bowl on her desk and popped it into her mouth. She was a heavy smoker, and candy was her only way to get through the workday in the no-smoking university buildings. I couldn't understand how she could eat candy all day and look like a famine refugee.

"You didn't expect it?" I asked.

Alice shook her head. "Every once in a while, he reads about some new way of handling students, and then he goes off on that tangent for a case or two. Trying it out. He's very progressive."

I lifted an eyebrow. "But normal procedure would be . . . ?"

"A complete audit of the paper's finances. Force Andrew to step down pending the decision whether to prosecute criminally or as a disciplinary matter. At best, he'd be expelled and required to sign a contract to repay the money. At worst—and that's what I thought this case was—he'd be turned over to the courts. Some of those students depend on their *News* article stipends to buy food."

Alice used her fingertips to push more body into her already full hair. "I asked Eugene why he wasn't doing anything. He got mad and said, because he didn't have to."

I knew my shock showed on my face.

"I know." Alice's smile was tired. "It doesn't sound like Eugene. Later, he apologized. Said he was going to do something, just not the usual procedures."

I looked down at my notebook. "He was giving Andrew special treatment?"

"It's his prerogative." Alice's tone grew sharp and defensive. "He has complete discretion over the disposition of such cases."

"Why would he make Andrew a special case?"

Alice shook her head. "He had a good reason. Eugene is not capricious."

She'd drawn into protective stance, and I'd get nothing further, so I thanked her. On my way out, the skeletal woman reached into the candy bowl again.

It was almost five o'clock when I returned to my office. Frank and Gil waited with news of Gil's interviews of *News* staff members, and Mary typed a summary for me to take home.

"I'm only missing two," Gil said. "I'll get them tomorrow." He held up a plaster cast of a man's medium-size shoe. "The techs were able to get these at the murder scene."

I looked at the white surface's crenellations. "Some kind of athletic shoe."

"Yes, ma'am," said Gil with a grin. "They're working with the Regional Crime Lab on identifying the brand."

"Good job," I told him, easing into my chair and leaning back in fatigue. I could feel the tension in my back. Before long, I'd wind up at the chiropractor. "Mary still seems to be speaking to me."

Gil looked perplexed. Frank laughed. "Mary wasn't real happy when Skeet told her Tina and her son were suspects. She didn't think Skeet should have questioned them because, after all, they're neighbors and friends."

I frowned. "Lots of people feel that way. They don't understand what our job requires."

"She was pissed because you acted like a cop instead of a woman. It was the only way for a good cop."

I grimaced as he made his first remark, but softened my expression when I realized he was trying to praise, not insult.

Gil looked confused. I wasn't used to this Frank, either. At any rate, he'd given up his war against me.

"How are things with the media?" I asked.

Frank shrugged. "I told them I'd bring them up-to-date on our progress in the morning. Have we made any?"

I sighed and rubbed my aching head. "We're aggressively pursuing several leads at the moment."

Frank nodded. "They won't like it. What the hell. They tracked down Tina's first marriage and asked questions like crazy. Were we questioning Tom Jamison, et cetera?"

"We haven't any reason to. He's the one who left. He divorced Tina before she met Andrew. Why would we suspect him?"

Frank gave me a knowing look. "It makes good soap opera on the news shows."

I sighed in exasperation. "What did you tell them?"

"We are questioning everyone who had any involvement with the deceased. I stressed 'everyone' so they could assume it included whoever they wanted."

"Good move." I rolled my head back and forth against the chair back. "Anyone know any reason we ought to be questioning Tom? He wasn't trying for custody, was he?"

Frank laughed unpleasantly. "From what I've heard, he didn't have much interest in the kid. Now that his little sweetheart's dumped him, maybe he feels real paternal."

I waved the speculation away. "Let them run after that red herring. We're looking at two solid leads I don't want them to hear about. Funny business with college funds and child pornography."

Frank whistled.

"How'd you find out about the financial stuff?" Gil asked.

"That's what the stolen article was about. I asked Scott Lampkin to duplicate it and bring it to us without telling anyone."

"You want a student to do that?" Frank's voice was severe.

"He knows what he did the first time. We could dig away and never know what triggered all this."

"Isn't he a suspect?" asked Gil. "Or did he have an alibi?"

"He didn't have any alibi at all, but he had something better." I picked up the plaster cast. "He's got to wear a size-thirteen shoe, at least. These footprints couldn't be his."

Gil shook his head with a rueful grin. "I see our future now. You and I wander the campus measuring people's feet."

Frank and I laughed.

"What about kiddie porn?"

"That's some weird research Andrew did for a psych professor. It may have no connection, but he was dealing directly with porn dealers and customers. Any of them can get rough if they feel threatened. It's a line to follow."

The phone rang. "I wanted to see how things are going," Jeremy said. "The chancellor's asking."

"We've been questioning people. We have leads. We're doing everything we can to solve this. That's the scoop."

"That's just what Frank told the press, Marquitta. What's really going on?"

I sighed and ran my hand over my face. "I told you high-level administrators may be implicated. They have to be investigated. So we keep it confidential until we know whether those leads pay off."

"Are you refusing to tell me what you're investigating?"

His voice had an edge to it. "Marquitta, I'm trying to help you. Don't make it impossible for me to defend you."

"Maybe you're the vice chancellor I'm investigating, Jeremy. I shouldn't tell a murder suspect what I'm doing. If you weren't guilty, you wouldn't appreciate me telling anyone else I was investigating you, would you?"

I could hear the irritation in my voice. I tried to control my temper.

"Investigate me?" Jeremy's voice rose. I moved the phone away from my ear. "Why . . ."

We both fell silent. I'd never known him to lose his temper before and chalked up a bit more damage to this case.

He took a loud breath. "You made your point, Marquitta. I'll explain it to the chancellor."

I sighed in relief. Jeremy was the only ally I had in the corridors of power. "I appreciate that."

"Even if you are putting a friend like me on your suspect list," he added with a slight laugh.

"When it comes to murder suspects, I have no friends. I can't afford it."

He lapsed into another brief silence. Suddenly he chuckled. "That's my girl. Absolutely incorruptible. I'll check in later. Maybe you'll have cleared me enough to talk to me."

"I'd have to clear all your colleagues, too, Jeremy."

He sighed loudly. "Good night, Marquitta. Get some rest."

"I take it the good vice chancellor doesn't like it that you won't give him details of the investigation," Frank said as I hung up.

I tried to smile and failed. "No. Of course, he's not someone we're looking at, but we have leads in the direction of two other vice chancellors, so I'd rather keep things just among us.

It's a shame because he's the only one trying to keep the chancellor in line."

I stood and walked to the large whiteboard topped by a narrow cork strip on the back wall. Clearing items from the cork, I surveyed the board below it. "Time to begin organizing the info we've already got. Frank, bring those photos of campus suspects."

I looked over at them. Gil looked as tired as I did, and for all his glib talk, dealing with the media on top of the department's administrative tasks had clearly taken its toll on Frank. And we were just beginning. Not for the first time, I wished for the resources I'd had at KCPD.

"I want Gil, with some help from an officer or two, to check with everyone in the offices around Andrew's to see if any of these people showed over at the *News* offices yesterday. None of them should have been there." I stared out the window at the silver ribbon of the Missouri River, putting my thoughts in order. "One of the VCs might have, but it would be fishy. The others . . . Andrew wasn't working for Oldrick anymore. Tina says she didn't. All the rest were on the outs with our boy."

I looked back. Frank and Gil nodded in unison. Grabbing a marker, I drew a schematic with dates and times surrounding the central event of Andrew's death. Lines connected names to Andrew and/or one another. Along the side, I printed my list of questions and drew lines to the names involved with each. It began to look like a complex spiderweb. Gil and Frank asked questions, made comments. I erased some lines, shifted others from one name to another. I could feel my brain click in on this case.

As we learned more, I'd fill the diagram, change it until peripheral people and issues were erased and only the essence of the case was left. One name would emerge in my mind and, I hoped, the evidence. Nothing was worse than knowing who killed someone and not being able to pin him. It had happened before. I always hated it. I needed to learn who had done this so I could prove it in court. I hoped to weave a tight enough web to do just that.

CHAPTER 7

It was after seven o'clock when I headed out of town on Highway 9. Later than I'd told Charlie. He sounded so pleased I was coming that I hoped it wouldn't matter. My cell phone rang. It was Gil.

"Wayne Hamlisch claims to have heard Tom Jamison threaten to kill McAfee."

"Did anyone else hear this threat?"

"Hamlisch says Stuart Morley and a student in the newsroom. Trying to track down the student."

"Check with Janice Carmo's boyfriend, Duran Hayward. When I talked with him, he was hiding something about someone older. I'll bet he knows something." I passed a lumbering truck, overloaded with cut limbs and brush.

"Which dorm is he in?" Gil asked.

"Carney. Talk with him tonight, and try to talk to Morley. If they corroborate, we'll go question Tom in the morning. I'll come along."

"Thanks." I could hear relief in his voice. "It's kind of sticky. Him being a dean and all."

I grimaced. "This is not going to make the chancellor happy." I felt immediately exhausted. "I'm on my way to KC right now. If we're on for the morning with Jamison, call me on my cell."

This would be tricky. Jamison had been dean of the business school for eight years and had a national reputation in his field. He'd just moved to the top of my list, but until we had hard evidence, I had to check out all the other leads. Andrew had worked hard at giving people reasons to kill him.

The closer I came to Charlie's, the more nervous I became. I'd hoped to put him out of my life. In the back of my mind, I knew he was getting older with no one to take care of him when he no longer could. No one but me.

Driving finally through the neighborhood where I'd spent childhood and adolescent summers felt like moving backward in time, slowed and weighted as if I swam deep under the ocean. When Mom left Charlie and took me to Oklahoma at age ten, my world ended. To lose my father, that shining man, a policeman who made the world better, was the worst that could have happened. I longed for summers to come so I could return to this neighborhood and be with my adored father. Once I'd graduated, I hotfooted it back to Kansas City to enter the police academy, imagining Charlie thrilled to have me join him in his sacred profession. It hadn't gone down that way.

I sighed, noticing the shabby houses and broken-down cars that had appeared only in the past five or six years as the neighborhood slid down the socioeconomic scale—and my father with it. The last time I'd been to Charlie's had been for his retirement celebration, a pitiful collection of old friends and colleagues. And me, of course. Everyone drunk, naturally, except me. Years of trying to get my dad dried out had left me with little desire for alcohol.

I'd been in shock ever since I heard he was taking retirement and not fighting corruption charges. Hadn't wanted to believe it. Every time I tried to talk to him, he clammed up, evaded the issue, or blew up at me.

There were officers I'd expected to see at Big Charlie Bannion's retirement party who just weren't there. Supervisors. Men who had served with Charlie, even partnered with him, before moving up the hierarchy. Men who'd always respected him. Only the oldest of buddies and the dregs had shown up for this party—and Sam, the son Charlie'd always wanted, whom I'd given him when I married and taken away when I divorced. Sam was drunker than I'd seen him since the first few months after I'd left. He spent the evening trying to get me alone. I spent it avoiding him. It hadn't just been Sam. The other men were drunker than usual, too. Charlie's situation was a drag on everyone's spirits. Even Charlie outdid himself, something difficult to do.

I always dreaded my father drunk. That was when he became cruel. Over the years, I learned to tough out his drunken attacks, not let them make me cry. I hadn't realized how sick of them I was until he started in on me in front of everyone that night. All the old insults. I walked out while Sam was trying to shut him up. When I woke the next day, I found I'd decided overnight to leave Kansas City and its police force.

I shook off those memories as I parked in front of Charlie's small house. *That was then, this is now,* I told myself. Things were different. I'd broken free of him, and he knew it.

When he opened the door, I almost gasped. He'd aged tremendously in six months. His broad shoulders had a stoop that hadn't been there even at his retirement party. He had lost substance, some inner core missing. His face was more lined than I remembered, cheeks sunken, skin graying, eyes cloudy. Holding the door open wordlessly, he followed me into the dilapidated living room.

"I ran into some things I had to deal with on a murder." *Why was I excusing my lateness?*

Nodding, he cleared old newspapers from the sagging couch. I put my purse beside me.

"Murders are like that," Charlie said, voice rough, as if he weren't used to talking.

I couldn't help staring. The changes were striking. What was wrong with Charlie? Were these terrible changes the result of finally being able to drink as much as he wanted without having to sober up for work? Was he drinking himself to death?

"Looking good," he said. "The new job agrees with you."

I sucked in air. "You don't look so hot, Charlie. What gives?"

He gave me a surprised glance. "You can tell there's something wrong with me?"

"You look ten years older. What are you doing to yourself?"

He batted the air with his hand, as if to dismiss the importance of the change. "Aw, it's a weird thing, these attacks that make me dizzy. Sometimes I get a little blind."

"That sounds bad." I shuddered.

He laughed, and it turned into a cough. "Scared me shitless the first time. Thought I was going to die. They say they're little-bitty strokes. Just warnings. I can see after they leave. They say I may not always get sight back. Might be left with a blind spot."

"Charlie, what can they do? Is there medicine? What have they told you?"

"Aw, they want me to take pills. Quit drinking and smoking.

Stop eating everything I like. That kind of stuff." He shrugged. "The 'if it tastes good spit it out' diet. Won't make you live longer. Just makes it feel that way." Slapping his thigh, he guffawed until he choked and coughed.

"Sounds to me like you need to be doing what the doctors tell you," I said in a firm voice.

"The hell with that!" His dismissive hand cut the air. "Tell me about this murder."

I sighed, knowing this mood. I'd have to talk about other things before I could bring up his health again. I began to summarize the murder and its investigation.

"Kiddie porn. Here in KC. I know that place. I probably know the photographers. What are their names?" Charlie looked eager, and color began to flow back into his face.

"You're retired. Don't mess in this case. You're sick. You need to take care of yourself."

"I can help. I still know my way around. You think you're better than your old man?" He glared at me.

"You were never a detective. Now is not the time to start a new career in investigation. That time's over." I glared back at him.

"You think my time for living is over," he yelled.

"It will be in short order if you don't start taking these doctors seriously, Charlie."

"Fuck off, Skeet!"

I bit my lower lip to keep from responding and shook my head. "I don't know why I bother. I should have known it would be a mistake."

His face grew pasty. "Shit, kid, I didn't mean it." He reached a hand toward me. "I'm . . . I'm real glad you came."

I leaned back with a sigh of exasperation. "Okay, Charlie." My phone rang. I stood up. "I'll take this in the kitchen."

I headed to the kitchen, listening to Gil. I wondered what I'd gotten myself into. Duran had indeed been the student in the newsroom cleaning out Janice's desk. All three witnesses admitted they'd heard Jamison threaten Andrew the day before he was killed.

When I came back to the living room, Charlie was on the floor, stuffing something into my purse. He twitched when he saw me. "Uh, I knocked your purse down. Sorry."

"That's okay." I reached for it, and he set its strap in my hand.

"I think I got everything back in." He shrugged. "At least I tried."

I checked the floor in front of the couch and checked my purse. "Looks like you got it all. Charlie, maybe Sam or I should go with you to your doctor. Sometimes it's hard to—"

"Hell you will! I'm no damn snot-nose kid who needs Mommy to talk to the doctor for him."

"I just thought that way I'd know what he told you to do and—"

"You could make me do it? You think I'm senile? I'll do what I damn well please about whatever he says." His face had turned red in a matter of seconds. That couldn't be a good sign. "You think I'm old and useless. Think you ought to put me on an iceberg like the Eskimos, huh?"

"That's it, Charlie. I'm out of here." I pulled out my car keys and shouldered my purse. "You do whatever you want. You always do."

I slammed out the door and squealed my tires leaving. How did you make a grown man stop killing himself?

Early the next morning, I joined Gil outside Tom Jamison's house in the upscale Wickbrook subdivision. Jamison's house was a sprawling California contemporary set on a raw hillside with a covered deck to the side that wrapped around to the second story in back. I couldn't resist comparing it with Tina's cramped bungalow.

"Maybe he'll have a solid alibi for the murder." Gil's voice was hopeful.

"Don't count on it," I cautioned. "Most people don't know they'll need an alibi so they don't have one."

"It makes it easier for everyone if they do," he muttered.

I laughed and rang the doorbell. Tom Jamison answered in a pale blue sweatsuit. He looked at me as if trying to place me. "You're chief of campus police, right? Bannion?"

I raised my eyebrows. After six months of chancellor's staff meetings, I expected a little more recognition. "Yes. This is my investigator, Lieutenant Mendez. We'd like to ask you a few questions."

Jamison frowned and hesitated. Suddenly, Gil nudged me. I looked at him, and he shifted his eyes in the direction of the side patio stacked with household goods. Hammered brass wall plates and a gilded French Provincial wall clock leaned against intricately carved cabinets and a fancy dressing table and bench. To the side and behind the table sat four large cardboard boxes packed with various items. A lighted makeup mirror topped one of them, flashing the sun from both its mirror and the light bulbs surrounding it. But what caught my eye and had obviously caught Gil's was the sun hitting an edge of something purple and translucent or crystal peeking out of the side of a box next to the door from the house.

It could have been something made out of purple glass, of course, but something about its shape didn't seem right for that. It was thicker and seemed just a small piece sticking up. Like the tip of an amethyst crystal geode.

Jamison's voice was querulous. "Why would you want to question me? I suppose it's all right, but I've had no notice of this. You could have—"

I interrupted him. "What are those items on the deck?"

Jamison's head turned. "Those belong to me. I'm going to give them to charity." He turned back to me sharply. "Does my ex-wife have something to do with this visit? Is she going to the university to cause me trouble now? I paid for everything out there. It belongs to me, and I have the right to dispose of it as I please. If I choose to give it to Goodwill, that's my prerogative. I don't have to let her have it. She hasn't got a leg to stand on about this, and her lawyer's told her that. Goodwill is sending a truck this afternoon to take all of this away and use it for a good cause."

He gave a self-satisfied smile, as if to say, *That'll teach her to mess with me.*

"Tina?" I asked.

"No, my other ex-wife." Jamison glared at me. "What is this all about?"

I pulled out my notebook. "Were you aware that Andrew McAfee was murdered the night before last?"

Jamison nodded. "I imagine everyone on campus knows. Horrible. I went to Tina's to see what I could do to help. She's in pretty bad shape. Brian's very . . . upset." His mouth twisted.

"Where were you Monday night between the hours of ten P.M. and one A.M.?" I looked up at him expectantly.

"Why should I tell you that?" He puffed up. "What do my whereabouts have to do with anything?"

"Dean Jamison, you threatened Andrew McAfee's life before he was killed, so you're going to have to answer questions, including where you were at the time of his death."

He shrank back. "I . . . I didn't mean it. It was just an argument."

"Where were you Monday night?" I reiterated.

He looked around wildly. "Here. I worked on an article and watched the news and went to bed and . . . Oh, God! I was here alone. All night."

I nodded. "Dean Jamison, I'd like you to come with me back to the office." At his panicked protests, I raised my hand. "This is not an arrest. We simply want to talk with you."

"I want my lawyer," he said, his skin ashen.

"Call him. We'll wait."

When he went inside to phone, I turned to Gil. "Good sighting! Call Dispatch when I take Jamison. Get an officer over here to keep watch. You hightail it to the DA's office. Get Beau Fletcher to write up a search warrant for Judge Felissen. Say we believe we might have the murder weapon, but we have to rush the warrant through because he's in the process of disposing of it. Have Sid confirm for her if you need to. Make sure you go to Beau, and make sure he takes it to Magda. She's our best bet. We don't want Randy sitting on it all week or, worse, leaking it to the press." I looked around the yard with its new plantings and back at the box on the deck. "Come back with county techs and impound that. Go over the whole house. The shoes might be somewhere in there."

Gil was so excited he bounced on his feet ever so slightly. "It's in there, isn't it?"

I nodded. "It sure could be. But it could turn out to be something else. Don't get your hopes up too high. Ordinarily, I wouldn't try for a search warrant on so little, but if Goodwill carts off those boxes this afternoon, we could lose it if it is there."

Breathing deeply, I waited on Jamison. This might be simple, after all. A form of domestic homicide. Poor Tina and Brian. What would this do to them?

Shortly after I brought Jamison in, his lawyer showed up. Lanky and balding, Marsh Corgill had sincere eyes that had convinced many juries his arguments were true. The slight lines on his large forehead reassured them he took things seriously. His soft, even voice that paused to select just the right word convinced them of his integrity. I liked him. If I were in legal trouble, Marsh would be the lawyer I'd choose.

Immediately, Marsh insisted that he and Tom have a private conference before questioning began. I'd left them in the conference room and gone to call Gil about the search warrant. Before I could dial, Tina Jamison burst through my office door past Mary's efforts at restraint.

"I told her you were busy," Mary explained, "but she wouldn't wait."

"It's okay." I hung up the phone.

"Skeet, you can't think Tom killed Andrew, surely?" Tina cried as Mary closed the door. "Not Tom."

I raised my hands to calm her. "Sit down, Tina. Calm down. We'll talk."

Devastated, Tina sat on the edge of a chair facing me. Ravaged face, hair barely combed, tailored slacks with a worn, stained sweatshirt, and sneakers. "What do you want with him?"

I sighed in exasperation. *Why* had someone dragged her into this? "How did you know we brought Tom in? We just got here. His lawyer just got here."

Tina wiped her eyes with a tissue. "Tom called me in a panic, talking crazy. He said you were arresting him for Andrew's death, but he was innocent. He said you'd give him the death penalty. Of course, I came."

I ran my hand through my hair. Why had he done that? Did he think Tina's pleas would help, or was he just used to looking to the old wife when things got tough? Either way, I didn't like it.

"First of all, Tina, we're not arresting him. We asked him to talk to us and answer some questions. That's all." I stopped and looked straight at Tina. "He decided to call his lawyer. I guess for his own reasons he thought he'd need one."

Tina shook her head vehemently. "Tom had no reason to kill Andrew."

"Maybe he was jealous of you." I sat back in my chair, looking at Tina. Grief-stricken over one no-good husband's death and frantic to protect another just as bad. How did these things happen to smart women?

Tina laughed and hiccupped. "That's ridiculous. Tom's the one who left me."

"Maybe he wanted you back, and Andrew was in the way."

Tina looked angry. "You don't believe that."

I tilted my head to look at Tina with speculation. "Maybe you were jealous. Did you know Andrew was unfaithful?"

Tina's eyes grew large, and tears began to form. She shook her head, looked at me angrily, and shook her head more vehemently. The tears stopped. For the first time since I'd notified Tina, the woman I knew, who'd thumbed her nose at the academic rumor mill, looked out of those eyes. "That's not true. Andrew was never unfaithful to me. You don't believe that any more than you believe Tom killed him."

I leaned forward over the desk. "I don't believe anything right now. I'm following leads to a killer. I'm looking for proof."

Tina raised her hands in entreaty. "I found some of Andrew's papers. Deposit slips for banks in Kansas City I didn't know about. Lots of money."

I felt that little click in the back of my mind. We'd gone through Andrew's papers at the office and found nothing. Checking into his papers at home had been on my to-do list. It just moved to the top. Maybe all these strings were going to tie together.

"All right." I stopped and figured times. "When I'm finished here, I'll come get the papers. In an hour or so. Will you be home?"

"Yes. Thanks, Skeet." Tina's voice was firmer.

"I'm going to check out everything," I said in a softer tone. "I want to find the killer, not just someone convenient."

Tina's tears began again, silently. I guided her out of the office, turning her over to Mary. "Go home. Wait for me."

Tina looked up, smiling through tears. "I will."

With a sigh, I closed the door and headed back to the phone to see if Gil had any news.

An hour later, I walked across campus to talk to Wayne and Stuart about Tom's threat. Something didn't click for me with Tom as the killer. Gil had obtained the search warrant, though he said Judge Magda warned against trying again for a hurry-up warrant. They found not only the amethyst geode in the box but a pair of running shoes of the type identified outside the murder scene. The lab found traces of blood on the rock base of the amethyst geode and on the running shoes. Currently, they were testing for Andrew's blood and for any fingerprints on the large crystal extrusion that had probably been used as a handle by the killer. They were also checking to see if the running shoes fit the footprints found outside the french doors. Tom refused to talk, on his lawyer's advice. We would have to turn him loose soon unless the techs came through for us.

At class-change time, the quad teemed with students and faculty hurrying from one building to another. A group of students passed, laughing and teasing. I saw Carl Haskins, half hidden behind a tree. He started yelling when he saw me, drawing everyone's attention.

"Hey, Chief. Is it true you arrested Dean Jamison for McAfee's murder?"

All motion ceased. Everyone in the quad turned to stare. I continued past Haskins at a brisk clip. "That's absolutely false."

"You arrested him at his home. The neighbors saw." He tried to keep up, but fell behind as my longer legs outpaced him.

"We haven't arrested anyone. Your informant is mistaken, Carl." I pulled out my cell phone and dialed Mary. "Have two residence hall security guards pull an extra shift, and put one in new Admin and one in Moller to keep all reporters out. Use a couple of officers until they arrive."

"Hey. Hey." Haskins' voice came from behind me. "You can't throw me out. Public's got a right to know. First Amendment."

I ignored him until I reached Moller and turned at the doors to bar his entrance. "The university is private property. You can't come on these grounds and disrupt things." My morning-shift sergeant, Milo Graf, turned the corner from the parking lot. "Sergeant Graf will escort you off university grounds."

"Hey. Public's got a right to know." Haskins backed away from Milo's advance.

"If you want facts, attend Captain Booth's press conference and stop these ambushes."

Trish Cassell showed up to guard the door as Milo gently but inexorably pulled Haskins away. "Come on, Carl. I'll take you to your car and see you off campus."

Stuart's office was arranged with military precision. Bookcase, filing cabinet, desk, and computer sat at absolute geometric angles to one another. His desk held a tablet at the exact middle point of its width, one fountain pen perfectly parallel to it. A desk calendar sat at a precise right angle to the tablet and pen. On a bookcase stood a photo of him in an army officer's uniform with a chest of medals. The walls were bare except for a vinyl, erasable planning calendar with lettering and figures in a small, neat hand. He could pick up his photo and move out tomorrow, and no one would know he had ever been there. I wondered if he was trying to re-create his old army office. How unhappy he must be surrounded by all these loosey-goosey academics! I could imagine the satisfaction with which he pulled Oldrick's research moneys.

Stuart put the manuscript he was reading in a drawer as I took a chair in front of his desk.

"According to what you and Wayne told Lieutenant Mendez, you were both coming from a meeting down the hall from the *News* offices when you heard Jamison's threat, is that right?"

"It was the Department of Accounting, across the hall from the *News* offices. We attended a meeting on new federal guidelines for grants accounting." He smiled with his mouth only. The slight hint of twang behind his precise words hinted of his birthplace, the Ozarks.

I nodded. "You both left at the same time?"

"I walked out first. He was right behind me. We had other meetings to attend and couldn't afford to stay and chat."

I doubted that Wayne would ever chat with Stuart. Stuart

was too friendless and solitary to rate Wayne's attention, unless he had something Wayne wanted.

"I had just entered the hall when I heard shouting," he continued. "From the *News* offices. Quite naturally, I ran to see what it was. I heard a loud crash. A chair thrown. Something like that. I was in the newsroom by then. I moved toward the office. To see if anyone was hurt."

"Of course." I looked up from my notebook directly into his pale eyes surrounded by stubby fair lashes. "Please tell me exactly what you saw and heard."

"A student in the newsroom looked as startled as I was. The door to the inner office was open. Tom Jamison stood just inside, yelling at Andrew McAfee." He stopped to look up at the ceiling for a second, as if rewinding his memory. "He said, If you hurt Tina, Andrew, I'll shoot you down like the dog you are." He looked at me. "Those might not be his exact words, but they're pretty close."

"There are slight differences in the wording, but you, Wayne, and Duran agree the threat was about Andrew hurting Tina, that he'd shoot him like a dog."

Stuart nodded. "That was difficult to forget."

"Did you see Jamison's face? What did he look like?"

"Just from half profile. Enough to recognize him. His face was red with anger. That's all I can say."

"What did you do after that?"

He shrugged. "I originally thought it an argument among students that I'd break up, but when I saw Tom, I quietly left."

"If it had been students, you'd have broken up the fight, but since a faculty member was involved, you just left?" I sounded cynical.

"It would be embarrassing for Tom to know we'd overheard. I didn't worry that anyone would be physically hurt. . . ."

His voice trailed off. He chopped one hand through the air. "It was a personal argument."

"You didn't feel there was any danger to Andrew?"

He thought for a second. His words were slow and carefully chosen. "Tom's anger was alarming. You don't expect violence from one of your academic colleagues, even if he seems explosive."

"I understand. If you'd heard someone else make that threat, would you take it more seriously than you did?"

"I would, but I know Tom. He's a civilized man. It was unusual to see him verbally aggressive like that. He's normally well spoken."

I scribbled in my notebook and then looked up. "Tell me about Alec Oldrick's research involving Andrew."

Stuart's full lips curved down, and his nostrils flared. "That." His tone dripped distaste.

"I understand you pulled the plug on it."

He rolled his eyes, then schooled his face into impassivity. "Oldrick has the right to research anything he wants. He obtained research funds under false pretenses. He was to gather his information through the Internet with a research assistant to help collate and photocopy."

"Instead, he took Andrew into the city to find subjects?"

"A place like that, full of criminals and perverts." Stuart folded his hands on his desk. "We can't have faculty endangering student employees in that way."

I nodded. "But Oldrick says Andrew and his girlfriend found the place for him."

"I don't believe that," he said slowly. "Even if true, it makes no difference. We have responsibilities to our students."

I glanced at Stuart and chewed the inside of my lip. "Why don't you believe Oldrick when he says that?"

"Because I've seen Andrew's girlfriend, and she certainly didn't look like someone who'd be digging up pornographers and pimps. She's attractive in a very wholesome way. Short red hair. Clean-cut face. I think it unlikely."

I focused on the description of the girlfriend. Oldrick had led me astray. It wasn't Janice Carmo. "Where did you meet her, Stuart? Do you remember her name?"

He shook his head. "I don't know her name. I never met her. I saw her with Andrew in a bar in Girlville. I didn't go over to them. I don't believe in fraternizing with students the way so many faculty do. It just leads to problems."

I smiled. "You're not really faculty, are you?"

He pulled himself erect and glared. "I am a member of the research faculty of this institution, as well as an administrator."

I tried to look properly contrite. "You'll have to excuse me. I'm still new to the academic scene. I thought you had to teach to be faculty."

"Certainly not. We have a number of research faculty who never teach." He gave me his cold smile again to show he held no ill feelings.

"I appreciate the time you've given me." I stood, offering my hand. Instead of shaking it, Stuart took it in his and held it too long. I pulled away from his damp grasp.

"This must keep you busy," he said with another smile that never reached his eyes. "I suppose there's no sense in my asking you to have dinner with me again."

"I'm afraid not. I often don't eat except with colleagues while going over leads."

His smile broadened and touched his eyes at last. "You're a hunter. I understand that. I grew up hunting. An old half-breed taught me how to live off the land. I still go out each season." The smile involved his eyes fully now. "It's in your blood. Cherokee, isn't it? We must hunt together sometime. A group of us hunt deer in the fall."

I grimaced. My relatives in Oklahoma hunted to put food on the table, not for sport. "I don't kill animals when I don't need to."

His smile broadened. "Because you hunt the most dangerous animal." His voice grew husky. His eyes dropped to my bustline.

"What I do is not a sport." My voice was sharp.

He nodded, and his smile disappeared, but his gaze remained on my breasts. "It's an obsession, isn't it?"

I whirled around to walk away. "It's my job, that's all. A very necessary job in today's world."

When I started toward the elevator, he called after me, "Skeet, do have dinner with me sometime."

I just kept walking. I'd run into his type before, intrigued because I was a cop, as if that made me some kind of domina-trix. He was harmless but obnoxious.

While waiting for the elevator, the phone call from Gil came. "It's the murder weapon, all right. The blood on the base is Andrew's. It's been wiped off down there, but the traces were enough for the lab boys." Gil sounded excited. "Guess what? The crystal extrusion held fingerprints. I guess he didn't bother wip-ing that part off."

"Anyone we know, Gil?" I let the elevator come and go since I might have lost the phone signal on it.

"Tom Jamison's. They were on file with the air force. And the shoes match the casts they took of the footprints."

I closed my eyes. Poor Tina. "Take it to the DA, Gil. They'll go for an arrest warrant. Ask Joe for a city uniform and pick Tom up. Take him to city jail and book him."

"We got him. Like you said we would."

I nodded to myself. "We got him, but I want to play out these other leads. It's no good if there's something his lawyer can bring up in court to get him off. We follow them all the way. Give the DA everything we find so he's ready for whatever they try."

"Yeah. I can see them dragging in the kiddie-porn number to say, 'How do you know it wasn't these big criminals?'"

"As soon as I finish with Hamlisch, I'm going over to Tina's. She's found odd things in Andrew's papers. I'll bring them back to the office to go over."

After Gil hung up, I left for New Admin and Wayne's large third-floor office, which was decorated with framed photos of Wayne as a college athlete with other more-famous athletes. His desk was covered with papers that overflowed onto the top of the credenza behind him.

Wayne led me over to the conference table his private office held. "What's this about?"

I accepted a chair. "I'd like you to go over what you heard Tom say again."

"Why?" His tone was suddenly challenging. "I did my duty as a citizen and reported it. That's enough."

I shrugged. "Stuart's been good enough to go over it again with me, so I'll use his testimony." I kept my voice calm and nonconfrontational.

He looked concerned at the prospect of having his version of events replaced by Stuart's and hesitated, as if to formulate what he wanted to say.

I didn't give him a chance. "Instead, answer some questions for me about accounting errors in the athletics-program books."

His eyes bulged like a stunned bull's.

"You were upset about these when they were brought to your attention," I said smoothly. "There was speculation that you might fire or demote one or more of the people involved."

His broad nose flared, and his face swelled and reddened. I wondered if this was what English novels referred to as "apoplexy." "My accountants are professionals. We're audited regularly. My accounts have no irregularities." He leaned across the round table threateningly. "You'd better watch out. You can lose your job for irresponsible talk."

I refused to move back from his looming face. I'd grown up with his type. If you're wrong, bull your way out by anger and intimidation. I'd long since learned to stand and face the Big Charlies of the world.

"You completely deny this?" I made my voice icy.

"You're damn right!"

I shrugged. "I'll bring back the papers showing these errors, and we'll discuss them then." I stood, turning in the process, forcing him to move back across the table to keep his nose from being smacked by my shoulder.

"Papers?" he repeated hesitantly. Then he resumed his aggressive tone. "Bring 'em on. *If* you can find any. You won't. My accountants' books are clean."

At the door, I turned to face him. My smile was deliberately cheerful. "I'll be back."

"Go to hell," he muttered.

My smile grew bigger, and I walked out through his suite, past assistants and secretaries, all of whom ducked their heads as I passed. *He must be hell to work for,* I thought in pity.

The accounts mix-up was more serious than Scott Lampkin

realized. Wayne wouldn't bully and lie about a real error or mix-up. Even if it was his own fault, he'd blame it on vulnerable subordinates. There was more to it. Something that threatened his position.

Andrew sure had a nose for the unsavory. What had he done with the information? Had he been struck down before he could do what he'd planned with it?

My next stop was Tina's. I'd gather Andrew's papers that had surfaced, see if I could figure out what he'd done. No matter what, when I had Scott's reconstructed research, I'd pay another visit to Wayne Hamlisch.

I began to think I wouldn't have this job for long. By the time I finished investigating, I'd have pissed off every administrator on campus. Maybe I'd have to go back to KCPD. But not to an administrative job. I'd return to Homicide, where I belonged.

I walked out into a sunny day that didn't do a thing for my mood. After I left the parking lot, I thought for a second a dark Lexus was following me. Old instincts kicked in. I stayed straight as College Hill turned into Marshall in Girlville, instead of taking the turnoff for my neighborhood. The car followed. As I slowed for a look at the occupant, it turned into the Salerno's Pizza parking lot.

Old habits tripping me up. This wasn't Kansas City. I ran it back in my mind, realized I'd worried because Wayne had a black Lexus. That was all. Picturing that fat bureaucrat tailing me like a hired killer would have made me laugh if my mood had been better. When I turned for my neighborhood, I'd stopped checking to see if any car was following, let alone a dark Lexus.

I brought Andrew's papers back to my office and began to go through them. I sorted them into categories in an hour, glancing at each only long enough to establish its type. I began to wade through each category, one at a time. I thought of people like Stuart dramatizing detective work, as if it's like the TV action shows. He should see me now, wading through papers and details like an accountant or a secretary.

The financial pile showed an interesting pattern. I found two Kansas City bank accounts that didn't include Tina. Andrew had been a big spender. I found evidence that he'd spent time at Kansas City casinos. At the same time as he blew joint-account money on gambling and night spots—those nights Tina thought he was working late—he also deposited regular sums of money in the two Kansas City bank accounts in his name only.

At first, I thought that was where the money from their joint account and credit cards went, but that had gone to casinos. Nothing matched the amounts he'd deposited in Kansas City or the times when he'd made the deposits. This was obviously money from another source. About the same time as the Kansas City accounts were opened, he started to repay the joint account and credit cards. He began repaying Tina as secretly as he'd begun robbing her.

I sorted through the categories painstakingly as the hours slipped past. Every so often, Mary entered to refill my cup with fresh coffee. Part of me noticed, but the bulk of my consciousness was on the trail I followed.

As the day ended, I turned to the last pile. Assorted papers that didn't fit any other category, research notes for Oldrick—these I set aside to go through when my mind was fresher—and Andrew's pocket calendar.

I leaned back in my chair. An orange-magenta sunset beyond the river rippled up through thin layers of pink and rose to purple-blue and charcoal clouds that had moved in while I sat at my desk. Standing and stretching, I moved in front of the window to watch the colors change minute-by-minute.

Mary came in. "It's five forty. I'm going home. Are you done?"

"No. I'm just going to go through his calendar and call it a night." I smiled at her and nodded my head toward the window. "Gorgeous, isn't it?"

She moved for a better view. "Pastor would say it's a visible sign of God's grace."

I looked back out the window. "I don't know much about God's grace, but I can't see anything like that without knowing there's some kind of sense in the world's design. My gran says creation has an order, and only humans are too stupid and self-centered to be blind to it."

Mary laughed. "She and Pastor would see eye to eye on that."

I thought about Gran making cornmeal offerings to the four directions at sunrise or asking permission from the earth before she harvested wild greens and herbs and didn't quite see that meeting of minds.

I turned from the window back to my desk, rolling my stiff shoulders. "Well, I'll continue my search for order in this mess."

I sat down at the desk and reached for the calendar. Once more immersed in Andrew's life, I waved a hand at Mary's good-night and began proceeding day by day from January 1. From the beginning, I noticed entries that didn't make sense: *January 6, midnight, water tower, $300. January 11, biz, $400. January 15, show, $150. February 4, 11:30, RWPark, $300. February 9, biz, $400. February 16, show, $150. March 5, midnight, nature preserve, $300 more. March 6, biz, $400. March 9, 3 $men, $400ea/ mo., calls, set up. March 15, show, $150.* I wrote them in my notebook. The amounts matched those that Andrew had deposited in the Kansas City banks and the dates coordinated.

I checked the week of Andrew's death. He had a *News* editorial staff meeting and an appointment with Mike Berman. Also meetings scheduled in the last two weeks of the month with Jamison, Oldrick, Stuart, and the three vice chancellors. I noted those meetings Andrew hadn't lived long enough to attend and underlined them. I flipped his calendar past the days to come that Andrew would never fill with tasks or meetings. At the back, I found notes, financial transactions.

show	$150
nw	$150
kp	$300
biz	$400
show	$150
nw	$150
kp	$300
biz	$400
show	$150
nw	$200
kp	$300
biz	$400
$$	$400
il	$400
stu	$400

I noted these also. Flipping through the rest of the calendar, I found a small key taped to the inside back cover. Safe deposit box, I'd bet. We'd have to identify the bank and get Tina's consent to open it. All this looked like blackmail, the first thing to make sense in this snarled mess. If Andrew had blackmailed six people, that answered many questions—and why he'd been killed.

I put the remaining papers in my briefcase, grabbed my jacket, and headed for the car. This would take a peaceful night with jazz on the stereo and time to knit and puzzle the whole thing out. I had only pieces, but I'd finally found a loose thread that might unravel the whole tangle.

CHAPTER 8

The darkest clouds had conquered the sunset by the time I left. A chill drizzle fell in sheets. My mind picked at the strands of the case as I hurried to the car. I was driving down College Hill toward town when my headlights picked up the form of Brian walking on the side of the road. He turned back toward the lights before moving farther off the roadway.

I stopped beside him, rolling down my window. "Need a ride?"

He nodded and got in, hunching down in the seat, wet and cold, looking upset.

I turned the heater up and started driving again. "It'll warm up fast. Doesn't your mom usually pick you up?"

He nodded glumly. "Always. If she can't, she calls me." He pulled out a cell phone. "That's why she got me this."

"She didn't call this time?" I felt a little prick at the back of my mind. Tina'd struck me as a devoted mother.

"You don't think she's had a wreck and is hurt, do you?" He turned his face up to me anxiously.

I shook my head and pasted on a smile. "Don't invent

problems. She's probably at the jail visiting your dad. I know she was going there earlier." A lot earlier, I remembered.

"Him. Of course." His voice was full of scorn. "Figures. She goes to the creep who dumped us and leaves me out in the rain."

"You're not worried about your father facing murder charges?"

He shrugged impatiently. "If he killed Andrew, he deserves it. I wouldn't put it past him. Just because he couldn't stand to see us happy."

My eyebrows rose in surprise. "I didn't think you liked Andrew that much."

Brian's shrug this time was more hesitant. "We got along okay. He made Mom happy. Things were bad after my dad threw us away. I didn't think Mom would ever recover. But Andrew came, and things were good again. Now, he's dead. Dad's in jail. Mom forgot me. . . ." He stopped. "It's crap. That's all." He sank back in dejected silence.

I decided to change the subject. "Why are you on the Hill?"

"Private lessons with Professor Garton." His face lifted.

"Garton? Isn't he in music?"

"He teaches me music theory and composition."

"You're a composer? All this time with you taking care of Lady, and I didn't know that?"

Brian blushed. "I'm not a real composer. I'd like to be some-day. I play the flute. I'm pretty good, but composing's what I really love." He hesitated a second, then confided, "Professor G. thinks I have a shot at a scholarship to Juilliard."

I made an impressed face. "Would you like that? Juilliard?"

"It's my dream, but my dad wants me in business or some more-academic subject."

"He doesn't think music at that level is academic?" I asked, incredulous.

Brian laughed bitterly. "He doesn't think music at any level is academic. He doesn't count English or French, either. Not for me."

"Are those also strong subjects of yours?"

"Yeah. He wants me to focus on business or law. Something like that."

I nodded in sympathy. "Mine's like that. Not an academic, but the same kind of attitude. It's tough when you're a kid, but it gets better as you get older."

Really? I asked myself. *Who are you kidding?*

He looked up at me with interest. "Did your dad not want you to be a cop?"

"No, and he was one all his life." I turned onto Ash and headed the last three blocks to home.

"Why didn't he want you to be one? My dad wants me to be a clone of him. As if!"

I grinned at his loud disdain. "Because I was a girl. He doesn't think women belong in police work."

Brian laughed in surprise. "You're kidding. I didn't think anyone thought like that anymore."

I laughed with him. "You'd be surprised. Many men—and even women—still think women shouldn't do certain things."

Brian shook his head in disbelief. I had an urge to ruffle his sandy hair—the way Big Charlie used to do when he was pleased with the little kid I had been. I turned my attention to the road. Soon, I passed my house and headed for Brian's, two houses down.

"It's okay," he said. "You can park at your house. I can walk home."

"I want to be sure you get there safely. Police blood, re-member?" I grinned at him again. I liked this kid. Too bad his family was such a mess.

As I parked in front of Tina's neat bungalow, my inner alarms started to blare. Brian grabbed the door.

"Hold it, Bri. Something's wrong here." I reached out to remove his hand from the handle.

"What?" He looked around frantically.

"Isn't that your mom's car?"

He nodded. Then his posture stiffened. "So why didn't she pick me up?"

"It's after dark. If she's there, why no lights?" I picked up the radio mike.

"Maybe she's hurt. We need to help her." He reached for the door again.

"No!" I used my command voice. Peering through the dark, I finally saw what I feared.

"Why not?" he cried.

"Your front door's ajar. I think we've got a break-in. The burglar could still be in there."

I called in on my radio and explained the situation. "I'm going in to check it out," I finished. "The boy will be in my car parked in front. Get me some backup."

"Sending them out now, Chief." The dispatcher's tinny voice paused. "By the way, Joe Louzon called. Tom Jamison hung himself."

Next to me, I heard Brian catch his breath. He might dislike Tom, but Tom was still his father. I knew how that went.

"His son's in the car," I warned Dispatch. "Just send backup."

I turned to Brian. "Are you okay?"

His eyes were big with shock and fear. "We can't do anything about him. Save Mom."

I stared straight at him. "Stay in this car with the doors locked. I'll check out the place and look for your mom. Whoever broke in could still be in there. I don't need you in his path so he can grab you for a hostage. Understand?"

He nodded soberly. I couldn't blame him for being frightened. I smiled reassuringly. "It'll be okay. Just stay locked in the car until I tell you."

I picked up my big flashlight before leaving. I listened for Brian to click the door locks behind me. Finally, I headed for the dark house, where the door hung slightly open. I pulled my Glock and shoved the door open wide, moving to the side of the jamb as I did.

I heard nothing. I clicked on the flashlight and beamed it into the room's darkness, then moved carefully through the doorway. The flashlight's beam bounced around the room, making it clear that someone had systematically trashed it. It looked worse than a regular burglary.

Looking for something? I wondered. Like the papers Tina gave me earlier? Or the blackmail proof Andrew must have kept somewhere? He had to have proof to make his victims pay. His word wouldn't be enough.

I checked the wall for the switch and flicked on the overhead light. I headed to the dining room, finding more damage. I didn't like this. Avoiding broken china and glass, I moved toward the kitchen.

Several steps before the door, it hit me—the strong, coppery smell of blood. I'd smelled it too many times in my life to mistake it. I pulled back the hand with which I'd been about to switch on the dining-room lights. Again, I grew still and listened. No sound.

I swung around into the kitchen so I'd be standing with my back to the wall. The ricochet of the flashlight beam briefly illuminated Tina's slumped body before it hit the sink full of dishes and the window wall beyond. Swinging the beam around the room to make sure I was alone, I flicked on the light and trudged to the table that supported Tina's bloody head. She had no pulse. She'd been tied to a chair and shot in the right temple.

I never quite got used to violent death, no matter how many times I encountered it, the smell of blood and body wastes, the empty, glaring look of the eyes, my outrage at the violation of another human being. I thought I'd put this behind me when I left the city. I'd just talked to Tina. She'd been grieving for Andrew, angry at Tom's arrest, proud of and concerned about Brian. It shouldn't be so damn easy to wipe out all that life.

I moved around the table, looking at the ropes carefully without touching anything. He tied her up for a reason. If he just unexpectedly encountered her, he'd shoot her but wouldn't tie her up. He wanted something—the same thing he searched for. Probably the papers Tina gave me that morning. Or something else Andrew had that he didn't keep at home.

He tied her up, probably threatened her to make her tell, with no intention of leaving her alive. Either she told him what he wanted or he decided she really didn't know anything. Then, he shot her. The scene's cold-bloodedness sent a shiver down my back. Everything so deliberate.

He used either a silencer or a mouse gun. Otherwise, the neighbors would hear. This wasn't like my old KC neighborhood where everyone was used to hearing gunshots. The sound would be noticed. *Have to canvass the neighbors, see if anyone heard. I'd bet not.*

This guy didn't take those kinds of chances. A whole different picture from Andrew's death, but the same care to avoid discovery. Unless someone else killed Andrew, and this was a new player looking for what Andrew had held over his head. I shook my head at the thought. How many people did Andrew blackmail? Would they all come out of the woodwork to kill, trying to get their hands on the evidence against them? Or was this all the handiwork of one determined person?

I heard sirens and turned toward the front of the house. It would all begin again now, the collection of evidence, the examination of the body, too many people hanging around and getting in the way, hoping to find something that would catch the killer. Turning back through the kitchen, I examined the back door, noticing the clean glasses on the drainboard as I passed. The counter was clear, but the space under the cupboards was packed full with mug racks, canisters, and small appliances. Just as the walls were covered with hanging utensils and tools. The kitchen was as crowded as the rest of the house. I recognized from my own life the signs of divorce, contents of a large house crammed into one much smaller.

Suddenly, I heard running steps and a shout behind me. I spun, raising my gun, only to find myself aiming it at a white-faced Brian. He'd stopped in the kitchen doorway, eyes wide in horror, mouth working as if to scream. Shakily holstering the gun, I hurried to him, blocking the view of his mother. Trish and Stan pelted into the room behind him.

"Sorry, Chief. He just ran into the house when we pulled up. We couldn't catch him in time." Stan glared at Brian.

"It's okay," I said. "Trish, secure the perimeter. Stan, I

haven't gone upstairs yet. Brian and I will go out and radio for evidence techs and the coroner." Motioning them off, I put my arm around Brian's shoulders. "Let's go sit down in the car."

I nudged him toward the door, but he stiffened and stared up at me. "Is she dead?" he asked hoarsely.

I nodded. "It's not something she'd want you to see, Bri. When you see someone's body, every time you remember them, that's what you see. Your mom wouldn't want to be remembered this way. She'd want you able to remember the good times when she was laughing and smiling."

"What did he do to her?" His voice sounded old.

"He shot her." I started to move him out of the doorway. "It was probably quick."

I hoped. Probably not, I knew, but he didn't need to.

"He tied her up. Why?"

I wasn't surprised at the detail he'd seen in such a short time. The whole scene was probably burned into his brain and would come back to haunt him again and again.

"Let's get you out of here. You've had a shock. You need to sit down."

Once again he resisted. "I need to know what that creep did to my mother." Tears finally snaked down his cheeks.

Taking a deep breath, I decided truth might be better than grim imaginings. "He tied her up and shot her. That's it."

He stared up at me in outrage and grief. I began to steer him out of the room. This time he allowed it. I maneuvered him through the front of the house and toward the car in silence, wondering whom I could call for him with his father gone. What would happen when he had to come to grips with that?

When we reached the car, I opened the passenger door. "Get in and sit down. I've got to talk to my dispatcher."

I went around to the driver's side, pulled out the radio,

and called in. I told the dispatcher to notify Joe and send Gil, the coroner, and county evidence techs. Sliding into my seat, I put away the radio. "Are you okay, Bri?"

He stared at me without speaking. *Of course, he's not,* I thought. *What a stupid thing to ask!*

"I'll stay with you until we get someone to take care of you. Have you got relatives anywhere close? I know you don't have any in town."

He shook his head. "No, my dad doesn't—didn't have any family, and my mom's only relative is a sister in California." His eyes widened. "Oh, no. I'll have to tell her. And what about the funeral? And . . ."

He broke off in tears. I held his head against my shoulder. I could feel his thin shoulders shaking with the violence of his grief. "It's all right. You don't have to do any of that, Bri."

I suspected not much would be all right again for this kid with his family destroyed by violence. I smoothed down his hair. He stopped crying as suddenly as he'd begun. Sitting up and wiping his eyes, he sniffed and coughed once.

"I could call Annette again. Maybe she could take you back to her house."

"Couldn't I stay with you?" he asked anxiously. "I won't get in the way."

I smiled at him and felt that strange urge to ruffle his hair again. "I don't think you would, but pretty soon we'll have a lot of officers here. We'll be working late. It's best if I find someplace for you to go."

He nodded with a bleak look. I pulled my phone out of its cradle and dialed Annette's home number. When I got her answering machine, I remembered she was attending a play at the university. I replaced the phone with a curse under my breath. "Is there anyone else you'd like?"

He shook his head. "Just you. Haven't you got room?"

"Sure, but I don't want you left alone. I can't stay with you. Maybe your minister?"

"We didn't go to church."

In desperation, I called Karen at home, and she answered on the third ring. "Could you come to my house? I've got Brian Jamison here. We've just found his mother dead. I've got an investigation, and he doesn't have anyone to take care of him. He wants to stay at my house. I don't want him to be alone."

"Of course," Karen said. I felt that sense of relief that she so often gave me. "I'll leave now. Be there in about ten minutes. I can stay with him until you get home. Poor kid."

Karen would know the right things to do for Brian and the right things to say. "That's great. Meet us in front of the house."

I turned to Brian. "You know Karen Wise of Forgotten Arts? She lives just outside town. She'll stay with you at my place until I get finished here. You'll sleep in my guest room. I'll probably get in late."

Brian nodded. "I probably won't sleep." He looked down and then back up at me. "Thanks, Skeet. I just don't want to stay with strangers right now."

I gave him a quick hug, wondering at a family so isolated that a neighbor was the only resort short of strangers.

Next morning, after too little sleep, I dragged myself out of bed and into the shower. Standing in the pounding hot water, I saw Brian's face when Joe came with me after midnight to tell Brian about his dad. I'd offered to do it, but Joe insisted on facing Brian, blaming himself for Tom's death.

Tom had left an incoherent note. He'd confessed to embezzlement, which Andrew had used to blackmail him. He'd hanged himself with a sheet. The guard might have found him in time, but the ambulance and EMTs had arrived too late to save him. I silently cursed Sheriff Dick Wold.

Brian stared at Joe. "Did he kill Andrew, after all? And if he did, who killed my mother?"

Joe said we'd cooperate to find out. He left me a boy with too much grief and too many questions to sleep. Thank God for Lady and Wilma. They kept to Brian's side like shadows, piling on him whenever he sat or lay down. He clung to them like furry life rafts. When I finally got him to bed, he jerked upright, crying that Andrew's funeral was the next day and how would he get clothes from his house.

I promised to take him to Walmart for underwear, slacks, and a shirt in the morning, telling him no one would expect a boy to wear a suit. I had no idea if that was true or not. I thought at least no one would say anything to him about it. If they did, I'd just slug them.

Still weary, I toweled off and dressed in the bathroom steam. I had a teenage boy sleeping upstairs and didn't feel right walking around in just a bathrobe. He'd be better off with al-most any other woman, who'd know what she was doing with a kid.

Carrying pajamas, robe, and slippers, wet hair wrapped in a towel, I stepped out, heading for my bedroom to dry my hair. The doorbell shocked me in the early-morning quiet. Dropping my clothes, I ran to get it before it rang again and woke Brian. I looked out the pane of glass in the front door to see Karen, Annette, and Miryam with bags and drink carriers. I let them in without a word.

"I stopped by the coffee shop to tell them about last night," Karen said, heading for the back of the house.

"You and Brian could probably use breakfast," Miryam added.

"God knows you probably don't have anything decent in your fridge or cupboards to eat." Karen's voice came from the kitchen.

Annette stopped as I closed the door. "If we're intruding, just tell us. We thought it'd be easier for both of you if we brought something, but that doesn't mean it necessarily is." She smiled and winked. "I know that, if none of the others do."

I laughed. "Karen's right. I don't have food for a teenage boy. Probably not even for a thirty-five-year-old woman."

We headed back to the kitchen after the others. Miryam set the table while Karen put butter, milk, and orange juice in my refrigerator. "Look at this! Two containers of whipped cream but no milk."

"I'll bet Brian likes whipped cream better than milk, just the way I do," I said defensively.

"This bag has cereal and sandwich bread." Annette set it on the counter.

"Ham and turkey." Karen put the same in the refrigerator. "That way you'll have something to eat when we're gone."

I sank into a chair. "Thanks, guys. I have no idea what I'm doing with a kid in the house."

Miryam dragged an extra chair from the dining room. We passed around muffins, bagels, and cups of coffee and herbal tea.

"How is he?" Karen asked.

"Still asleep. He couldn't get to sleep for a long time last night." I popped the lid on my coffee and drank greedily.

"No surprise there," muttered Annette.

"He's got Wilma and Lady with him. They know something's wrong, and they won't leave him." I stared away for a second, reliving the late hours of the night.

"Animals are very sensitive," Miryam said as she licked icing from her finger. "They have powers to comfort afflictions and heal emotional hurts. They're great souls who've chosen their current forms in order to serve humanity."

Annette rolled her eyes. "They're females. They think he's their kitten or puppy. Females of all species respond to pain in the young. Look at us."

"I'm glad they've given him some comfort. I'm not very good at that." I grimaced. "I'm not a real womanly, motherly sort of woman."

Everyone laughed.

"Brian sees something special in you," Karen said. "That's why he insists on staying with you. Don't sell yourself short, Skeet. You're more than what Charlie tried to make of you."

"What happens now? Did the guy who killed Andrew kill Tina? What about Tom? I thought he killed Andrew. His suicide sure makes him look guilty." Miryam pouted prettily. "I'm confused."

Annette snickered. "You're always confused."

"And you're mean in the morning until you have your coffee," Miryam replied serenely. "Caffeine is a drug."

I smiled. "I appreciate your help, guys, but I really can't discuss the case with you."

"Of course," said Annette eagerly. "But we can discuss it with you and tell you anything we know or find out."

Miryam beamed happily. "We'll be assistant detectives."

"Absolutely not." I made my voice as firm as I could when I felt like laughing. "I appreciate your offer to help. Whoever killed Tina is vicious and ruthless. I can't allow you to get involved with this investigation. I really don't need you running around trying to detect behind my back, either." I smiled to soften my words. "This is serious, not make-believe. You have no idea—"

"Do you think he tied her up to torture her?" Miryam asked with suppressed excitement.

"No. Probably to threaten." How did she know Tina had been tied up?

"How long do you think she was tied up while he searched?" Annette asked. "That shows real nerve. What if a neighbor had come to the door?"

My head started to spin. "How do you guys know details of the crime scene?"

Miryam smiled. "Carolyn's niece is married to one of the county guys."

"My next-door neighbor's son-in-law is a morgue attendant who made the run with Sid Ambrose," Annette added.

"It's not like Kansas City," Karen said. "You can't keep anything quiet around here. I know you're right. This person is too dangerous for us. People will still speculate."

I put my hand up to run it through my hair, only to knock off my towel turban. "Hell."

Karen picked up the towel and handed it to me. "How many other people were blackmailed by Andrew?"

I just stared.

"The suicide note at the jail said Andrew was blackmailing Tom," Miryam explained.

"Don't tell me. Someone's related to or neighbors with a guard at the jail." I looked around the room for deliverance. "How do cops out here ever solve anything if they're so busy blabbing to everyone in town?" I froze for a second. "Oh, shit. The news media will have it if you guys do. I've got to warn Frank and the chancellor." I ran out of the room for the phone.

Behind me, I heard Miryam's plaintive cry: "I think Skeet's a little upset."

"No kidding," Annette answered in a dry voice.

I called Frank's house first. "Have the media come after you with details from the crime scene last night? And Tom's suicide?" I asked abruptly when he answered.

"They've tried, but I just tell them I'll give a briefing later this morning. What's going on?"

"I just found out that some county and city guys have been shooting their mouths off with details all over town."

He sighed. "That's small-town life for you, Skeet. Nothing stays secret."

"Tell me our guys have been quiet about it."

"Sure, but the only ones of our guys who've been at the actual scenes were you and Gil."

I took a deep breath to calm myself. "Okay. I wanted to warn you that the media probably have a lot of details."

"I don't have to confirm or deny any of them."

"I'll call Joe and Dick Wold and ask them to gag their guys," I said.

"They can try. Will you be in the office today? Mike Berman left a message with the office after you left last night that he's bringing over the stuff from payroll you wanted."

"Probably not until later. I've got the funeral for Andrew in the morning, and in the afternoon I've got Tina's autopsy. I want you to meet me at Dick Wold's office. We're going to have to ask him for some help. Mike's stuff is for my interview with Scheuer. If he actually makes it. It can wait."

"The lab guys called, too." His voice was strained. "The murder shoes . . . And those shoes were the murder shoes. They confirmed that. Going through the inventory of his house, his were all longer. They went to the jail to make sure. Only . . ."

"Only he was already dead." I tried to restrain the rage welling up inside me. "He was framed, and we fell for it. Now he's dead."

Frank was silent for a minute. "It wasn't your fault. It wasn't our fault. The fool killed himself, dammit."

Now it was my turn to be silent. If I opened my mouth I'd scream and curse, and that was no way to act in front of one of my men. I had to gain control of myself. I'd erupt later, sometime later. Finally, I spoke in a cold, calm voice. "Someone knew about those fingerprints on the geode and set Tom up. We have to go back and find out who."

"I'll see you this afternoon then."

I hung up, wondering at his calm acceptance. After a moment, I stuffed my guilt and rage over Tom's death deep inside and focused on the leaks. Before I could talk myself out of it, I dialed the chancellor's home. "We've got one dean dead with a suicide note admitting embezzlement and blackmail, one widow and ex-wife murdered." I decided to hit him with everything in one big dump, hoping to shock him enough to keep him from blowing up. "The media will have that from the personnel at the jail and hospital. I've found evidence of McAfee's blackmail that indicates at least seven victims on campus. That, the media should not have. I have to track these down before they blow up in our face. Before we have another killing."

"Oh my God," he moaned. "How will our capital campaign survive this?"

"Chancellor, I'm going to ask the sheriff for help from his

investigators. If we don't get this dealt with, you're going to be asking how will the college ever survive."

There was a long silence on the other line. Finally, he said, "Do what you have to do."

I hung up to find Karen and the others leaving the kitchen, pulling on wraps.

"We've put everything away, Skeet," Annette said.

"What is all this?" Brian appeared, bleary-eyed, at the bottom of the stairs, Lady and Wilma like two escorts at his sides.

"Friends just brought us some food. They're heading out now."

Karen gave me a hug and started for the door. Annette walked over to Brian and hugged him, though he stood stiff as a stick. "I'm going to the funeral. Do you want a ride?"

"Skeet'll take me." He looked at her, puzzled. "I didn't know you were friends with Andrew."

She shrugged. "I wasn't. I figure it's the least I can do for Tina."

Brian's face softened. "Thanks, Annette."

She hugged him again and headed for the door, where the others waited.

"Food's in the kitchen. Go help yourself." I gestured with my head, and he stumbled sleepily along. I turned to warn my friends one last time. "No messing in this, guys. It's dangerous. Could get you killed. I'm asking for your promise."

Miryam and Annette looked solemn. "Okay," Annette said as she left.

"Skeet, I know I could help—" began Miryam.

"Promise her," Karen said in a voice of iron.

"I promise," Miryam said plaintively. "You don't have to worry about me." She slipped out the door.

"Thanks." I hugged Karen.

"Just keep yourself safe. That's the promise I want."

"Always. I'm a good cop. First thing we do is protect ourselves. Can't help anyone else if we're down." We hugged again, and Karen left.

I walked back to the kitchen. "Did you find everything all right?"

Brian nodded, his mouth full of muffin.

I smiled. "Think I'll go back to my room to finish getting ready. They interrupted me."

He swallowed quickly. "Skeet, can I ask something?"

"What?" I took a chair so he wouldn't feel rushed.

He choked a little, swallowing again, and looked down, then back up at me. "He tied her up. Was he trying to get her to tell him something?"

I sighed and looked straight into his eyes. "Most likely."

"Did he . . . did he hurt her?"

I shook my head. "No sign of anything like that."

I could see he was holding back a flood of tears. I wanted to tell him not to think about it. But Brian was made of stronger stuff than that. He needed to face things straight-on.

"He wanted information. He probably threatened her, trying to get her to tell him." I watched his face to see if he understood. "Probably Andrew's papers that she gave me."

He stared at me.

"Think about it. A little woman who's always lived a peaceful life. Nine out of ten people will tell what's wanted right away. There's nothing wrong with that. It's only in books that people hold out when their lives are threatened. But he didn't come to my house, searching, even though it's so close."

He looked down at the floor until I lifted his face to look into mine. "Think about it, Bri. Tell me what that means."

130

He stared wildly at me. Then understanding crossed his face. "She didn't tell."

I nodded. "Your mother was a brave woman."

He nodded. "She must have been."

I thought of the soft-spoken, frail woman I'd talked to earlier. "You remember that when you think of her dying. Remember she was a really brave woman. I sure will."

Brian's face lifted, as a few soft tears traced his cheeks. He wiped them and took a drink of milk. The exchange seemed to have satisfied his need for information. He took another huge bite of muffin and broke off a piece for Lady, who sat at his feet.

I headed for my bedroom. Chances were that Tina just hadn't known the information the killer wanted. Probably Andrew's proof stash. Brian didn't have to know that. Let him have something to hold on to while his world fell apart around him. Besides, for all I knew, Tina did hold out, tried to keep from giving him my name. My whole body tensed at the thought.

I put on my Homicide loafers. No time for high heels. I had a killer to catch.

CHAPTER 9

Yesterday's clouds and off-and-on rain had disappeared into a bright sunny day. Parking in the cemetery with Brian beside me, I couldn't wait for this spring to end with its roller coaster of weather. Spring had always been my favorite season. Before.

We left the car and hiked over to the canopied grave site. I appreciated my loafers on the still-mushy ground, even if they weren't ideal funeral wear. The number of people surprised me. I supposed not many would bother coming to Andrew's funeral.

The funeral director seated us in the front chairs since Brian was Andrew's only kin. I wondered at all these people with no family. I had only too much. Not only Charlie but the Oklahoma family—Gran, Mom, my half brother and half sister. Not to mention the aunts and cousins. I often wished I could be alone in the world. Sitting in the family seats for Andrew McAfee because there was no one else made me wonder if I truly wanted that.

Jeremy Coulter looked elegant, sloppy Wayne Hamlisch beside him. Usually the funeral of a student didn't merit the attendance of two vice chancellors. I assumed the chancellor wanted them there. Stuart Morley and Alec Oldrick glared at each other over the grave. I could understand their presence. Andrew had been Oldrick's research assistant, and Stuart certainly seemed to have had Andrew's welfare at heart when he ended Oldrick's research.

To my surprise, Miryam came with Annette. She wore black chiffon and should have looked completely out of place. Instead, she managed to look like a fragile Hollywood widow. Some media types attended and television crews that Joe's men were keeping at a distance. I bet myself one of them would interview Miryam as next of kin.

My secretary, Mary, stood with Annette and Miryam. Mary and Tina had been work friends. The head of the university's media-relations department and Frank were present, which made sense, given the media. Gil and Joe Louzon stood off to one side in the back, scanning the mourners as carefully as I was.

A couple of students stood awkwardly to the left. I wondered if they were *News* staff or some of the friends he'd partied with. One girl wore a garden-party hat and cried on the shoulder of one of the boys.

As the minister droned, I looked beyond the cemetery to the abandoned railroad spur ending at the old Eichorn place and the wildlife sanctuary behind it. Derelicts sometimes rode the trains into town and walked the tracks to the deserted house. They camped out in its backyard, overlooked only by the sanctuary's animals. In bad weather, they moved into the house to keep drier, though its walls and roof were no longer whole. Periodically, Joe cleaned them out. The campus and town wanted to believe the murders were the work of one of those hapless guys.

Now, trees leafed out, and ancient daffodils peeped through

grass and weeds already overgrown in front of the ramshackle house. It had a kind of charm in this spring light.

My eyes flew to the wildlife sanctuary and relieved my thoughts from the week's bleak deaths. Something about wild places always made me breathe easier and loosened a tight loop around my chest I usually never noticed. Gran would have said it was because of the Cherokee in me. She always said stuff like that. Trouble was, she was usually right.

I hoped Brian was looking that way. He sat quietly beside me. His tears had all been for his mother. They were cried out now. I patted his hand as we stood for the final prayer, and he gave me a grateful look.

Finally, the minister finished. People came to Brian to offer condolences. I remained by his side. He might need me if some fool said the wrong thing, and I'd guard against any reporters who got past Frank.

Joe joined me. A frown crossed Stuart's face. Ignoring him, I smiled at Joe.

"How are you guys doing?" he asked. He offered his hand to Brian, who shook it loosely.

"It's hard," Brian said. "I don't know what I'd do if Skeet hadn't taken me in."

"Plenty of folks would be happy to have you. It's no big deal." I gave him a little hug. His face was so bleak.

"Brian would rather not have them," Joe said. "Right?"

Brian nodded, looking wretched.

Joe smiled. "Kids know where they'll do best. I think you made the right decision."

A woman who'd worked with Tina took Brian's hand, cooing consolation, and he turned to face her.

"How are you holding up?" Joe asked in a quiet voice.

I shrugged. "He's a good kid. His mother had a sister in Hollywood. I called the department out there to have LAPD notify her of Tina's death and tell her to contact me about Brian."

Joe gave me a pained look. "He's all alone except for her?"

"Mother and stepfather murdered. Dad a suicide. There's no one else." I shook my head. "I never saw such a family for having no living relatives. Why didn't someone make plans for this kid? When you know you haven't got family to take him in, you ought to do that."

"Too many folks think they'll never die, or at least not any time soon." He looked over at Brian. "I'll bet Tom had life insurance and such for Brian."

"I'd better have Marsh Corgill go through Tom's papers and start the estate ball rolling for Brian—and his aunt when she comes." I closed my eyes at the thought.

"You need a break from this. So does he." Joe gestured to Brian, who was greeting the university people.

"I need a break in the case, but Brian needs a break from it." I worried about the lines that had formed overnight between the kid's eyebrows. He was only fourteen.

"What are you planning day after tomorrow? It's Saturday, remember?"

"I may go into Kansas City to check on my dad and talk to an old friend from Homicide about an aspect of this that leads into the city."

His face grew serious. "An aspect we're not going to mention with everybody around us?"

I nodded. "Brief you later."

"Marquitta. How are you holding up?" Finished with Brian, Jeremy now stood before me.

"Fine. Making progress." I gave him a tired smile.

"You certainly showed the chancellor what you were made of. You had the murderer in jail in two days. I call that fine work." His smile was brilliant.

Wayne appeared at his shoulder, sullen as ever. "Let's head back. I've got work to do."

Jeremy lifted his hands in a graceful, apologetic motion. "We rode over together. Duty calls. Take care. You, too, Joe."

"He seems ready enough to name one of his colleagues a murderer," Joe said.

"To him—and the chancellor—if Tom killed Andrew, it's over. The media heat's off the university. Tina was killed in town." I shook my head. "Wait till they find out the media's boiling over. Those reporters are smart enough to figure out these murders are connected."

"Skeet, how are you holding up?" asked Stuart.

If I heard the question one more time, I'd . . . I wouldn't be holding up very well. "Just fine, Stuart." I forced a smile. It wasn't his fault everyone else came up with the line first.

I turned to Joe. "Do you two know each other? Joe Louzon, Stuart Morley."

"I don't believe we've met," Joe said, holding out his hand.

Stuart hesitated almost imperceptibly, then shook hands. "I've heard of you, Chief."

The two men chatted politely as Carl Haskins approached.

"No, Carl," I said before he could speak. "Don't you go near the boy."

"Hey." Carl lifted his hands in a show of offended innocence. "Just want to see if he'll talk to me later. I wouldn't interview him here."

"Not with me around, you won't. He won't talk to anyone now or later. Keep moving."

"Hey. Just doing my job." He glared.

I frowned back at him. "Move on." He backed away, heading for the cluster of reporters surrounding Frank.

Turning back, I found Joe and Stuart deep in conversation.

"I've haven't had a chance to go out in deer season the last few years," Joe said. "I usually spend my time off with my kid. I miss tramping through the woods in the fall."

Stuart nodded and smiled. The smile involved his eyes and actually made his face pleasant. "I wouldn't miss it. Takes me back to my roots. You ought to try to join us this year." He looked over at me. "I've already asked Skeet."

Joe looked wistful. "I wish. I don't really spend enough time with Julie now."

"Is that your little girl's name? Pretty name." Stuart had relaxed and looked so genuine that for a moment I almost forgot who he was. "Speaking of girls' names, Skeet, did you get the name of Andrew's girlfriend?"

I tilted my head. "No, I haven't been able to find her."

"She's here. Over there." He pointed to where the group of students had been, now all vanished. "I guess she left already. She was wearing a big awful hat. Gaudy."

"Get away!" Brian's voice was high with anger and fright.

Turning, I saw Alec Oldrick holding out his hand to the boy. I moved forward to block them from the reporters. "What's wrong, Brian?"

"He's Oldrick." He turned with raw appeal on his face. "I told you. Andrew warned me about him."

Oldrick looked embarrassed. "I only wanted to offer my

condolences." He stepped closer to Brian. "I was a friend of Andrew's. We got along quite well."

"Why did he tell me to stay away from you, that he didn't ever want you to get your hands on me?" Brian moved away from him to stand partially behind me. "He knew something bad about you. Maybe you killed him and my mom." He sobbed and shook with fear and anger.

Oldrick's big voice sounded almost as young as Brian's. "I swear—"

I interrupted him. "Go on back to campus for now. I'll take care of Brian."

Brian leaned against my shoulder. "Can we go home now?"

"Yes, Bri." I put my arm about him, and Joe took his other side, so the curious crowd could hardly see him. Between us, we walked him to my car, where we put Brian inside, both still blocking any camera. Joe stayed outside Brian's door while I hurried around and got in.

"Looks like we've got a lot to catch up on," he said.

Brian had calmed at the sight of the car. "I'm sorry. It's just . . ."

"You were thinking about what Andrew said." I patted his hand.

"Saturday, why don't we both go to Kansas City and take Brian and Julie with us? I can take them to a movie or the museum. Someplace fun. While you talk with your detective buddies. Then we'll have a nice dinner and come back. It'll give both of you a break from all this." Joe leaned into Brian's window to ask, "How does that sound?"

Brian nodded. "I'd like to get out of town for a day. If it's okay with Skeet."

He looked at me as if I were his only solid ground in a

world turned to swamp. I felt my heart turn over sickeningly. What could I possibly do with or for this kid?

"Sounds like fun," I said, faking a smile. "I've got to make the trip anyway."

"I'll call to set the time and where the kids would like to go. Be thinking about that, Brian, okay?" Joe slapped his hand against the side of the car as if it were the side of a horse, and I took off.

After a few silent minutes, Brian looked over at me. "I'm sorry I lost it. It was stupid to think he'd try anything with all those people around. For sure not with you there. I just thought, What if he thinks I know where the papers are?"

At his words, I felt fear invade my core. What if the killer did think that about Brian? Where could I put him and know he'd be safe against such a ruthless adversary?

I drove straight to Forgotten Arts, Karen's shop on the town square. She had agreed to keep Brian in her back office for me. Suddenly, I didn't want to leave him at home with just Lady and Wilma.

In the front window stood an ornate Saxony spinning wheel, draped with color-drenched hanks of hand-dyed yarns. More skeins of yarn were piled on the floor. A small frame loom leaned against the wall, displaying a half-finished tapestry of silvery river, flaming autumn hills, and thunderous sky. A bell hanging on hand-spun red wool tinkled as I pushed the door open.

Karen sat at an upright spinning wheel, turning a fluffy mass of teal-green mohair into yarn. "There you are." She stopped the wheel and wound a length of unspun mohair over the top peg to keep it from unspinning when she let loose of it.

Woven and knitted samples hung on racks of knitting and

weaving yarns throughout the store. Toward the back, floor-to-ceiling shelf units held a rainbow of weaving yarns.

I tore my eyes from the highly colored and textured display. "Thanks for keeping Brian."

Karen smiled warmly at us. "You can use my office in back, Brian. Read or do homework."

"Or play video games?" His grin was sheepish.

"What does Skeet say?" Karen looked my way.

"Just for today." I loved that grin. Things were so dark for this kid. If a few hours of video games could restore that smile, I was all for it. That probably made me a bad guardian. I didn't care. I wanted to see the haunted look leave his eyes for a while. "Tomorrow, back to the books."

He nodded. "Sure thing."

Karen laughed. "Back through that door. Watch out for the cat, though. Kelly rescued her from the streets. She's still feral, with very pointy claws." Kelly worked in the store part-time. "There's soda in the refrigerator if you're thirsty."

Brian hurried in the direction she pointed.

"This'll keep him out of sight." I sighed heavily and looked around at Karen's fiber goodies. "I don't know what I'm doing with him, but would the foster system protect him any better?"

"He's doing remarkably well. A major reason is that he has you in his life." Karen separated a strip of teal mohair from a big coil of combed fiber. Unhooking the yarn coming out of the wheel's orifice, she laid the ends of her unspun mohair over the loose ends of the yarn. Her foot tapped the treadle, and she waited for the twist from the yarn to catch the unspun fiber before pulling it out from the wheel, rolling out thick spots in the yarn with her free hand. I loved to watch her spin. The magic never grew old.

I looked around the shop, warm with color, texture, and the artistry of her samples and wall hangings, and smiled. When Jake died and Karen left her career as police psychologist to open a store for knitters, weavers, and spinners in the boondocks, I worried. But people came from Kansas City to buy from her. She developed a thriving Internet business. Her Chilean shepherd took care of a flock of angora goats and Romney sheep on her farm. Yarn from those sheep and goats that she spun and hand-dyed hung all over the shop, a big seller.

"You've made a whole new life for yourself here, haven't you?"

She gave me a sad smile. "Not the life I had with Jake. It never will be. But a good life. I'm learning to be happy again, little by little."

I nodded. "Later, I may ask you for a consult. I haven't got enough now. When I do, I'd like your best guess on the profile of this killer."

Karen shook her head. "I don't do that anymore. It's the only way I can make this work for me. Keep the cutoff clean."

I sighed. "Okay. Play safe house for Brian. That's enough."

She reached up to brush hair out of my eyes. "You'll find this killer and stop him."

I hugged her and left with the door ringing behind me. At least one of us had faith in my detective abilities.

That afternoon, I sorted through the rest of Andrew's papers. Mary found the Kansas City bank where Andrew had his safety deposit box. I started proceedings for a search warrant, a complicated matter because it was in another legal jurisdiction. I also arranged to confiscate Oldrick's research records.

Before I had a chance to leave for the morgue and the county courthouse, Jeremy called. "Marquitta, the chancellor is pressing for information."

I sighed in exasperation. "I'm a little busy. Two murders to solve? Remember? I've explained why I'm keeping this as confidential as I can."

"Trust me on this." Jeremy's voice was unusually serious. "Give me something I can use to appease and calm him down. Meet with me."

"Jeremy—"

He overrode my complaint. "Show up, Marquitta. I'm trying to protect you, but you make it incredibly difficult."

"I'm sorry. I do appreciate it." I paused to take a deep breath and expel my impatience. Jeremy was my only real ally among the chancellor's advisers. I didn't want to undercut his help.

"That's not important." His tone brushed aside my apology and gratitude. "My telling him you've met with me and given me what he wants is what counts. Take the time."

Frustrated, I ran my hand through my hair. "I'll meet you at five."

"Good." Jeremy sounded relieved. I must have been in more trouble than I knew. I hung up and headed out the door. How much longer before I was fired? I had to hurry before I was sent packing. I was the best chance we had to jail this guy and keep anyone else from dying. If I could only do it while I still had the chance.

Sheriff Dick Wold's small eyes gleamed beneath his gray crew cut. His mouth twisted when I entered the courthouse conference room where he sat with Frank and Randy Thorsson, district attorney. I'd asked Frank to meet me here after the autopsy because he and Dick were old friends, and I wanted to ask the sheriff for some help with the case.

The three men had been laughing together at some joke when I entered and the laughter cut off. Frank offered a friendly greeting. Randy was pompous. Dick just bared his teeth.

"If it isn't the tall chief," he said, nudging Frank with his shoulder. "Get it. Tallchief." He chortled. Frank looked uncomfortable.

Randy giggled before making his face stern. "Dick, I know you meant no harm, but that was inappropriate. I hope you weren't offended, Skeet."

Behind him, Dick smirked. I sighed at having to go through the prove-yourself-to-the-boys hoops again and made myself smile. "Dick was being literal. I am two inches taller than he is."

Frank hid a laugh. Randy looked confused while Dick scowled.

"You are tall for a woman," Randy said.

"She's taller than every man in the room but Frank," Dick snapped. "Even you in your elevator shoes."

Randy drew back, affronted. Only five foot six without the shoes, he was two inches shorter than Dick.

"My height's not what brings us here today," I began.

Joe burst through the door. "Sorry I'm late. Throwing off the newshounds." He smiled at me, nodded at the men, and headed for the coffee urn.

I felt better. Now we'd dispense with the macho garbage. Get an agreement worked out. I wanted to get back to the trail of blackmail I was following.

"With this second murder," Frank said after a nod from me, "we could use another investigator to help. We got Skeet and Gil, but Gil's inexperienced. Joe's guy is out right now. Maybe you could loan us one of your investigators?"

I sat smiling politely. Joe sipped coffee, nodding in agreement. Even Randy nodded.

Dick leaned back in his chair and spread his legs wide, pursing his lips. "Frank, I'd like to help you, but my men are occupied. It's all I can do to let my techs work on this. We're swamped." He dropped his head to look upward, jowls splayed out against his thick neck.

"What is this? Sudden crime wave in Deacon County?" Joe asked.

Dick smiled and pulled a nail file from his pocket. He began to shape his nails with careful attention.

Randy leaned forward. "Dick doesn't mean he won't give help. I'm sure he feels that, as a higher authority, he should be in charge of any investigation in which his men are involved."

"Higher authority!" Joe slammed his Styrofoam cup on the table, spilling coffee.

"Not what I mean." Dick continued to pay attention to his nails, but a sly grin crept across his face. "You couldn't pay me to be in charge of this fucking mess."

Randy looked puzzled. "Think of the good publicity—"

"Think of the bad publicity. The squaw and her Mex detective arrested the wrong guy, who killed himself in Joe-boy's jail. You want some of that, Randy? 'Cause I sure as hell don't." Dick looked up from his manicure.

"We were set up." Frank leaned over the table to point at Dick. "Your techs screwed up. The shoes weren't his."

"You see?" Dick pointed his nail file at Randy.

I raised my hands to calm Frank and Joe. "I don't blame your techs or us. Your techs found out about the shoes eventually. It was bad luck Tom killed himself before that."

Frank and Joe subsided. Randy opened his mouth, but I continued. "Tom didn't kill himself because he was abused in Joe's jail. He killed himself because he'd embezzled, paid blackmail, threatened Andrew's life, and left his fingerprints on the murder weapon. Mostly because he was unstable."

Randy turned to Dick. "You're right. You'd have to be in charge, so that kind of thing couldn't happen. Make it a county case." He nodded knowingly. "Good publicity for an election year."

Joe shot out of his seat. "The hell with this. I'll work with you, Skeet. I used to be a pretty good investigator."

I stood up beside him, as did Frank, across the table. "Sounds good to me. Dick, I retract my request for county help, other than your evidence techs. If you want to pull them, go ahead. I'll use KCPD and tell the media why."

Frank moved around the table to join Joe and me. "I don't believe this crap, Dick. We're trying to stop a cold-blooded killer, and you're talking politics."

"What the hell'd she do to get you on her side?" Dick's face turned an angry red. "She giving you some all of a sudden?"

I laid my hands on Frank's and Joe's arms to calm them. "That's too stupid for an answer. Randy, I hope you realize what a political liability you've got here."

I shoved both men ahead of me through the door as Randy bleated behind us, "Skeet, don't leave. We can work this out."

"That SOB," Frank muttered once we were outside.

Jaw stiff from gritting my teeth against angry remarks I'd not allowed myself to make, I knew from painful experience what would happen if I let myself get drawn into a pissing match with idiots. "We'll solve the cases without them."

"I'm shorthanded," Joe said. "But unlike Dick, we're not having an invisible crime wave in Brewster."

I smiled. "Thanks. Both of you."

We walked out of the courthouse together. A late-afternoon train hooted and rattled through town, momentarily drowning out anything anyone tried to say.

I looked at my watch and cursed. "I have to meet Jeremy so I can keep the chancellor off our tails." I looked up at Frank. "Karen's bringing Brian by on her way home. Will you tell him to stay inside my office until I come for him?"

Frank nodded, and we separated. I wondered how many ways Dick would find to sabotage my investigation now.

Smiling, Jeremy indicated a chair in his handsome office as he listened to someone on the phone. "That's all settled then," he said brightly. "Good talking to you, Gordon." He laughed and hung up the phone to stare out his window at the crenellations of Old Central, next door. I realized he'd been doing that the whole time he was on the phone.

"You know, Marquitta, I like old Dolph Brewster." He turned toward me with a strange look on his face. "We need some of Dolph's cunning and daring. Cursed with daughters, he trained them in his businesses and married them to men willing to take the Brewster name. He didn't hesitate to think out of the box."

I rolled my eyes. "I heard he was a bad guy. Stole his fortune from the Chouteau fur-trading family? What does this have to do with my murder investigation?"

"The Chouteaus were in-laws, partners. Devious in their own way. He went them one better." Swiveling his oxblood leather desk chair, he turned his attention to the town square below the campus, like a setting for a toy train. "In Brewster I'm as important as my father and uncles in their New England hometowns. I want to keep it that way."

"Jeremy—"

He put up a hand to quiet me, lost in deep thought. I looked around at his collection of sea glass. Noticing, a big smile broke on his face.

"A taste of home I picked up on the Cape during vacations with my family. Who will write me out of all wills immediately if this little problem blows up in our faces." He shrugged with natural grace. "I've become a true Coulter success. The only true Coulters, as far as my family's concerned. To be successful in exile was hardly my dream. Still, I've no intention of giving it up."

Why was Jeremy telling me this? He never gave out personal information. This particular personal information seemed painful.

"The chancellor and I have been informed that the murder on campus was not solved with Tom's arrest, that both murders are still open cases. Is that so?"

I nodded.

"Marquitta, it's important to both of us that these murders be solved. Take me into your confidence. If I must keep things from the chancellor, give me some ammunition to keep him at bay." He sounded so humble that I felt like an idiot for keeping him in the dark, my only ally among the powerful.

"Jeremy, strong trails lead to your colleagues. Not necessarily murder, though that's certainly possible. If I bring you up-to-date, you have to give your word you won't tell them—or anyone but the chancellor."

He smiled at me, holding his hand on his chest. "Cross my heart and hope to die?"

I laughed. "Let's hope not." Leaning forward, I gave him all the information I had.

Afterward, he shepherded me out the door with an arm around my shoulder. "Don't worry about the chancellor," he murmured in my ear. "I'll keep him out of your hair. I know you can find this killer and clean up this mess. Go do your work now."

I walked out of New Admin with a sense of relief. I'd done the right thing. I wouldn't have the chancellor at my heels any longer. I took a deep breath of the cool, spring air and set out to do my job.

CHAPTER 10

I had planned on finding a family for Brian until his aunt could come for him. That changed with the possibility that the killer might be after him. When I woke the next morning, I felt we'd done a decent job of protecting him while we worked the two cases we now had.

Last night, after a fast-food supper eaten with Brian at home, I'd arranged after-school care by phone with Joe and Karen. On Saturday, Brian would be with Joe and me in Kansas City, out of the line of fire. That was as far ahead as I dared look.

I wished again for the resources I'd had in Kansas City. Extra staff trained for hard-core action, safe houses, the whole structure of a metropolitan police force. Along with the blessings of peace in a small town came institutional incapacity for dealing with violence.

Still, I had a security plan for Brian so I felt good at breakfast. Until I saw the front page of the Metropolitan section of the *Kansas City Star*. Carl Haskins finally had a byline in the *Star*. He'd used me to get it.

He chronicled the arrest and suicide of Tom Jamison so

that I appeared to be the villain who'd driven an innocent man to his death. Worse was his research into my past. He laid out the accusations of bribery against Charlie and the Internal Affairs investigation that had ended when he retired. He tied in my resignation of a high-level position on the Kansas City force to become a police chief at Chouteau University, using terms like *fled in disgrace*.

Rage poured through my body. I wanted to hit something. I reread the piece. My stomach dropped at the thought of all who would read it. I ripped it in half and stood with half the newspaper in each hand. Nausea joined the rage. Dropping the halves to the floor, I ran to the bathroom. Kneeling, I vomited the breakfast I'd just eaten. I cursed methodically between heaves. Carl Haskins, the *Star,* Charlie, Tom Jamison. Most of all, I cursed myself and the murderer. I swore I'd find him and take him apart.

When the vomiting stopped, I sat on the tile floor, tears streaming down my face. I didn't know when I'd started crying. I never cried. I couldn't believe I was letting Carl Haskins make me cry.

I remembered I wasn't alone in the house. I didn't want Brian to see me this way. He'd done too much comforting of adults in his life. I had no intention of putting him in that position. But I couldn't seem to stop. I sat on the floor of my bathroom, letting tears come, thinking up new curses, pouring them out to get rid of them so I could deal with things again.

After a long time of sobbing, hiccupping, drying eyes, and starting all over again, my crying jag was finally over. I could breathe again without getting the tremors that signaled more tears. I stood, washed my face, brushed my teeth. In the mirror, I looked like hell. Brian was bound to know something was wrong. When he read that article, he would blame me for his father's death and want nothing more to do with me, solving the problem of what to do with Brian.

I blew my nose and unlocked the door to return to the kitchen. Lady stood outside in the hall and shoved her head into my hand with a sympathetic whine. "Thanks, girl," I said softly and headed to the kitchen as Wilma padded down the hall toward me.

At the table sat Brian and Karen, torn paper lying across the table in front of them. Brian avoided my eyes, but Karen inspected me slowly. "Feel better?"

I shrugged. "I don't know. I couldn't seem to do anything else for a while."

"That jerk," Brian muttered.

"Which one?" I asked with a tremulous laugh.

"That reporter. He had no right to print those things." Brian still wouldn't look at me. I felt my stomach turn over again.

I shrugged. "They're unfortunately all true. He didn't lie. Though he did make them all seem worse than they are."

Brian looked up, his eyes brimming. "I'm sorry. He used my family to screw you, used my crazy dad to make you look bad."

"He used my family to screw me, too." I tousled his hair. "Look what my own crazy father gave him to use against me. You've nothing to be sorry about. I should be apologizing to you."

Karen stood, crumpling the newspaper into a ball and putting it in the trash. "Neither of you has anything to apologize for. You're not to blame for what your fathers have done. Or the way unscrupulous people use their acts. I brought this for you." She held up a red T-shirt that said, *I knit so I won't kill anyone.* "I bought it for your birthday, but now seems a better time."

I laughed with a little shiver of a sob at the end of it. "When did you get here?"

"I saw my paper and took off. When I got here, Brian said you were throwing up and screaming." She smoothed my rumpled hair. "I told him it was good for you. You carry too much inside. Time to let some out."

I shuddered. "I don't like letting it out. It was horrible. I felt totally out of control."

"You can't always be in control, Skeet." Smiling, Karen pulled out a chair. "Sit down. I'll make some cocoa to settle that stomach. I might even give you whipped cream. Brian could probably use one, too."

Dropping into the chair, I looked over at Brian. "I probably scared you to death. Right?"

Brian hesitated and shook his head. "I was just worried about you."

Karen set the filled kettle on the stove. "It's only a newspaper story. People will forget soon enough."

I took a deep breath. "I can't let it get to me. I've got more important things to do."

With serious eyes, Brian looked at me and nodded. "You can't let this guy get away with it."

"She won't." Karen pulled cups out of the cupboard. "Skeet'll make him pay. Count on it."

I smiled my gratitude for Karen's faith, wondering how justified it really was.

When I drove to work later that morning, I headed for New Admin instead of Old Central. Since I couldn't do anything about the *Star,* I'd pour my energies into hunting down the person who'd set up Tom and me and killed Andrew and Tina. I told Gil to find out whom Duran had told about Tom's confrontation with Andrew and question them. I'd take Stuart and Wayne.

To keep from brooding, I decided to confront them first thing. Wayne's secretary told me he was gone until the end of the day. Stuart, on the other hand, was out of his office but on campus. I trekked over to the Jewell Harnett Library. I wasn't sure where Stuart did his research, but I only had to search four floors.

Most of the library was under ground in the limestone caves the college rented to businesses that wanted stable temperatures and humidity, but the fourth-floor entry of the library was aboveground, opening on a hall hung with Indonesian tapestries and lined with display cases holding rare books and manuscripts. These fascinated me, but this morning I passed them by. The rest of the fourth floor contained the main circulation desk, two reference rooms, the periodicals section, and the main reading room. If I didn't find Stuart here, I'd search the study carrels and small reading rooms on the other floors or the maze of the stacks.

I headed to the main reading room first. If I were Stuart, I'd choose it over the reference rooms always crowded with students. Students avoided it for the small reading rooms or individual carrels where they could sneak in food and drinks.

As I entered, my gaze went to the wall of windows opposite. The hills it framed were covered with the tender green of spring and dotted with occasional splotches of bright color—dogwood, forsythia, redbud. The view was why I preferred this room to the others. This morning, though, I could give the beauty of the hills only a quick glance before turning my attention to the room itself.

At one end, an elderly professor flashed me a familiar smile, and I returned a nod. My gaze swept across the room to see a back bent over a table. A step farther into the room gave me a glimpse of the side of the face, and I sighed with relief. At least one thing was going my way this morning.

I walked over to Stuart and touched him lightly on the shoulder. His head jerked up, and he turned with a frown. In front of him I saw a stack of outdoor magazines and swallowed a grin. I'd caught him playing hooky under the guise of research.

The professor at the other end of the room gathered papers and books and left the room. I pulled out a chair and sat down at Stuart's table.

"I need to talk with you," I said softly. "We need to revisit Tom Jamison's threat. Everything you saw and heard. Everyone you told about it."

Stuart carefully slid his notepad to cover the stack of magazines and faced me. "I don't understand. I've told you everything I know."

"Who else did you tell? Someone who knew about this argument framed Jamison for Andrew's murder. That person was the real killer." I stared at him intently.

Frowning, Stuart pursed his lips and leaned his head back in thought. "I did mention it to Tony Morelli when I got to his office for my next meeting." He gave me a defensive look. "I wouldn't ordinarily go around talking about it, but it had just happened."

"Did you tell anyone else?" I groaned inwardly. Tony Morelli. Dean of the College of Arts & Sciences. Another campus big shot. Oh boy!

He shook his head. "I was sorry I told Tony. It felt like a betrayal of my colleague. It was out of my mouth before I thought about it." That surprised me. Stuart was always so controlled. I couldn't imagine anything coming out of his mouth that wasn't exactly planned. He looked down for a second and then back at me. "You don't run into something like that every day in our circles. I suppose I had to talk about it to someone."

I nodded. "I'm sure you're not the only one who did. We have to find out how many were told. One of you witnesses or someone one of you told is the murderer." I watched his face carefully as I spoke. His eyes widened the barest bit at my words, but he kept them focused steadily on my face. "One more thing, Stuart. Where were you between ten and one on Tuesday night?"

He stiffened. "Do you really think I killed Andrew?"

I shrugged. "I don't know what you did or didn't do until I know where you were."

"I was here at the library until eleven P.M. Closing. Then I drove over to Art's on the square for a nightcap. I was there until closing, talking with Art. It must have been about one A.M. when I left."

I nodded and wrote it down. "So you got there—when?"

He shrugged. "I left here at closing. Eleven P.M. I drove straight over there. Probably eleven fifteen P.M. or so. Art can tell you. Or Twyla. The waitress."

I stood and put away my notebook. "Thanks for your help."

Stuart stood and held out his hand to shake mine. "Get him, Skeet. Hunt him down. We can't have this animal running around killing people."

"I intend to." I slid my hand from his damp grip and left the reading room. When I reached the entry hall, I looked back to see Stuart still standing in the doorway, watching me.

•   •   •

"I've got it!" Scott Lampkin said.

I was in my office at midmorning when Mary ushered him in. I'd left instructions with the office that, whether or not I was there, if Scott came looking, they were to let him into the squad room and send him to Mary. Only Mary, Gil, and Frank knew what Scott was doing.

I smiled at him. "You've got the same thing you had before the theft?"

He nodded with a big grin. "The accounts. Just the public-consumption ones, of course. I never had the real detailed ones. The notes from my friend in Accounting. I told her I'd lost them from before. Everything Andrew stole. It's all here."

He slapped a stack of papers of varying sizes on my desk. His grin widened even more. "Plus . . ." He held another stack of large computer printouts over his head. "Something I didn't have before. I begged my friend in Accounting for their stuff in this area, and she got me copies."

"Way to go." I stretched out both hands, and he set the papers in them. "This will really help us."

"All I ask is that you let me write my story when all this murder stuff is over, okay?" He looked like an excited little boy in an oversized body.

I laughed. "I'd never try to stop you. But not until we've got this all wrapped up."

"Of course." Scott's grinning face sobered. "I heard about Andrew's wife. I was sorry to hear that. Nice lady. Whatever Andrew may have done, she didn't deserve to die for it. I won't print anything until you give me the go-ahead."

"Thanks, Scott." I called Gil and Frank into the office and asked Scott to explain to them what he'd found.

It was Gil who asked the best questions. I'd thought it

would be Frank, with his years of work with the department's accounts, but it turned out Mary had always done most of the detail work. It also turned out that Gil's degree was a double, criminal justice and accounting.

"I wasn't sure I'd make it through the police academy. I needed a fallback. My folks weren't thrilled about my becoming a cop. The accounting was reassurance for them."

"It'll sure come in handy now," Scott said. "I've done bookkeeping for my dad's business, but these accounts are real complex. Some debits seem to add to some accounts, and some credits seem to be debits in certain situations." He looked serious. "As I was looking over these copies, I thought maybe this was more than just accounting errors. Maybe I was right about a criminal exposé in the first place. But I'd never be able to prove it because this is such a stupid, complex system."

Gil nodded. "A complex system is always easier to rip off than a simple one. That's what one of my accounting profs told us. Simplicity offers security."

I saw Scott out with more thanks and turned to Gil. "Have Mary make copies of all this. I want you both to go over them with a fine-tooth comb. I'm meeting Scheuer this afternoon. I've got payroll records to flaunt in his face and see what reaction I get. Let's keep these accounts secret until you two have made them tell us everything."

Looking grim, Frank shook his head. "This is bad business. You'll have vice chancellors burning your ass. You can't go after them. Not all of them."

I shrugged, trying to look unconcerned. "We're not going after all of them. So far, Jeremy Coulter doesn't seem to be involved."

"A good thing, too," Frank replied. "He's the brains of the three. If he's involved, we're in deep trouble."

"So far we're clear." I forced a laugh. "Hell, Frank, if this keeps up, you may get a new boss." I let the smile leave my face. "Just so long as they let me put this killer behind bars first."

Gil shook his head. Frank looked taken aback.

"Come on, guys. Get out of here. To work. It's not my funeral yet." I waved them from the room with both hands and started to go over the payroll statements I'd take to my meeting with Scheuer. Whether I liked it or not, I was playing in the academic top rungs now.

CHAPTER 11

On my way to Scheuer's office, I stopped to talk to the librarians on duty the night of Andrew's death. One of them had talked with Stuart when he came in early in the evening. Another had had a conversation with him at closing time, thanking him for not waiting, as everyone else did, until they were locking the doors. Gil was checking the second half of his alibi with Art and Twyla at Art's Bar and Grill. Maybe we'd get another person ticked off our whiteboard list.

Where Wayne Hamlisch had sports memorabilia plastered all over his office, Eugene Scheuer's walls were covered with metal-framed, blown-up photographs of multiethnic groups of smiling students engaged in various kinds of fun.

Alice Fremantle waited inside when the secretary ushered me in. I expected Alice to leave, but she stayed seated at the side of Eugene's big desk.

"You know Alice, of course," Eugene said, smiling hopefully and rubbing his hands nervously. His mostly bald head was shiny with perspiration under the fluorescent lights. "I thought she could take notes for us."

Alice smiled at me with her eyes narrowed.

I smiled back, trying to keep my eyes wide and threatless. "Of course I know Alice, but we need to speak privately, Eugene. After all, this is a criminal investigation."

Eugene's face lost some of its color. His hands twisted together and apart now. "A . . . a criminal investigation. Why . . . what—"

I interrupted him out of mercy. "I'm investigating two murders, Eugene. I need to ask you questions about matters connected with these murders. When I'm finished, I'll ask Alice her questions in private, as well."

Surprise crossed Alice's face while Eugene just looked sick.

"I . . . I don't think so," he said. "I want Alice here to take notes and be a witness."

"I understand if you feel the need to have a witness," I said. "In that case, I'll ask you to come with me for questioning and call your attorney."

Eugene's eyes swelled. "Come with you? Attorney?"

"Yes," I said. "Normally, people who are not directly suspects don't feel they need their lawyers, but if you do, you're certainly welcome to call yours on the way."

"But . . . but . . . I don't think I need my lawyer. I just want Alice to stay and witness . . ."

I shook my head. "Only attorneys allowed to be present during official questioning."

"Oh." Eugene looked lost. "Alice, I guess you'd best go back to your office." He twisted his hands more rapidly.

Alice stood, notebook in hand. Her hostile expression had turned to one of apprehension. "I don't know why you'd need to speak with me again."

"Just to confirm a few facts." I smiled. "It won't take but a few minutes once I'm finished here."

With a nod, Alice left the office. I turned to Eugene, whose hands snaked around each other repeatedly, and laid my copies of the payroll records on the desk in front of him.

"Why did you refuse to take legal action, or any kind of action, against Andrew McAfee when Mike Berman presented you with clear evidence of theft and embezzlement?"

Eugene stared at the records as if at a rabid animal. "I'm not sure I know what you mean."

"Do keep in mind that I will talk with Alice after our conversation, and I will remind her of the penalties for perjury." I gave him a severe look. "Perhaps I should remind you of those penalties. You're not under oath here, but you will be eventually."

"No. No. N-not necessary." His voice was a high-pitched squeal. "I just didn't realize what you were talking about at first."

"Now, do you remember that Mike Berman, in his position as faculty adviser to the *News,* brought you evidence of serious wrongdoing by Andrew McAfee and was initially assured that it would be investigated and prosecuted? Then, the day after you met with Andrew, Mike was informed that no charges would be filed?" I watched his hands squirm as I spoke.

"Yes, I remember now." He was breathing heavily. "After talking with Andrew, I felt he deserved a chance to make restitution and amends." He smiled weakly. "He had no other black marks on his record. He was willing to repay what he had taken, and under those circumstances there was no sense in punishing him further."

His voice grew stronger as he spoke, as if the speech were

rehearsed and brought him confidence he didn't have when he had to ad lib.

"I'm sure in your line of work, you are fixated on prosecution and punishment, but I find, when dealing with basically good students, forgiveness and a chance to make amends and start over are more effective." He smiled at me, his hands barely rubbing against each other now. His color was back, and he looked confident.

"Well, Eugene, here's a news flash. Andrew was blackmailing highly placed people on this campus. We have his records. We will be investigating all those people, no matter how highly placed." I smiled at him. "Because the blackmail alone gives a perfect motive for murder, so everyone he was blackmailing is a murder suspect. Do you understand?"

His color had again faded. His hands twitched and twisted. "I . . . I don't want to talk to you anymore. I'm not feeling well. I've been ill. I think I need to go home now." He actually was looking sick, but I didn't think it was anything physical. He grabbed his phone.

"Send Alice in here right away. I'm very ill. I need her to drive me to my doctor." He looked up at me. "We'll have to finish this another time."

Alice came bursting through the door. "Eugene, what is it?"

He stumbled toward her. "Alice, I'm so sick. I have to go now."

"Certainly." She put an arm around his shoulder to support him and cast a poisonous glance at me. "What did you do to him? He's not been well. Look at him."

Picking up my papers, I headed for the door. "I told him the truth. You'd better take him where he wants to go. But, Eugene, I'd suggest your lawyer rather than your doctor. An M.D. won't be able to help you. We *will* talk again later."

My next stop was Alec Oldrick's Psychology 110 classroom in Ormond Hall, a first-floor lecture room that held over a hundred students, who came barreling out when class ended. I waited for the first rush to die down before entering and standing at the back of the large lecture hall.

A phone call had established that Dean Tony Morelli had been out of town for Andrew's murder, but before leaving, he'd told Oldrick about Jamison threatening Andrew. Oddly enough, according to Morelli, Oldrick's fears of not making tenure were unfounded. It seemed the powers that be thought highly of his research.

Now, below me at the front of the room, Oldrick talked to students waiting in line before his desk. After most of them departed, I made my way down to Oldrick. Only three students were left, clustered around him, popping questions, all concerned with paper length and number of references.

Oldrick looked away from them and noticed me standing patiently. "Okay, guys. That's the deal. No exceptions. No more than one Internet reference. At least seven references. Ten pages minimum to fifteen pages maximum. If it's written well enough, I might allow you to go over fifteen pages, but it had better be solid and not puff. You're never to go under ten pages. No amount of discussion will change that."

A miniskirted blonde wailed, "But, Dr. Oldrick, only one Internet reference? That's medieval."

"Man, I write concise. I'm not some long-winded academic. I've never had to take ten pages to explain anything in my life." A skinny white kid with dreadlocks clenched both fists in righteous indignation.

The third student, overweight and pasty-looking, made a

163

moue of disgust and walked away past me. "Give it up," he muttered. "He used to be someone you could work, but he's gotten all hard-assed since they murdered his research assistant."

I nodded, thinking it was good I wasn't a student of Alec Oldrick's right now. I don't mind research, but I hate to write papers. I'd probably have as much trouble as the kid in dreadlocks getting ten pages down on anything.

The other two students turned and left, grumbling to each other. I moved closer to Oldrick. "I need to ask you a few questions." I noticed new students drifting into the room.

Nodding, Oldrick picked up his book bag from the desk. "Can we talk on the way to the Union? I always get a decent cup of coffee after class. The department's brew is awful."

Two large groups of students burst through the doors at the back of the room, and the sound level shot up dramatically as we climbed the steps, dodging students. When we exited to the hall outside, the noise level only rose as dozens of students scurried between classes in talkative groups.

Once outside, the noise and crowds decreased. A few single students here and there raced across the quad for their classes as the last of the groups of students vanished through the doors of buildings. Three guys sat cross-legged on the grass under a tree, talking quietly, and a woman student sat alone on a bench reading while two teaching assistants discussed something in French in the middle of the quad.

As we headed toward the Chouteau Union, I asked, "Can you tell me what you were doing between ten and one the night Andrew was killed?"

Oldrick shot me a surprised glance. "Am I a suspect? Why? I liked Andrew. I wanted him back as my research assistant."

"Tony Morelli told you about Tom Jamison's threat to Andrew."

Oldrick looked at me as if weighing whether or not to lie. "It didn't surprise me. Jamison is—was a prime example of the oppressive boss system here, and his threats to Andrew were just a part of that."

I watched him closely. "Did you tell anyone about it?"

Oldrick looked surprised. "No. Why should I? It was just more of the usual trash."

Of course, I thought. Oldrick was too self-involved to worry about anyone else. "Let's go back to where you were that night. Ten P.M. to one A.M."

He cleared his throat. "I have a faculty-senate committee meeting on Mondays that always runs late, and a few of us always go out for drinks afterward. That's where I was until . . . oh, one thirty, maybe."

"Which faculty committee is this and who's the chair?"

He looked startled that I would ask anything further. "Well, it's the bylaws committee, and Rud James of History is the chair."

I thanked him and headed back to the office to compile the information Gil and I were amassing. I hoped we were making progress. After a few steps, though, I stopped, feeling I was being watched. I turned to find Oldrick still staring after me and, behind him in the doorway to the Union, Stuart Morley. I was discovering just how unpleasant this peaceful university could be under the surface.

I got back to the squad room before Gil or Frank. At the heavy wooden table with the coffee machine and a box of doughnuts were gathered officers from the evening and morning shifts. As I approached the table, Bill Morton, the evening-shift sergeant, continued regaling the others with his tale. "Naw, they caught them. Live on camera, so to speak."

"Something that happened this morning or on evening shift, Bill?" I asked.

"Evening, Chief." Middle-aged with a potbelly and a mostly bald head, Bill had a talent for entertaining.

"Go ahead," I said. "Your version will be the funniest bit of the report, won't it?"

Bill laughed and used his belt to pull up his pants, which constantly slipped down over the bulge of his belly. "You know those new digital overhead projectors? They're built into all the new classrooms. You just pull a handle, and they swing down so you can put your stuff on them."

Everyone nodded.

"Well, a couple a bozo Omega Chi Delts got the idea to play with one of 'em in an empty classroom last night about six o'clock. One of these guys pulls down the overhead, flips the switch to turn it on, pulls out his pecker, and lays it on the little flat window to show it all enlarged on the big screen on the wall and monitors up in the corners."

Everyone laughed. Stan Hovis said, "Some guys'll do anything to make it look bigger." The others sniggered.

"Anyway, they all think this is real cool so the others whip out theirs to do the same thing. Only thing is, it's all hooked up to the classroom next door for one a those overflow classes during the day, and that one isn't empty."

"You're kidding," I said. "Who was in it?"

From the giggle that went through the group, the evening officers had already heard the punch line.

"A night adult-education class in it with a bunch a old la-dies who start screaming 'cause suddenly on all the monitors in the corners a their classroom these guys' dicks are showing up! Way bigger than life! Greeks!"

Everyone burst into laughter.

I shook my head. "Bad as the Greeks can get, remember what the blue-haired, tattooed, and pierced crowd can come up with. Like that kid on the roof last month."

Everyone groaned, laughing at the memory of the student stuck without pants on top of Old Central's four stories, unable to get himself down. Just then, Gil came through the exterior, locked door.

"What have you got?" I asked him. "Get some coffee first and a doughnut."

He smiled and pulled out his notebook. "I'll save it for when I leave. Stop at the Herbal for coffee and a cinnamon roll."

"Dolores won't have any left." I knew how fast her homemade goods sold each day.

"I asked her to save me one," he said with a shy smile. "She'll have one."

"Sure, she will 'cause she knows Gil's sweet on her, right?" Stan said with a wink.

Gil blushed. I took pity on him. "Okay, tell me what you've learned in your time in the halls of higher learning."

He fumbled with his notebook and dropped it. As he bent to pick it up, his hand knocked foam cups flying. Trish and Milo knelt to help pick them up. Gil got to his feet, face flaming.

"That's our Gil," said Stan. "Keep it up. I got a bet on how many things you can knock over in a day."

I gave him a hard look, and he straightened from his slouch. "Just kidding. No harm meant."

Gil ignored him, staring at his notebook. "Wayne Hamlisch has an alibi. He was home with his wife from eight thirty that night till six thirty the next morning. Mrs. Hamlisch confirms this."

"That's bullshit!" Stan said with a laugh. "I know for a fact that sack of guts wasn't home with his missus because on my final rounds at ten thirty, I saw this car steamed and bouncing in Ormond parking lot. Thought I'd caught some students in the rough and ready, but it was old Hamlisch and Cherry Abrams from Accounting, half naked and screwing away like mad."

Everyone but Gil and I started laughing. I looked at my investigator.

"Hamlisch's alibi is phony," he said softly. "He doesn't really have one for the time of the murder." The laughter died out around us, and everyone suddenly looked serious.

I nodded, grimacing. I was seeing everyone's tawdry little secrets because murder had thrown a light everywhere. It was depressing to see how numerous and trashy they were.

That evening, Brian and I sat in the living room, he practicing his flute, I knitting a pair of socks. I had managed to get Brian's flute and music stand, schoolbooks, and some clothing out of the house where Tina had died. At the end of a difficult day and week, I found Brian's classical flute music as relaxing and conducive to thought as my favorite jazz. Finally, I had a chance to let my mind wander the tangled paths of the case.

The fire crackled. Lady stretched out at Brian's feet as he sat, playing, and Wilma snuggled on the couch by me, face and ears pointed toward Brian. Sitting in front of the fire with my hands working an automatic sock pattern, I began to put names to the list of payments I'd found in Andrew's calendar.

I'd locked up all his papers at the office where bulletproof glass and armed officers were on duty 24/7. I didn't want anyone else killed for them. I'd memorized the listing of payments, though, along with other key items. So I could let my mind wander and untangle the muddled strands.

Based on what I already knew, "nw" could be the rip-offs of the *News* writers. Then, "biz" must be Tom Jamison, the business-school dean, with his financial misbehavior. I set down my sock for a moment and made a note to have Gil track down Jamison's misdeeds when he finished with the accounts Scott had given us.

Returning to my knitting, I focused on the list again and thought "kp" must surely be someone Andrew blackmailed over the kiddie porn, perhaps Oldrick, perhaps someone else he'd found in that connection. Possession of child pornography didn't carry much of a sentence, but it could be a career destroyer.

That left "show," "$$," "il," and "stu." "Stu" was pretty obviously Eugene Scheuer, the VC for student affairs. Andrew had had some kind of hold over him to make the charges on embezzling the writers' pay go away. I had the feeling Eugene would break and tell me what it was if I could question him for any length of time without the protective Alice.

I wasn't as clear on who "$$" might be. Probably Wayne Hamlisch, VC for money, among other things. He also had something fishy going on with accounts. He would be a harder nut to crack than Eugene, but I sensed that something lay hidden there. Also, both vice chancellors had had appointments with Andrew shortly before he died.

All of Andrew's blackmail seemed to fall into lines of financial misconduct, except for "kp," but I thought a successful financial blackmailer might find room to expand his business if he somehow found a connection between a solid citizen and child pornography. Andrew had been given that kind of opportunity.

Thinking of Oldrick's choice of such a controversial field for research, I wondered if the professor had an interest in the field that predated his need to publish. I'd not done a lot of work in that area because the Special Victims squad, part of the Sex Crimes and Juvenile Unit, handled all that, but child-porn consumers, like pedophiles—and there was a big cross-over between the two—generally looked like normal, everyday types you'd meet in any neighborhood. Could Oldrick or another professor at this nice, quiet school be involved in that kind of thing? Still, I couldn't see Oldrick paying blackmail. He seemed to have accepted that his career was effectively over. According to Morelli, that wasn't true, however.

Had Andrew run across someone else he recognized from campus in the course of that research? And if so, whom?

I put down my knitting when Brian went to bed and turned to the copies of the questionnaires that Andrew and Oldrick had filled in. I'd had Gil pick them up from Oldrick earlier in the day. I read the first and wondered why Oldrick bothered. Would some stately academic journal really publish an article discussing how many times someone got an erection watching kiddie porn?

It was getting late, and I flipped quickly through the rest of the stack, looking for anything that stood out in some way. At the end, something niggled at the back of my head, and I picked them up and started flipping through again. All of them bore the same computer time/date stamp. Oldrick and Andrew were supposed to have gathered these a few at a time over a couple of months, but all twenty-seven had been done on the same day with only a matter of minutes between them, as if they had stumbled into some big gathering of men who watched child pornography. What was that about?

I made another note to check into it. I looked back at my list of payments for "show." Had these questionnaires all been filled out at some showing of a child-porn flick? I remembered Oldrick saying that he paid his subjects. Did he pay them in their favorite coin? That would make for ideal blackmail.

These were the questions I would start answering in the morning.

The last entry, "il," stumped me. Apparently, another blackmail victim, but I couldn't come up with an idea of who or why from the letters alone. "Illegal," "Illinois," "illiterate," "illusion," "illustrate"—I couldn't think of any others. I made another note to check immigration and home-state status on everyone involved and the dictionary for other "il" words.

After struggling with it for almost an hour like a recalcitrant crossword-puzzle clue before I climbed into bed for the night, I was plagued by the feeling that the letters connected to someone I should know, in the way a familiar name slips the tongue and leaves the mind searching for something that vanishes just ahead of the senses.

Throughout the night, I woke believing I'd found the answer, only to have it melt away like any nighttime fog. I lay in bed afterward, my mind circling, trying to pick up that elusive trail.

CHAPTER 12

I was glad to get up and shower in the morning and wake Brian, even though I'd had little sleep. When Brian and I met Joe and Julie at Pyewacket's for Saturday brunch, I was determined to put the case out of my mind until after I'd dropped off Joe and the kids in the city. During our meal, full of excited questions and exclamations from Julie and more restrained but no less enthusiastic comments from Brian, I failed. The case kept trying to dominate my thoughts.

After breakfast, the four of us headed for Kansas City in my Crown Victoria. The kids were excited about the day, Brian because he'd always wanted to see the restored Union Station with Science City, Julie because anything that let her spend time with her idol sounded wonderful.

I pulled out of the town square where we'd had breakfast and onto Beecher, followed by a dark Lexus. Then I turned again on Marshall to pass through Girlville and catch Highway 9 south out of town. The Lexus made the same turn. Laid out on steep hills, houses looked down on me as I drove past. Brewster was a stepped terrace garden growing houses.

Behind me, Brian focused on his handheld video game. Blips, beeps, and tiny screeches accompanied the movements of his fingers on the game's surface. Over that, I heard the campus calliope chiming from Old Central where it towered over us on College Hill. On the other side of Girlville from the town square now, we passed the city police department, jail, and city hall, all mashed together into a little concrete box.

"Are you sure you want to leave town with all this hanging over you right now?" I asked Joe, pointing my chin toward the municipal building as we passed by. "What will Mayor Harvey say?"

Joe smiled at me. "Trying to persuade me to back out? Harvey's not going to say anything. My men, yours, and the county guys are working in the labs and on leads. It won't do any good to have me hovering over their shoulders."

"Brian, can I please play with you? Please, please," Julie wheedled from the backseat.

Brian's voice was patient and polite. "I'm sorry, Julie. You can't. It's just designed for one person."

"Well, can I watch, then? Please." Julie sounded desperate for some way to share the experience with her hero.

"Sure. Here." I heard Brian shifting in the seat. "Can you see the screen now?"

Looking over at Joe, I asked, "You're pretty laid back, aren't you?" I wondered how he could just dismiss the murders from his mind.

Joe's smile faded. His forehead developed a crease slightly above and between the eyebrows. "Do you mean that as a compliment or a criticism?"

I shrugged and smiled uncertainly. "I'm not sure. Karen's

always telling me I mustn't let the job take over my life, become my life, but . . ."

"But you think I don't take the job seriously enough, maybe?" Joe's crease had turned into a full frown.

I glanced into the rearview mirror and noticed the same dark-blue Lexus behind us on the highway. "I didn't say that."

"Didn't you?" He stared out the window for a minute at the passing landscape on his side of the road, sprawling industrial parks.

"What's that little guy doing?" Julie asked as more bleeps came from the game. "He's just running into nowhere."

"He's searching for treasure or weapons or potions to increase his strength or heal him," Brian replied absently.

"For when he fights a monster?" Julie's voice grew excited.

"Yeah." Brian sounded preoccupied.

Joe turned to look at me. "I'll tell you something, Skeet. My job is very important to me. I take my responsibilities to the citizens seriously. But nothing's more important than my daughter."

I was silent as I watched the steep limestone cliffs covered with bare-branched trees on my side of the highway turn into the ubiquitous road construction of Riverside, part of the flood-control work going on in and around that town for years. I wondered how I'd come to this point with this conversation. Stupid.

"I wasn't trying to second-guess you, Joe. I just can't imagine having something or someone in my life more important than the job." I paused to let my words sink into my mind and added in a wry voice, "I guess that was my contribution to my divorce."

Joe nodded. "I've known cops like that. They're usually great cops, but they end up burned out or put out to retirement, alone and bitter. Neither's a good prospect, Skeet."

I smiled at him quickly. "I know. That's why I left KC and came here. To try to get a real life other than the job."

"Make him fight a monster now, why don't you?" Julie sounded bored.

"I don't control when monsters come up," Brian explained. "They just pop up on their own, and I fight them. Right now, I want to get everything I can before one comes."

I noticed the dark Lexus turn off at the North Kansas City exit and breathed a little easier. I hadn't been aware that I was nervous about its following until it moved off. God, it was like last Wednesday, when I'd thought Wayne Hamlisch was following me. Talk about paranoia.

A subdued roar issued from the game behind me.

Julie squealed. "Oooh! There. Can you beat that one?"

"Sure," Brian said confidently. "It's not a real strong one. I've got more strength and hit points than it has."

"Oh, it got you." Julie's voice was breathless.

Brian laughed. "Not bad. Now, see." A peal of tinny music sounded from the little machine he held. "I got him. Now, to heal myself and see what I picked up from the fight . . ."

The miles clicked by with only silence in the front seat. I found myself staring out at the white mass of the Kansas City Port Authority built out over the river and decided to return to the conversation.

"But, you see, Joe, when I've got a guy who's killed two people, I don't know how to take off until he's caught."

I tried to smile an apology at him. I didn't know why I was so insistent on pursuing this.

Joe looked at me soberly. "Well, then, I guess we'd better talk about the case. Wouldn't want this to get too social."

I hadn't meant that, but since I wasn't sure what I had meant, I just nodded.

"Tell me about the suicide. Did anyone see him before he did it? Could anyone else have gotten in the cell with him and strung him up?" I kept my voice soft enough not to be heard over the kids' conversation.

"Do you think you could fight a monster in real life, Brian?" Julie's voice sounded dreamy.

Brian snorted. "Shoot, no. There aren't any monsters in real life. If there were, I wouldn't be able to fight them because I don't have any weapons or potions or extra strength. This is all just make-believe, Julie."

Staring at me, Joe shook his head. "No one went into the cell. He was taken out to the visitors' meeting room for three different visitors. First, his lawyer. Then, his ex-wife. Finally, Jeremy Coulter from the university. About his benefits and employment status." His frown was back. "I know we're not KCPD, but we do have good jail procedures."

I nodded. "I wasn't questioning them. Unless someone's given a reason to be on watch, they can always do it." I noticed the Downtown Airport passing behind his head. "Jeremy came to see him? I guess he handles a lot of delicate stuff for the chancellor."

"Well, I'd like to know just what he said to him," Joe muttered.

I nodded. "So would I."

The kids were giggling about the game as I crossed the Broadway Bridge into Kansas City. The bleeps came faster.

"You got that one, too," Julie said, wonder in her voice. "You are so awesome, Brian."

"Better shut it off, Bri," I said as I pulled off Broadway onto Pershing Road. "We're about there."

Two blocks later, I pulled into the big front drive of Union Station to let Joe and the kids out.

"You're sure you guys will be okay until about four or four thirty?" I asked.

"It's okay." Joe dipped his head toward me. "If they get bored with Union Station, we've got Liberty Memorial and Crown Center in easy walking distance."

Julie pointed at the network of skywalks that hovered above Main Street and Pershing Road. "Can we use those to get there, Dad?"

"That's what they're for."

Both kids looked pleased, but Joe looked as if the pleasure had gone out of his day. Feeling guilty, I drove off as the three of them entered the huge front doors of Union Station, chattering excitedly.

I was glad to see some of the gloom lift off Brian, if only for an afternoon. He faced such a mess that he needed every bit of release from constant tension and stress that he could get. I was grateful to Joe for suggesting this outing. I hated the fact that I'd put him on the spot for it. What was wrong with me? He was trying to help me with this new responsibility I'd blindly accepted for Brian.

My mind once again shied away from the constant question of what I was going to do with a fourteen-year-old. Better to focus on who'd murdered his mother and stepfather.

Kansas City's Country Club Plaza sits forty-some blocks from downtown on the edge of Brush Creek. Built in the 1920s, its buildings resemble famous palaces and towers in Seville. Full of decorative tiles, fountains imported from Europe, and public art, even in winter its streets are never deserted. On a sunny spring Saturday, crowds of shoppers and strollers filled the sidewalks.

I joined them, walking from a parking lot walled in Spanish-tile-studded brick, to the Classic Cup, the restaurant where I was to meet Dan Wheelwright. The Classic Cup offered cozy seating near a large fireplace in winter and a sidewalk café in seasonable weather. I hoped Dan had been able to score a table outside.

To my delight, he waved at me from the fenced terrace as I entered the restaurant. I headed out to the sidewalk tables and found myself gathered into a strong hug. Stepping back, I looked at my friend and former boss.

Only slightly taller than I, Dan had clear gray eyes and fine features that always reminded me of aristocratic RAF pilots in old black-and-white movies. His hair had been graying all the years I'd known him, yet never seemed any grayer than when I'd first met him. In fact, Dan looked the same as when I'd last worked with him, three years earlier. I almost forgot we no longer worked together on a daily basis.

"I think Sally's been giving you drinks from the fountain of youth. You never seem to get any older."

Dan's warm smile grew even larger. "I was definitely aging fast until Sally. I think happiness just slowed it down some."

Dan's second wife, Sally, was much younger. Many on the force had assumed that this marriage would end in divorce the same as his brief, first marriage, but Sally and Dan were a love match and, three teenagers later, still one of the few happy couples I knew.

"How is your lovely lady?" I asked after ordering coffee and raspberry cheesecake. "What's she doing while you're here?"

"Shopping with the twins. Twin girls was not the smartest move for my pocketbook." Dan's smile was rueful. "It's not long until prom night, and this year my girls are going." He shook his head. "Who can believe those babies are in high school?"

"That can't be. Just yesterday I spoke to their Brownie troop."

He laughed. "And scared them all to death about strangers and drugs. I don't think any of those girls ever forgot that." He wiped long fingers across his forehead. "They're starting to date, Skeet. That's tough. Danny's been dating for a year or so, but he's . . ."

"A boy. Guess you'll have to get used to handing over your little girls to some pimply youth who just learned to drive. Like Danny boy." I grinned at him. "Sauce for the gander and all that."

Dan laughed at himself. "You got me there, kid."

The waiter arrived with my coffee and a refill for Dan's, along with cheesecake for both of us.

"Gotta have tons of cholesterol, it tastes so good," Dan said as he took his first bite. "Sally's got me on this low-cholesterol diet. This is a treat."

"Don't tell her I corrupted you."

I savored the creamy taste on my tongue and directed my attention for a second to the people passing by on the street before me. A group of tattooed Art Institute students in black leather laughed as a white-haired couple in their Sunday best strolled past. Across the street, behind three laughing Indian women in colorful saris with a stroller and a sullen-looking teenager, I could see the Roman faun fountain brought from prewar Europe.

"It's a beautiful day." I sighed. "Now to pick your brains. I only have so long before I have to pick up my friend and the kids."

"What's this about you taking in a teenager?" Dan asked.

"He's a real stand-up kid with nowhere else to go. Plus he's in danger from the one who killed his folks." I shrugged. "I knew him. It seemed a good temporary solution."

"These murders. What kind of help do you want from me?"

"There's a KC connection. The original victim was a blackmailer, and the second victim, his wife, was killed because the murderer was trying to find his records. He kept them in a bank here. Getting a search warrant. Most of the blackmail deals with financial scams, but there's a connection with child pornography in the city. This blackmailer was researching in kiddie-porn circles here."

Dan held up a hand. "You know damn good and well that's Special Victims stuff."

"You know Alvin Dressner's the guy I'd have to go through with Sex Crimes and Juvie. How likely is that? You know what an SOB he is."

Dan shook his head. "You never got along with him."

I stared at him in disbelief. "The man's a callous misogynist. He should have been shoved off that squad a long time ago."

Dan nodded. "They've got a good rate of clearing cases."

I stared down into my cup of coffee with a frown. "Only because of the good people working under him. Most hate his guts." I looked up at him. "Dan, he won't help me, even if I go over his head to the chief. He'll find some way to dog it. You could get the information I need."

"That's one thing you never learned," he said sadly. "Sometimes you have to close your eyes to things you can't do anything about in order to get your job done."

"I'd even be nice to that jerk myself to get what I need, but he already hates me."

"You're right. Alvin would mess up your case and let a murderer go free in order to screw you." He shook his head again. "What do you need?"

"Thanks." I smiled and laid my hand on top of his. "There's a kiddie-porn ring operating out of the skin shop between KC and Independence. I need to know the names of the operators. I've got leads to a possible photographer for the ring. I'll follow that up next week, but I need to know where to look for distributors, pimps, muscle. Trying to find someone who can connect one of my suspects with the ring."

"How am I supposed to get this out of Alvin?" He looked skeptical.

I waved my hand grandly. "Tell him you're cooperating with an out-of-town homicide investigation, and you need it. The truth."

"That might work." He still looked unsure of the wisdom of doing what I'd asked.

I leaned toward him. "Dan, this guy tied up my teen's mom and shot her in the head in her own kitchen. I was taking him home when we found her. He saw her that way."

"Shit, Skeet!" He pushed back his half-eaten cheesecake. "You had to tell me, didn't you?"

"I've got to stop him before he does someone else." I felt a little guilty. "I wouldn't ask you if I thought Alvin would be straight with me."

Dan sighed. "I'll see what info I can get for you."

I took a drink of coffee and sat back in my chair. "I really appreciate it."

Dan drew the remainder of his cheesecake back to take a bite. "It's worth it to get this. Tastes so good it's got to be pure fat, don't you think?"

I laughed and forked up a bite of my own. "I don't care as long as it tastes like this," I said before I put it in my mouth.

"You're still young. You don't have to worry about these things." Dan took a sip of coffee and regarded me with a quizzical stare. "So who's the guy who has your endangered kid right now? You must think the kid is safe with him or you'd never have left him."

I nodded. "Joe's the town chief of police. A good cop. He's

armed, and he'll watch out for Brian. He's got a little girl of his own, a single dad. He's taking both of them to Science City as we speak."

Dan lifted one eyebrow while he considered me. "Is this serious? You and this guy?"

I held up my hands in denial. "We're just friends. Colleagues." I shrugged. "He'd like to date, and sometimes I think it would be nice. But we're real different."

"How?"

"You know me, Dan. I live for the job when I'm on a case. You're the same when a case is hot. Like a bloodhound."

Dan raised his eyebrows, as if to say, *So?*

"Joe's good, but he doesn't have that same drive. Says family comes first. I respect that, but . . . You never let your family pull you off a case."

"Wait a minute. Apples and oranges here. He's a single dad?"

I nodded.

"Then he can't afford to take the attitude I take," Dan continued. "Remember, I've got Sally keeping the home fires burning and taking care of the kids. A damned ungrateful job it is, too. My first wife left 'cause she couldn't take what she called my 'obsession' with my work."

I grimaced in sympathy. "It played a part in my divorce, too. Sam couldn't stand anything being more important than him. Even temporarily."

"You've got a gift for detection, Skeet. You're just genetically disposed to find answers and re-create order out of crime. You can't help yourself really. It's usually men I see with that gift. Going to take a special man to be able to live with it." He lifted his coffee cup and regarded me over its rim. "Maybe a man who understands law enforcement and still puts his family first?"

I laughed and made an imaginary pistol with my fingers and fired it at him. "Touché."

We both laughed, settled back in our seats, business finished, to relax, talk about old friends and comrades, and enjoy the colorful scene before us.

My mood was mellow when I arrived at my old man's house. I was pleased to see that Charlie looked better than he had the last time I'd visited, his clothes clean, his hair cut, his eyes clearer. His appearance still wasn't healthy, but it was a definite improvement. Maybe it did some good for me to check on him, after all.

He ushered me inside with wide, swinging gestures, appearing to be in a good mood himself. "Hey, Skeet. Ain't this weather something? How're you doing? How's that murder coming?"

I smiled and took the offered seat on the sagging couch. It had already been cleared of newspapers in preparation for my visit, I noticed.

"It's a gorgeous day, all right, Charlie. How are you? Are you taking the medicines the doctors gave you? Have you had any more problems?"

He frowned. "Naw. I'm doing great, kid. That was just some . . . some thing that hit me."

"You haven't stopped taking the medicine, have you?" My voice was wary.

I knew Charlie. Overconfidence would lead him to stop the minute he started feeling better.

He waved an unconcerned hand. "I'm still taking it most days. Don't worry. I'm okay."

I forced air through my teeth in exasperation. "Charlie, you've got to take the medicine every day like the doctors told you. And stop drinking and—"

"And get lots of exercise and eat a low-fat diet," he said in a high-pitched, singsong voice, obviously meant to imitate his doctor. "I know. I know."

I took a deep breath. "Charlie—"

"Don't worry," he interrupted me. "I take it all the time, except once in a while when I forget, and I'm getting some exercise, walking around a lot while . . . Well, I'm walking a lot more. Not laying on the couch watching the tube so much."

"Oh. That's good, Charlie." I reminded myself that small steps to health were probably the best, in fact, the only, way for Charlie to make the changes necessary. He would never be able to do it all at once.

He looked at me from the corners of his eyes, and I knew he'd done something that he knew was wrong. He gave me a big smile, shaky at the edges.

"The other day when you were over," he said, "I did something you won't like." I could hear in his voice a warning of excuses and swindles to come.

"What was that, Charlie?" I asked, keeping my voice calm.

He gave me a sheepish glance. "I opened your purse while you were in the kitchen on the phone the other day and read over your case notes. Good job, by the way."

"What? Snuck into my purse and read my case notes?"

"I think I found your guy," Charlie interrupted me with a self-important air.

"What have you been up to?" I clasped my hands together tightly to keep from going for his throat.

Charlie shrugged and gave me a smug grin. "Just a little investigating, kid. There's this little ring of kiddie-porn operators that sort of headquarter in Midtown. They move around a lot to stay out of sight of the cops."

"What has this got to do with you violating—"

Charlie just rolled on as if he hadn't heard me. "They use kids about ten to sixteen. Seduce 'em. Bribe 'em. Drug 'em into it. Some of the kids they just buy from junkie parents."

My outrage fizzled at his tale. I'd seen all too much of what druggie parents did to their kids.

He shook his head and spit on the floor. "All kinds of animals out there, Skeeter. Sell their little girls for a hit." His expression grew dark. "Sometimes the head guy lets one of the local customers be the guy in the shoot for an extra payoff. And one of these johns is a guy they call the Professor on account of the way he talks. They think maybe he taught at some college out in the boondocks."

"I wonder if it could be Oldrick. Is he getting more involved in this research than he told me?"

Charlie shrugged. "If it's him, he's gotten a lot more involved. My snitch tells me one of the kids tried to fight one day, and this guy got rough enough that the little girl wound up dead."

I felt like hitting something. "This needs to go to Dan Wheelwright right away. You shouldn't be messing around with it."

Charlie laid his big hand on my shoulder for a moment, then continued his story. "The Professor paid humongous bucks to have them take care of the body and get him a new ID and then, supposedly, he left for Mexico."

"What if he didn't?" I asked. "What if he just didn't want them coming around looking for easy blackmail?" I stopped for a second, puzzled. "But how did Andrew McAfee get enough to blackmail him?"

Charlie grinned at me, looking like a giant, drunken leprechaun. "There's a picture of this guy's face among the porn shots, according to my snitch."

"That's got to be it. When Andrew researched for Old-rick, he found it and recognized whoever it is. But where did he put it?"

I stood and paced back and forth. "He's got a safe deposit box. That's where all his evidence is. At one of his KC banks. I'm working on a warrant to get into it."

"Don't worry," Charlie said expansively. "I'm going to get a copy of that dirty picture for you."

"Wait a minute, Charlie. How did you get someone to talk about this? Why are you so sure your source is telling you straight?"

He waved his hand grandly. "He's got a wife and kids, but he's on the down low. You know, with other guys. And I caught him at it. I know where his family lives, and I've just held on to it until I needed him. You'd be surprised what these guys will do to keep their families from finding out their dirty little secret."

"Charlie! That's blackmail now that you're a civilian!"

"It's what every cop does with snitches to get info. Threats or bribes. You know that, Skeeter."

"You're not a cop any longer. You're a private citizen."

He snorted. "I'm still enough of a cop to get you the evidence you need."

I took a deep breath and tried to slap my anger down. I looked over at him. He wasn't a young man anymore, and he looked twice his age. "Charlie, you've done a good job here. But you went about it the wrong way, and you've stumbled onto something a little more dangerous than either of us realized. You need to hand this over to Homicide. I'll call Dan—"

"The hell you will! If you think I'm going to turn over my leads and my snitch to that—" Charlie's face grew red.

"Charlie, you can't do this. You're not a cop anymore, re-member? And when you were, you never handled anything like this. Not even when you were young and healthy. Are you trying to give yourself a stroke? You never should have gotten involved in this in the first place."

"And if I hadn't, you wouldn't know any of this now, would you, Miss Hotshot Investigator? Don't sell the old man short here. I've still got what it takes to bring this scumbag in."

I tried to reason with him. "You can't do this. This isn't your case. It's not your job. It's mine—and now that we know about this kid's death, Dan's."

Charlie's mouth turned down in the sullen, stubborn way I knew too well. His jaw hardened, lower lip rolled out.

I dropped my face into my hands. Then, I looked up at him in furious disbelief. "You loony old man. You wouldn't have had any idea where to start if you hadn't stolen a look at my interview notes."

He erupted in rage. "Who the hell are you calling loony? I found this when you couldn't, Miss I've-got-a-degree Detective. You ain't shit."

"So you know some of the bums on the street. Probably old drinking buddies. And you used blackmail to get it. That's a crime, Charlie. I hadn't come to KC to even look yet because I'm pursuing this case with low manpower and following all the leads. I'd have gotten around to this, especially since I've asked for help from Homicide and Sex Crimes and Juvie."

"Alvin Dressner? He hates your guts. He'd help the killer get away just to spite you."

"That's why I asked Dan to get the information from him." I wheeled to face him. "I'm not stupid, Charlie. I'm a damn good cop."

"Hell, you're not a patch on the old man. I was the cop you never could be."

"That's right. Crooked and resigning under suspicion. Damn

right, that's the kind of cop I never want to be." I saw his face whiten with shock as I said the words, but I could no longer stop myself. "Why the hell do you think I left the force here? How could I face anyone?"

His face crumpled. "Skeet, I . . . I—"

My anger was too overwhelming to let him finish. "Don't bother trying to apologize. Just keep out of my way. I don't need some old warhorse trying to prove himself by messing with my case. You've got no business screwing around with this. You're retired and you're sick, for God's sake."

Anger brought some color back to his stricken face. "I'm not too feeble to take care of myself. Not so old you have to put me out to pasture yet. I can still take down a perp."

I grabbed my head in frustration. I worked hard to soften my voice. "Hell, Charlie, if you tried, you'd have a stroke."

"Well, why don't you just shoot me, then?" He was roaring now. "Just put me down like a damn dog who's gotten too long in the tooth, why don't you?"

Grabbing my purse from the couch, I stomped to the door. He called me back as I reached for the knob.

"Skeeter, don't go. I'm . . . I didn't mean to yell."

I looked back at a man once big and intimidating who had begun to shrink inside his skin with age and disease. I saw years of tending an increasingly feeble tyrant stretching before me. The joys of family.

"Charlie, I'm leaving before either of us says something that simply cannot be forgiven. Because that's about to happen. I'll call Dan about this news of yours and tell him you'll come see him with the information."

He started to say something, but I wouldn't let him. "You do that. You lay the whole thing out for Homicide. You give them all the information and contacts you have. Because this isn't about Big Charlie Bannion Supercop. This is about a murderer who's killed two people, maybe more, and it's your job as a citizen, if not a cop, to give the police any information you have that will help them get him."

Before he could answer, I slammed out of the house. I didn't look back until I was in my car heading down the block. He stood in the doorway, looking small and exposed in the rearview mirror as I put him behind me.

CHAPTER 13

I expected to park and wander around in Union Station to find Joe and the kids, but as I passed the front entrance, I spotted them standing in a little cluster at the door and honked. My relief at seeing them surprised me. I hadn't consciously worried about their safety, but now that I saw them, casual and smiling, I realized that at some lower level of consciousness, I had feared some disaster happening to them—or at least to Brian.

I left Charlie's earlier and in greater emotional turmoil than I'd planned. I drove around aimlessly from one Kansas City neighborhood to another until it was the earliest time we'd set to meet. In the process of driving from Midtown to Westport to the Gold Coast to Brookside and the other areas of the city that I knew so well, I dissipated the anger and depression that had overcome me at Charlie's house.

Still, in the back of my thoughts had been a nameless fear about the teenager for whom I was unexpectedly responsible. I hadn't realized what it meant, taking on that responsibility, and I probably didn't want to have it, but I couldn't imagine giving it up to someone else until this was all over. Brian had come to matter to me in a way I couldn't explain even to my-self, and I didn't think anyone else would take his safety as seriously as I did.

The fact that I trusted Joe with him rose up like Dan's comment. Another piece of news from my inner self I'd rather not have had. Like my sudden awareness of Charlie's vulnera-bility and the knowledge that I'd take care of him as he grew less and less able himself, facing my unconscious confidence in someone with whom I didn't want a relationship left me gloomy. My psyche seemed to be telling me things this afternoon that I really had no wish to know.

I pasted a smile on my face as the others climbed into the car. After the string of realizations I'd just had, I would have preferred to drive straight home and rid myself of Joe Louzon and his endearing little girl, fob Brian off on the animals, and sink myself into the relief of smooth jazz, beautiful sock yarn, and an evening of untangling the murders. Homicide seemed so much easier to deal with than all these relationships. If this was what getting a life outside work entailed, I understood now why I'd avoided it for so long.

"Wow! Union Station is great. And the IMAX was awe-some." Julie's smile bisected her face, and, as usual, her pony-tail had strands of hair straggling out underneath and on the sides. "Brian's idea to come here was brilliant."

I shot a glance at Brian, in the backseat, who smiled down at Julie with the natural condescension of an older brother or cousin.

"I was afraid when I saw you all out front that it had been a failure," I admitted to Joe.

"No, we were just trying to decide if we had enough time to take the walkway to Crown Center." He smiled at me as if the awkward conversation we'd had coming to the city had never happened. "We'll have to come back sometime."

"That would be great," Brian agreed. "Could we, Skeet?"

"Sure. Maybe next time, I can join you." I stared at myself in the rearview mirror, wondering who'd just said that. What was I doing making plans for the future with this kid who would soon be moved to the kind of home he needed with a real parent substitute?

"I hope you're all hungry," I said weakly. "Jack Stack is right around the corner."

I drove along Main Street where it spanned the railroad tracks, then turned left at Twentieth Street where the burnt-out hulk of the venerable Hereford House sat next to the boarded-up dingy white Midtown Hotel, home of prostitutes, junkies, and mentally ill street people with tiny disability checks. After a block, I turned onto Wyandotte, down a grimy street that seemed almost more a broad inner-city alley.

Joe looked questioningly at me. "Is this an area where we want to take the kids? Will it be safe?"

I gestured to art galleries on each side of the street, Project InSect with giant painted butterflies on the right and The Crossroads Blues Gallery with rusted steel sculptures out front among battered parked cars and motorcycles.

I laughed. "It's the city, Joe. Gentrification. Trendy galleries next to slums. And at the end . . ." I gestured at the long, low building painted barn red that blocked the road in front of us.

Wyandotte ended at the blocks-long Freight House. I turned right and drove to the far western end, where almost half of the original building was now Jack Stack.

"Man, this is neat," said Brian. "It looks really old."

"It is. It became the freight house once Union Station was built in 1914, but before Union Station was built, it was the old Kansas City railroad terminal." I pulled to the end of the building and around to the back.

Broad patios flanked the entrance with wrought iron umbrella tables and chairs where couples and families sat. In the middle of the western patio, a statue of an iron longhorn steer looked lost among the parties of people.

"Can we sit on the patio, Daddy?" asked Julie. "I want the one with the cow."

"That's not a cow. It's a bull. Can't you tell?" Brian's voice was full of good-natured teasing.

"Let's see what's inside first," Joe said quickly, before Brian could explain the difference between a cow and a bull. "You might like the inside even better."

"I think you will," I promised.

Brian pulled open the heavy front doors and held them for the others. Inside, the foyer had five-by-ten-foot photos of locomotive wheels on each side.

"Oh, look. A pig. Isn't that cute?" Julie ran to the carved wooden pig that stood shoulder-high to me holding out a thick wooden platter next to the inner entry to the restaurant. It looked down at Julie with a serene expression like a pig Buddha.

"Rub its nose for luck," I said, demonstrating with a quick swipe across the polished-smooth snout. "Everybody does it."

Julie reached up to pat the nose gently. Joe made a quick swipe the way I had. Brian rubbed back and forth several times with great deliberation.

"I figure I need the luck," he explained with a blush.

The interior was lit from large windows along the side

walls and from three huge wrought iron chandeliers with elec-
trified kerosene lamps dangling.

"You were right, Dad," Julie said, looking around at her
surroundings as a hostess ushered us to a long booth of dark
wood and leather. "It's even better in here."

"Julie, look at that." Brian pointed at the two-story-high
old-brick interior walls across from us that held immense
framed artworks—two huge collages of primitive farm paintings on wood, frames and all, mixed with paint-peeling carved
porch railings and pillars and old rusted teakettles, frying pans,
andirons, and graters.

"Look behind you at the cows." Julie pointed past Brian's
head to the wall behind. "Oops. Probably they're bulls, aren't
they? I can never tell the difference. How do you?"

I twisted to look at the two oversized paintings of massive
steers behind her and Brian.

"Size," said Joe blandly. "Bulls are much larger than cows."

With a small grin at me, Brian closed the mouth he had
opened to reply.

Jazz played over the music system, and downtown Kansas
City's skyscrapers were visible through the tall windows.

Brian twisted his head around to see everything. "This
place is brilliant, Skeet."

Joe nodded vigorously. "They've done a great job of pre-
serving not only the structure of the original train station but
the feeling."

As the waitress brought drinks for all of us and took our
orders for smoky barbecue, grilled vegetables, baked beans,
and cheesy corn bake, I felt tendrils of tension lifting from me
and drifting away in the cool, dark atmosphere. Feeling suddenly peaceful and contented, I stared at the downtown sky-

line and sipped my ice-cold soda while waitstaff and patrons walked past us on their way to other booths or tables.

Brian and Julie happily chattered on about the building and decor, and Joe looked relaxed and pleasantly surprised. Maybe we could have a peaceful meal together before we went back to Brewster to face the tangle of murder and suicide.

"Hey, Skeeter. Didn't expect to see you here."

I jerked at the words and looked up into my ex-husband's eyes. Sam had stopped beside us as a hostess tried to guide him and the woman following to a table or booth beyond ours.

"Like old times," he said with a rueful grin. "This was always one of your favorite spots."

The petite blonde behind him pursed her lips in irritation. Sam brushed back a lock of golden hair with an automatic gesture that I would always recognize as his, even in the dark.

"Sam," I said. "Do you remember Joe Louzon? You two met the last time you were in Brewster." I nodded to Joe.

Sam's mouth twisted. "And his lovely family? Two kids. A real family man."

I jerked my head toward Julie. "His daughter, Julie." I set my hand lightly on Brian's shoulder. "Brian Jamison. Brian's staying with me since his parents' sudden deaths."

Sam's eyes grew big. "So part of the family's yours? I'd never have figured that."

The woman behind him tugged at his sleeve. "Sam?"

He looked surprised, as if he'd forgotten about her. "Oh. Tammy, this is Skeet, my ex."

I nodded toward her. "Tammy."

Tammy's downturned mouth stretched straight across her face in a gruesome caricature of a smile. "Nice to meet you, I'm sure. Sam, honey, the girl's waiting to take us to our table."

"Why don't you go ahead? I'll be there shortly." Sam waved his hand without looking back at her.

With a vicious glare at me, Tammy followed the hostess past us.

"I don't think she's happy at going on alone. You'd better head after her, or there'll be hell to pay later." I carefully kept my voice neutral.

Sam shrugged carelessly and gave Brian's shoulders a light shove. "Hey, scoot over, buddy. Let me sit down for a sec. Okay?"

Brian moved closer to me. From the closed look of his face, I was certain it was not okay with him.

"Sam, we're having dinner here, and you've got someone waiting for you. Why don't you just call about whatever it is later?"

"How often do I get to see you in town, Skeeter?" he asked in a laughing tone of voice that I dreaded. He used it for camouflage, and I worried what it hid right now.

"Skeeter?" Julie asked. "Like in *mosquito*?"

Sam turned the blinding wattage of his best smile on the little girl, who couldn't help grinning back at him. "Sure. Didn't you know? Her mama called her Marquitta, and her daddy thought it sounded like *mosquito* so he started calling her Skeeter when she was little. That's where Skeet comes from."

Joe's face turned to carved wood. Brian's mouth tightened to a thin line, and his whole face shuttered itself and drew all signs of emotion inward. But Julie delighted in the story and the full glow of Sam's attention.

"Oh, Skeet. That's so cute." She brought her hands together as if to applaud. "Why don't you still call yourself Skeeter instead of Skeet?"

I took a sip of my drink to cool my raging throat before

speaking with precarious control. "Because I hate the nickname, Julie. I don't like my first name, and I absolutely hate that nickname, so I'm stuck with just Skeet. I don't mind it compared to the others. Sam knows how I feel about that nickname, so it's not very nice of him to tell you all, is it?"

Sam feigned a hurt look. "I've always called you that when I was being affectionate. I would never use it against you."

I stopped trying to control my features and let my displeasure show. "Exactly what do you want? You've got one minute to tell me, and then I want you to go to the table where your date is waiting and leave us alone."

I saw an answering fury light Sam's eyes. I remembered the kids and regretted giving in to the anger that was always my downfall. I could see he was about to say something hateful, and I had no intention of letting him spoil the afternoon.

"On second thought, I don't want to know what you want. I want you to leave us, or I'll call the manager over and have you thrown out."

His face livid, he began to shout, "You'll—"

I continued speaking as if he'd never opened his mouth. "If you ever want to see or speak to me again, go. Right now." I gestured behind me with a wave of my hand in the direction his companion had gone.

I was tired of this. If he intended to embarrass me in public every time he saw me, I'd just refuse to see him.

He read the determination in my expression. Anger drained from his face. "Aw, Skeet—"

"Not one word," I said, feeling as grim as I must have looked. "I will not allow you to invade my life like this."

Recoiling from something he saw in my face, Sam rose from beside Brian. "I'm . . . sorry. I didn't mean—"

"Good-bye, Sam." I resolutely turned my attention back to Joe, Julie, and Brian.

Joe's face had a quiet, threatening aspect. Julie looked confused and frightened. Brian had pulled himself up between Sam and me as if to protect me physically. After a second, I heard Sam move off toward his own table.

I let out a deep breath and looked around. "I'm the one who's sorry, guys."

Joe smiled at me. "Not your fault. I do know how it goes, remember?"

I had heard gossip about Julie's mother, who had finally left Joe and Julie for someone else after fairly public infidelities. Joe had mentioned her only once, saying she liked to make scenes, was addicted to drama.

Brian moved back to his original position. "It was my fault." He sounded disgusted with himself. "I shouldn't have moved over and let him sit with us."

I turned to him. "It wasn't your fault. He counted on the fact that none of us wanted to create a scene. I finally called him on it. I've had my fill of scenes."

"I don't know what you ever saw in him." Brian shook his head in wonder. "You seem so smart."

I laughed. "I was a lot younger and dumber, but marriage to Sam aged me and smartened me up real quick."

"I thought he was nice," Julie said in a subdued voice, holding on to the edge of the table with both hands. "He's real handsome. Like a movie star or something."

I could imagine how exciting Sam must seem to an eleven-year-old girl. I smiled at her and reached across the table to pat her hand. "Handsome is as handsome does, Julie. He can be a nice man when he wants to be. The problem is, too often he doesn't want to."

Joe ruffled Julie's hair with his big hand. "I think the best thing is to forget all about it so Skeet doesn't feel bad. We want her to have as much fun as we did today, don't we?"

Julie's big smile returned, and she giggled. "Yeah, we do."

At that moment, the waitress returned with our meals. I welcomed the necessary confusion of getting the different platters and side dishes to the right people and providing extra bowls of barbecue sauce and drink refills. Once we were alone again and eating, the shadow Sam's presence had thrown over us dissipated, and our conversation returned to the fun Julie and Brian had had at Union Station and Joe's descriptions of the weird goings-on at the Kansas City barbecue contest held each year at the American Royal.

That shadow didn't dissipate from me as it did from the others. It couldn't be Sam. He was an old irritant. Something else was dragging me down. As if, deep inside, I knew that the dirty infection of evil back home continued to spread even while we enjoyed an innocent moment of fun away from it.

The sun set with a spectacular glow beyond the silver ribbon of the river as we arrived back in Brewster. We could hear Lady barking the second we turned onto Ash Street. When I pulled up beside Joe's car in back of my house, Lady was trying to climb the fence.

"What's wrong with Lady?" Julie asked.

"That's not like her," Brian said. "She's so good about being left in the yard. She's not a barker."

"The neighbors will be furious if she's been doing this for long." I also wondered at the collie's unusual behavior. "Maybe she's mad at me for taking you away for the day, Bri."

"She never barks when I go to school and you go to work."

His young face looked serious and troubled. "I hope she's not sick or something."

"She looks pretty active and healthy to me, the way she's throwing herself onto that fence," Joe said. He was the first one out of the car, and he stretched his long body in the dying light.

Brian headed straight for the fence and Lady. "Here, girl. We're home now. Everything's all right."

Shutting my car door, I turned toward the back of the house and knew suddenly that nothing was right.

"Brian, come back to the car right now," I called out sharply. I pushed Julie back into the seat she was leaving and shut the car door on her.

"What's wrong?" Brian asked, hurrying to my side.

"What is it?" Joe turned and looked in the direction of my stare.

I pointed to the broken glass in the window of my kitchen door. "Bri, you get back in the car with Julie and lock the doors. Now."

He moved to obey me, and I took a step toward the door.

"Joe, do you want to take the front?" I took a second to work my front-door key off my key ring and hand it to him.

"Maybe we ought to let the dog out to sit in the car with the kids," he suggested.

I nodded and opened the back gate, grabbing Lady's collar and pulling her toward the car. She kept barking and lunging toward the door of the house. "No, girl. You stay here with the kids."

I opened Brian's door and thrust Lady at him. As he took possession of her with quiet words, she stopped barking and began to whine. I shut the car door and strode back to stand beside Joe.

"I'll give you a couple of minutes to get around the front and get it unlocked," I said.

I put on gloves from the kit in my trunk and handed some to Joe. Then, I pulled my Glock from its holster and waited for Joe to pull his gun.

"I'm not carrying, Skeet," he said.

I looked at him in disbelief.

"Today was a family outing." He stared at me. "You took your gun on a family outing?"

I shook my head. "I always carry my gun while I'm working a homicide. Go back to your car and call for backup."

"It's okay. He's probably gone. I'll—"

I glared at him. "Call for backup or stay in the car with the kids. Better yet, take my car and drive the kids away while you call for backup."

His face flushed. "Skeet, I can handle myself."

"Joe, this is probably the guy who did Andrew and Tina. Tina, for sure. He had a gun. He may be waiting in there for me to come home so he can torture me for the whereabouts of what he's looking for. No way do I take an unarmed man into a situation like this." I'd turned back to the door and kept my eyes on it as I spoke to him. "Grab the shotgun in my car."

He stood beside me for a minute, and then walked away. After a few seconds, I heard the unmistakable squawk of a police-band radio. I heard him coming back and prepared myself for the rush into the house where who knew what was waiting.

"I'll take the front," he said. I turned to find him holding the Remington 12-gauge from my car.

I looked into his eyes and nodded. "I'll give you a minute or two to get into position. Then I'm going in."

He moved silently around the side of the house. Counting off seconds, I advanced on the kitchen door. I carefully clicked it barely open and stepped back, switching the gun into my right hand. I yanked it open, banging it back against the house wall, and leaped to the other side of the door frame. There was still enough light from the dying sun to see that the room was empty, so I stepped cautiously over the broken glass in the doorway and flipped the light switch just inside the door.

I paced carefully through the kitchen and into the dining room. No damage confronted me here as it had in Tina's small house. My great-grandmother's glasses and my aunt's vases were still in the glass-fronted china cupboard I'd bought to hold them. I felt a sense of relief.

"Here, Skeet," called Joe from the front hall, to my right. I hurried through the dining room to find Joe kneeling at the foot of the stairs over a slumped body.

"What the hell?" I moved in for a clearer look at the body. Wayne Hamlisch stared up at me over a bloody chest.

Joe stood up and sighed. "It looks like he fell or was pushed and then shot at close range."

"My office is upstairs," I told him. "If he was looking for papers, he'd look there. They'd look there."

Looking back down at Wayne, I heard sirens in the distance. "How many killers have we got here, Joe?"

Later that night, closer to morning, I pulled my car off to the side of a dirt road surrounded by fields and pastures. Cutting off my headlights, I set my head against the steering wheel. I was just short of the long gravel driveway to Karen's house. I should have kept going. But I felt so empty that it frightened me, as though I'd lost everything inside myself—my purpose, my courage, everything that made up Skeet Bannion seeped away in the course of the night.

A paw touched me lightly on the cheek, claws withheld, and Wilma Mankiller gave an inquisitive mew. Grabbing her, I buried my face in her warm fur as tears burst forth.

"I'm sorry, sweetie," I whispered among the sobs. "I'm so sorry."

After finding Wayne's body, I hadn't even thought of the cat I'd had for eight years. I'd been in investigation mode. I called Karen to come take Brian and Lady, but Brian refused to leave without Wilma. To the dismay of the county techs, I walked through the house, searching everywhere, calling, "Here, Wilma! Wilma Mankiller!" without luck. I persuaded Brian to leave with Karen only by promising I'd find Wilma and bring her with me.

The night and the investigation dragged on. When I was finally free to go, I made one last, desperate round of the house, calling for Wilma. A faint mewing at the top of the stairs across from the study, which was blocked off with crime scene tape, led me to the built-in linen closet with its set of deep drawers. The one nearest the floor must have been cracked open by the killer or Wayne at some time in searching, and Wilma had crept in to hide among the sheets. Later, someone had closed it on her. So, Wilma survived.

I kept apologizing to her until Wilma twisted out of my arms and leaped down onto the passenger seat with an impatient cry.

I laughed unsteadily. It was as if Wilma had said, *Get a grip, girl.* That was one of the things I'd always valued about her. She had no sympathy with hysterics or self-flagellation. Like all cats, Wilma was reality based.

Turning on the interior light, I fumbled in my purse for tissues. I wasn't getting mad enough, having two crying jags in as many days. After I wiped my face dry, I turned on the car and finished the short drive to Karen's.

Though it was the tail end of the night when I arrived at her farmhouse, Karen was still up. I found her in her lavender-scented kitchen, waiting in her robe with her long hair down, to make hot chocolate for me and tea for herself. She offered a huge welcoming smile. Trying to smile in return, I set Wilma Mankiller on the floor and dropped into an old wooden kitchen chair as if I were a stone.

"Good. You brought the cat. Brian's been worried sick she might have been hurt by the killer, or let out and run away or something." Karen turned the burner on under the teakettle. "I told him cats are smarter than that, but he'd pretty much worked himself up over it." She pulled mugs down from the cupboard. "He's had good reason to learn to fear for those he loves."

"How's he doing?" I asked. "It's just too much, the way death is following him around. None of it's his doing. He's just stuck in the middle because of the adults in his life." I shook my head. "I should have called family services and had him taken to a foster home. Now he's been involved with another murder."

Karen sat back down across from me. "He wanted to stay with you. It was good for him. You were good for him. How were you supposed to know this would happen?"

I looked down at Wilma, who was curled into a ball on my feet.

I can't even take care of a cat, I thought. *What am I doing with a boy?*

"I'm calling the police in California in the morning. They've never let us know if they contacted his aunt or not, and we haven't heard anything from her." I reached down to stroke Wilma's fur. "We need to get him out of here and into a real home."

Karen looked at me with grave eyes. "You need to do what's best for Brian."

I nodded. "That's the best thing. A home with relatives."

"He doesn't even remember this woman. His mother hadn't heard from her in years. Remember?"

I shrugged. "She's still got to be better than me or a foster home."

Karen stared at me in silence until I bent down to pet Wilma again. "You have to do what you think is right," she finally said.

I straightened up and tried to smile at my best friend. Even the muscles of my face felt too fatigued to work right.

"I've got some clothes for Brian and me out in the car. His schoolbooks and food for the animals. I didn't feel like carrying it all in right now." I felt as if my mind had been sandpapered. I'd never had my own place turned into a crime scene before, and I felt assaulted at a deep level.

"Why should you?" Karen asked. "The morning will be soon enough to do it, and right now Brian desperately needs chores, things to do to keep busy. You're exhausted."

She stood gracefully and moved to the counter next to the stove, where she had the two mugs standing ready. She took down hot chocolate mix and a tea bag.

"I'm sorry I don't have whipped cream for you," she said. "But you know it's not good for you anyway."

Her long, graying hair fell around her face, and she looked at me with kind eyes that always seemed to see more than anyone realized. Because of Karen, I had learned to scrutinize my feelings and my actions.

The kettle shrieked for the few seconds it took her to move it from the burner and pour the steaming water into the mugs. Setting it back on an empty burner, she stirred the cups in silence.

"This has been a difficult day for you, hasn't it? Even before the body, I mean." She turned to hand me my cup and remained standing, leaning back against the counter. "You saw Dan. You saw Charlie. Two different kinds of grieving for the past."

I set my mug on the table and stirred it without paying real attention. "Seeing Dan was great. It reminded me how much I miss working with him and the rest of the team. I should never have left Homicide. Just trying to please the unpleasable Big Charlie Bannion. There's no way for me to be good enough for that man."

Karen shook her head with a sad look in her eyes. "You don't have to be good enough for him. You only need to be good enough for Skeet. But you've internalized so much of his judgmental outlook that you can't really be good enough for yourself, no matter what you do."

I stared at her for a long moment. Finally, Karen smiled and walked over to stand beside me, putting her hand on my head. "But you're exhausted inside and out. Now's not the time for me to play therapist, as Jake used to say. I'm sorry."

"That's okay." Reaching for my cup, I blew on the steaming chocolate. "You've got to keep your hand in. What's the use of having a dysfunctional best friend if you can't use her to stay in practice?"

Karen moved to stand in front of me. "You're not dysfunctional. You're one of the most competent people I know. You're just very hard on yourself, Skeet. Way too hard."

I grinned at her and took a cautious sip of my chocolate.

"You'll give me any compliment as long as you can ignore the part about using me as a practice guinea pig, right?"

Throwing her head back, she laughed deeply from the belly. "You've been learning from my mother. I should never have introduced the two of you."

She walked over to the counter, picked up her tea, and brought it to the table. "Seriously now. This case is getting personally dangerous. The killer invaded your home with a gun. If you'd been there, he would have shot you instead of Wayne Hamlisch."

"The difference is I carry a gun, too. Wayne didn't. And I know how to use it to protect myself. You needn't worry about me, Karen."

"I know you're armed. That provides no protection against someone breaking into your house and lying in waiting to shoot you. Even if you get a shot off at him, you're still wounded or dead." Her face looked suddenly older, all of her sixty years. Her voice sounded heavy and sad. "I couldn't bear to lose you, my dear. Not after losing Jake. You have to take this seriously."

I looked at her dark, softly round face and saw the grief for Jake still swimming in her black eyes. Karen was closer to me than my own mother ever could be, even if she'd wanted to be—which she didn't. When I'd come to Kansas City straight out of high school to start the police academy, Karen took the place my mother threw aside to marry and have a new family. Coreen just wanted to start over and undo all the mistakes of her life, Big Charlie and me included, but Karen took the new police recruit under her wing in her role as the academy's consulting psychologist.

Karen and Jake never had children. They'd treated me as a daughter, and I had so many happy memories of meals and conversations and always laughter with them. Jake's accidental death was acutely painful for me and catastrophic for Karen. For the first time, she leaned heavily on me—instead of the other way around—to get through the weeks after his death. When she'd moved and found a new life, I was all she chose to bring from the old one.

Now, Karen's fear hung in the air between us, and I couldn't just dismiss it.

"You're right. I'll be on alert now. I probably need to pull out my Kevlar vest and start wearing it. Just in case."

Karen's face lightened. "Would you do that? It just makes sense. He can still hit you, but he's much less likely to do real damage."

I grinned at her. "I'll do it. But I get to curse you for the discomfort and gripe about the weight the whole time."

Sighing, Karen took a sip of her tea. "Curse all you want. Just stay in one piece. That's all I ask."

After not nearly enough sleep, I woke to find that Karen had put Brian to work bringing in everything from my car. Lady and Wilma lay on either side of him as he sprawled on the couch in the living room with his schoolbooks. He grinned at me when I passed him.

"You found her. Karen said you would."

Shrugging, I nodded. "Never worry about Wilma, Bri. She's a survivor. She'll always make it through."

"Still, it's a good thing she has you to watch out for her," he said. "It's a good thing for me, too." He reached out and circled my hips with his arms, pulling me into an awkward hug. I patted the top of his head. I didn't know what to do with this kid, but I needed to do something fast.

In the kitchen, the heart of Karen's old farmhouse, I found her sitting at the table drinking tea, just as I'd left her, except dressed and with her hair in its habitual long braid. "Want some breakfast?"

I shook my head. "First thing I do today is call those L.A. cops to get someone on the stick about notifying Brian's aunt so she can come get him out of all this mess. Take him to a real home."

Karen shrugged. "He feels he's found a real home with you."

"It's just the pets. She can buy him a dog and a cat. Hell, I'll buy him a dog and a cat to take back to California with him."

"You know better than that." She gave me the look that meant she thought I was being deliberately dense. I pretended not to notice it and grabbed the phone.

It took dealing with three people at LAPD, none of them happy to take my call, but I finally found the guy I'd originally spoken to about contacting Veronica Ginandes the morning after Tina's death.

"Did you reach her and give her my number to call?" I asked. "It's important she come get her nephew. She's his only living relative, and he's been through hell."

"Nothing like the hell he'd go through if she did come get him," he replied with a drawl. "When there was no trace of her at the address you gave, I ran her name through the system. They know Ronnie real well over in Vice. She's a junkie and a hooker. Just got out from doing three months in jail. Word is she's right back on the streets. Lady, you don't want to dump this kid on her. He's better off in foster care."

"You're sure this is the same woman?"

He heaved a loud sigh. "The Vice guys confirmed she used to live at that address." He enunciated and emphasized each word, as if I were deaf or just stupid. "Back then, she just used. She wasn't hooking yet. Penny ante model and actress who didn't get much work and just hit the skids. We got a million of them out here. Every pretty kid from Kansas and Kentucky comes out here to get famous and rich. Most end up like this gal. She's got nothing for your kid, believe me. He's better off in an orphanage, even. Now, I got no more time for this, okay?"

I nodded, and he hung up as if he'd seen it. I had been counting on this mysterious aunt to swoop down and rescue Brian—and me. Now what would we do?

Karen just looked at me when I asked her how to break the news to Brian. "Skeet, this is not going to bother that boy. As long as he has you, he'll be fine."

"But after this is all over. What happens then?"

"Take it one day at a time. For now, he's just fine. As long as he believes he can count on you."

I shook my head. "I'm the last person he should count on. I've got no business with a kid."

Karen shrugged. "He has with you, it seems."

Monday morning dawned cold and cloudy gray, one of winter's last swats in the face. I wouldn't have minded so much if the weekend hadn't been warm and sunny. They finally let us back into my house the evening before, though the evidence of crime scene work was still all around us. I made Brian get up and run with Lady and me.

"Come on." I danced from one foot to the other in the early morning's brisk wind as I tried to keep warm. "I can't leave you here alone, and you wouldn't want that anyway."

He hunched up in his sweat pants and T-shirt with a jacket over it. "It's too early and too cold to go running. I don't want to."

"So. I don't want to, either." I slapped my hands together, swinging my arms wide. "Come on."

I headed off, walking at a vigorous pace to warm up on the way to the River Walk Park, where I would run. Brian followed disconsolately, pulled by Lady's leash as she bounded at my side.

"If you don't like doing it, why do you run?" he grumbled.

I swung my head back in his direction. "Because there are times you need to be able to move faster than the bad guys or for a longer time than they can." I turned back to face ahead and sped up my pace into a racewalk, swinging my arms.

Lady lunged forward, and Brian stumbled closer to my side. I looked over at him briefly. "Police work isn't all paperwork and phone calls, Bri. And it's not just guns and car chases, either. I've had to chase someone or run away from someone when the ability to run and keep running kept me or someone else alive."

We cut through the parking lot behind the little group of shops and restaurants that had sprung up beside the entrance to the wildlife sanctuary. Beyond the cluster of buildings, I could see the park bounded by the river on one side and train tracks on the other. Lady could see and smell the same, and she began to pull at her leash in growing excitement.

"You're going to have to speed up, Bri. Lady loves to run in the park in the morning."

As though she understood what I had said, Lady barked happily and headed toward the park. Laughing at her excitement, Brian began to stretch his legs into a faster, longer stride. Lady yipped again in sheer joy, and he began to run in earnest with her as they passed the buildings and entered the park. Lady leaped into the air, barking, and flipped her head back as if to ask if we were going to join her. I began to jog until we reached the river walk and then I stretched my jog into a steady running pace.

Brian and Lady dropped off the path and headed over to the antique carousel that dominated the center of the park. I continued to the fork in the path that determined the ultimate length of the circuit around the park. Normally, I would continue on the path that ran for another half mile beside the river before curving back toward the park, but with Brian and Lady at the carousel behind me, I turned left onto the crosspath that would take me over to the train-track side of the park and back around to the starting point.

If I ran the shorter loop, I could keep an eye on Brian and still do my miles. I'd just have to make more complete circuits than I did on the longer loop.

My eyes kept flicking to the carousel as I ran. Brian and Lady roughhoused and chased each other, clambering on and around the restored figures of horses, mermaids, and lions.

He was so good for Lady. I had to admit I never took this kind of time just to play and wrestle around with her. Rounding the turn that sent me back toward the park entrance, I saw Brian sit on the outer edge of the carousel floor, breathing heavily and tossing a stick for Lady to fetch.

I didn't feel so guilty now. Even a fourteen-year-old could be worn out by dog energy. Lady suddenly began to bark in earnest. While I drew closer to the carousel, Gil Mendez pulled his car into a nearby parking spot, stepped out, and walked over to join Brian on the carousel. Both of them waved at me. I waved back and increased my speed.

What was Gil doing out here at this hour? I left the path and sprinted across the grass to join them, aborting my full run.

By the time I reached them, all I could do was throw myself onto the grass while I filled my aching lungs with oxygen. The grass was cold and wet with condensation, but the metal carousel would be just as wet and even colder. I lay on my back against the grass, and Lady romped over and poked her wet nose at my face.

"All right, girl. I'll sit up in a minute. Give me a chance to catch my breath."

"Maybe you're getting too old for this, Chief." Gil grinned. His usually immaculate clothes were wrinkled and rumpled, and he looked as if he hadn't slept last night.

I smiled back at him. "I've always been too old for this. Even when I was eighteen. Either I do it, or waddle after crooks and hope they fall down so I can catch them." I sat up, leaning back on my arms for support.

Gil laughed. "Lots of cops do just that."

"That option's looking better all the time." I pulled my headband off and wiped my face with it before standing. Tucking it into the pocket of my sweats, I lifted one foot onto the edge of the carousel floor.

Brian threw the stick and raced Lady to it. They began to play tug-of-war a few feet away from the carousel. I smiled and nodded at Brian to show I appreciated his giving us privacy.

"What do you have for me, Gilberto? You look like you've been sleeping in your clothes."

"Sleep? What's that?" He shrugged. "I'd only dream in numbers. I've got the goods on two vice chancellors and a dean and I'm pretty sure about another vice chancellor, but I can't prove it." He lifted his hands. "So you see why I came to dump it all on you. Too rich for my blood."

"Hah!" I wanted to curse my luck, but I couldn't think of any curse strong or bad enough.

Gil dropped his hands into his lap. "The good news is that the dean and one of the vice chancellors are already dead and can't come after us. The bad news is that the others aren't."

"So Jeremy Coulter's involved, too?"

He nodded. "I'm pretty sure, but he's the one I don't have the goods on. I'd swear he had to be in on it, but there's no paper trail to him the way there is to the others."

I bit my lip while I thought. "Maybe he wasn't involved. He's too smart to get into something like this."

"He was definitely too smart to get caught at it. Unlike the others. Hamlisch, Scheuer, and Jamison. I got the goods on them all. Coulter was involved with the whole thing. Just not with the actual criminal stuff as far as I can find anything." He looked frustrated.

I sat down beside him on the carousel. "So maybe he's not crooked?"

He stretched out his feet and examined his snakeskin boots. "I've traced him through the whole hinky setup with fake holding companies and fake vendor accounts. I just can't find him in the actual illegal stuff, but he's there up to the last second. He wouldn't be in all the other unethical stuff if he wasn't going to get the illegal profit."

"Hell!" I stared at the river and its opposite shore for a moment. Wisps of fog rose in dancing tendrils above the surface of the river and rendered the line of woods on the Kansas side indistinct, impressionistic. Dammit, I liked Jeremy.

"I've got to go home before I come into the office, Gil." I indicated Brian and Lady, who'd fallen in a heap together on the grass. I stood up and called out, "Get off that wet grass, Bri. Come on, we're going home. School awaits."

Turning back to Gil, I lowered my voice. "Get some breakfast. Better yet, bring us some, too. We need to talk this out before we get to the office. Nothing stays secret for long there."

He stood and shook wrinkles out of his slacks. "I'll hit The Herbal." He grinned. "I keep trying to make time with Dolores. Now, I can do it on the clock."

I shook my head and laughed. "She's too good for you, Gil. Give it up. Besides, she's going the *curandera* route."

He faked a look of offended dignity. "So? I can be traditional. Ask her to give me a love potion."

"She's a healer, not a witch."

"*De corazon*. She's a *bruja de corazon,* a witch of the heart." He struck his own chest, then stepped out of his mock dramatic persona. "I'll pick up breakfast for us and meet you in a half an hour or so. Plenty of coffee. But, hey, Brian doesn't do coffee, does he?"

"He's not supposed to," I answered, preoccupied with considerations of Jeremy's probable guilt or innocence.

Gil looked at me sharply. "Yeah, well, we've got a lot of folks all of a sudden who're doing things they're not supposed to."

Once we'd dropped Brian at school, Gil and I drove straight to Eugene Scheuer's office. When Alice found us, she rushed into her office and slammed the door.

"Calling Eugene," I told Gil.

"Think Scheuer will rush in here to deal with us, or will he bolt?" he asked.

"He's definitely the bolting type. I don't think he'll run yet. He doesn't know for sure what we have."

Gil nodded. "What do you think he'll do when he finds out?"

I thought for a second. "He'll crumble. That will be our best chance to get Jeremy. I think he'll toss us anyone he can to try to get a better deal."

That was the type of guy Eugene was, but I wondered if it would really play out that way. He knew university politics and the way the chancellor felt about negative publicity, especially on the heels of the deaths of another vice chancellor and a dean. Eugene might feel that he could wangle a face-saving deal out of the chancellor. No criminal charges if Eugene left his position quietly and paid back some of the money. This couldn't happen if I proved Eugene had anything to do with the murders, but the problem was I didn't have anything other than motive to tie him in to them.

We'd been sitting in Eugene's suite for almost an hour when he came barreling through the door. He had obviously showered, shaved, and dressed as carefully as he usually did, but his face was a match for Gil's in its obvious exhaustion and lack of sleep.

"Skeet, Alice said you needed to talk to me right away. Is it something about Wayne's death?" Eugene kept his hands rigidly at his sides. "Shall we go into my office?"

Alice opened the door to the inner office and began to follow us. I fixed her with a warning glare. She stiffened.

"Do you want me to take notes, Eugene?" she asked, leaning around me to make eye contact with him.

"I don't think you'll want her in here while we're talking," I said before he could answer.

Eugene looked at me and nodded. Avoiding Alice's pleading look, he gestured for her to leave. I closed the door behind her and approached him as he stood next to the conference table. He had already begun to wring his hands together.

Taking a seat at the table, Gil pulled the accounting-department printouts from his briefcase. Eugene glanced once at them and then turned his gaze out the window.

"You might want to sit, Eugene," I said as I pulled out a chair and sat. "We're going to be here for a while."

"What . . . What is this all about?" Eugene threw himself into a chair and laid his hands carefully still on the table before him.

"We have proof that you conspired with Wayne and probably Jeremy to embezzle funds from the university, Eugene. Andrew McAfee knew it and blackmailed you."

I actually had no proof that Andrew had blackmailed him. Until I got my search warrant for Andrew's safe deposit box, I'd have no direct evidence of the blackmail itself. But I didn't see any reason to let him know that.

Eugene's face drained of color, but he kept his hands under control, to my surprise. "That's quite ridiculous. What is this so-called proof?"

I signaled Gil with my eyes. He picked up the printouts and looked directly at Eugene. "These documents show that you, Hamlisch, and Coulter set up a holding company."

"There's absolutely no reason that we shouldn't do that," Eugene protested. "There was no conflict of interest with our university positions. It was for investment and tax purposes." He appeared remarkably calm. He'd lost his color, but his hands remained still, and his voice was firm and controlled. I found this surprising after my earlier encounter with him.

Gil nodded. "That's right. Then you set up multiple intermediary companies with accounts that fed into the holding-company accounts, and you obtained approved-vendor status for some of these companies and billed the university for non-existent goods and services. We have proof that you siphoned off large amounts of this money before it ever reached the holding-company account, as did Hamlisch."

Eugene grew paler and gulped compulsively. "You're mistaken. What do police know about accounting?"

"This officer has an accounting degree." I smiled deliberately and pointed at Gil. "I'm certain that the district attorney's office will be able to follow the clear trail that Gil has found in the accounts—and that Andrew McAfee found before him—and make it visible to a jury. Or to a judge, if you decide to forgo a jury trial."

Eugene brought his hands together and began to twist them around each other. He looked down at them as if they belonged to someone else and dropped them back to the table-top.

"I don't expect the chancellor will want this to go to trial, do you, Skeet? Not with the capital campaign coming on. I expect he'll just want me to give up my job and sign an agreement to repay the money." Eugene looked almost resigned. He sounded as though he had rehearsed what he was saying. "I think we should talk to him before we do anything else."

"You haven't got anything to deal with. Unless you're willing to testify against Jeremy."

Eugene's lips curved into a tiny, sad smile. "I'm afraid I can't do that, Skeet. I could testify forever on Wayne Hamlisch's guilt. He's the one who started it all and brought us in. But Jeremy didn't do anything illegal or wrong."

I shook my head. "He signed the papers for the holding company the same way you did."

Eugene gave me a smug look. "But you didn't find any trace of his having taken any money from the fake companies, did you? No, you didn't. Because Jeremy was never involved or even knowledgeable about that part of it all."

I leaned forward across the table. "Eugene, even if you can work your deal with the chancellor, you'll still lose your job and your profession. You'll be unable to find a job. You'll be ruined. Why should you protect Jeremy? I'll bet he's the one who set things up and got you involved in the first place."

"You'd lose, then. It was all Wayne. First, he came to us and wanted us to do the holding company, which made good financial sense. It was only later that he suckered me into the illegal stuff, and neither of us ever let Jeremy know about that. We knew it wouldn't fly with him." He turned his mouth down in a bitter expression. "I only wish I'd been as smart or as honest."

I shook my head. "Don't go down protecting him, Eugene."

He stood up and headed for the phone on his desk with a careful, controlled gait, holding his hands stiffly at his sides. "I think it's time now for us to talk with the chancellor. If you want to keep your job."

I was furious. The chancellor fell in with Eugene's scheme. No criminal charges, just a gentleman's agreement to leave his position and repay 50 percent of the money he'd stolen. And guess who was going to broker it? Jeremy Coulter. I was convinced now that Jeremy had talked Eugene into confessing and covering for him. Why not? Everyone knew that Jeremy handled the chancellor's most important correspondence. It would be simple for him to get Eugene the kind of letters of recommendation that would see him in a new high-level position at some other university in a matter of months.

I argued for pressing charges. I pointed out the connections to Andrew's death, but the chancellor was happily convinced that Tom Jamison had committed that crime and handily tidied himself away. I wanted justice. The chancellor wanted convenience.

I spoke to him alone and told him of our suspicions about Jeremy. I explained how we could apply the threat of arrest to press Eugene to incriminate Jeremy, but the chancellor refused to believe that his favorite staff member could be guilty of anything wrong, let alone illegal.

"After all, Chief," he said, "Jeremy's Ivy League. You can't really suspect him of wrongdoing, surely?" And that was the exact moment when I realized what the letters "il" in Andrew's list meant. I simply nodded and left the chancellor's office with Gil as the university legal team arrived.

Now, I stood at Jeremy Coulter's office door alone while his secretary announced me. I had sent Gil back to the department office, not wanting him to be involved.

"Marquitta, I'm so pleased to see you." Jeremy ushered me into his domain.

He did appear genuinely glad to see me. I walked in and took the seat he offered. He folded himself gracefully into the chair next to mine.

"I only have half an hour before a meeting with the chancellor that's just come up. I hope we can take care of your business in that time. If not, you can reschedule with Helen." He aimed a warm smile at me.

"I suspect your meeting is connected to this meeting." I ignored his smile.

He smiled with less warmth. "Are you going to tell me about it?"

"We've tracked the embezzlement schemes you were involved in—with Tom Jamison and with Wayne and Eugene. You were all blackmailed by Andrew McAfee."

I waited in silence. Most people can't stand silence and will speak simply to fill it up. This was one way suspects gave themselves away. I'd learned this technique from Dan Wheelwright.

After a long moment, Jeremy gave me a quizzical smile. "You're serious. You really believe this."

I kept watching him in silence.

"No, Marquitta. I haven't embezzled any money." He looked straight into my eyes. "I can see why you think I have. However, I knew nothing about Tom's use of our company for embezzlement until he told me in the jail."

He admitted that ill-timed visit. Of course, how could he hope to hide it since it was recorded by the police department?

"As for this scheme with Wayne and Eugene you mention, I know nothing of what you're talking about. Are you simply assuming that because one holding company was used to steal from the university that the other must be doing the same? It really is just for investment and tax purposes."

"Eugene's already confessed." I left the statement hanging in the air without any follow-up. Let him worry about exactly what Eugene had confessed.

He looked at me with a sad expression. "Whatever he's confessed, it can't have had anything to do with me. I've done nothing illegal, Marquitta, no matter what you seem to think."

He stared at me for a second and then dropped his gaze to his hands, relaxed on the table. "I thought we were friends."

I sat in the reproachful silence without responding. He was so good at this. He almost made me believe he was innocent. I reminded myself of Tom Jamison, who'd thought Jeremy was a friend. I was certain the man before me had manipulated Tom across that line into suicide to save his own skin.

Finally, he lifted his head to look straight at me again. "Tom, Wayne, and Eugene seem to have placed me in a very awkward situation. It doesn't look good for me, does it?"

I shrugged. "Wayne and Tom are dead now. That situation's a little more than awkward."

"You can't think I have anything to do with their deaths," he cried, showing his first real concern.

"They're not the only ones dead." I made my voice as cold as I felt whenever I thought of Tina's death. "Embezzlement. Blackmail. It's so ugly. You'd do anything to make it go away."

His jaw firmed up, and his mouth tightened into a straight line. "It is indeed ugly, and someone might do anything to make it go away, obviously even murder. But not me."

I raised my eyebrows to show my skepticism.

"I have not stolen. I have not paid blackmail. I have not killed anyone." His eyes narrowed. "You haven't a shred of real evidence against me. This is all a bluff. Eugene may have confessed, but he hasn't implicated me in any way."

And I'd like to know why not, I thought.

Jeremy laughed in genuine amusement. "Did you think you could come in here and fool me into admitting to all those crimes? Marquitta, I'm disappointed. I'm innocent, but if I weren't, why would I just admit it all to you?"

"You were involved in the embezzling. I think you were the senior partner in both cases. You were the one with the brains. You can't expect me to believe that Wayne or Eugene thought it up."

He laughed with delight. "I'm guilty because I'm intelligent? God, that's priceless."

I ignored his laughter. "You found Tom Jamison in a precarious state of mind after he'd been arrested, and you worked on him until he was suicidal."

Jeremy's face sobered. "Tom was not an emotionally strong man. I suspect no one is to blame for his suicide but Tom."

I stared at him. "That was your big mistake. If you hadn't had to do something to shut Tom up permanently, I might have bought all the rest of it, suspicious as it looks."

Suddenly, he relaxed and smiled with the same warmth he'd shown when I arrived. "No, you wouldn't, Marquitta. You're too good a cop for that. You might have wanted to believe me, but you'd have had to doubt me because of the suspicious circumstances."

I stared at him in surprise. Why would he start telling me the truth now? Was he going to confess? Why?

"You know, I really do like you, Marquitta," he said. "You can't do anything about your doubts because you have no evidence. But I could convince the chancellor to get rid of you."

Before I could react, he waved his hand negligently. "Oh, don't worry, my dear. I wouldn't do that. You're one of the few people at this benighted institution who isn't a total fool. I know you've too much intelligence to repeat your accusations to anyone else unless you found proof. Which you won't."

"So you're willing to have the police chief of your campus believe you're definitely guilty of embezzlement and having caused a suicide and possibly guilty of multiple murders?" I asked incredulously.

"I have great faith in you, Marquitta. I know you'll find the murderer and arrest him, and then you'll know I'm not guilty of that. As far as the embezzlement and the suicide go, you can believe what you want. There's not any way you can prove anything." He smiled at me again.

It was as though he'd admitted right out that he'd embezzled and driven Tom to suicide, and he was taunting me with my inability to do anything about it.

"Come now, we'll still be friends," he said with a laugh. "We have such high opinions of each other."

Feeling sick, I rose from the table and left the room in a daze. As I walked out, Jeremy continued to speak to me in a cloud of normal, courteous, friendly phrases that I now knew he'd been using as camouflage for years.

As I walked out of New Admin, still kicking myself for trusting Jeremy the way I had, my phone rang with a call from Gil.

"Guess what?" he said. "Oldrick is a member of that faculty senate bylaws committee, but he didn't show for the meeting or the old guys at the local bar thing afterward. You said you thought it was phony. Well, it is."

Whoopie. Score one for me. I could read transparent Oldrick. It was just the real pros like Jeremy I tripped up on. "We'll pay him a visit, Gilberto. Find out what he was really doing. I'll meet you at the office in a couple of minutes."

As I hung up and passed by Moller, Stuart Morley ran out the front door, calling my name. I stopped and waited for him to catch up with me.

"Skeet, I need to tell you something." He was breathing

only a little harder than if he'd walked, and I wondered if he was also a runner. "It's about Oldrick."

"So tell me, Stuart." I readied myself for another tirade about Oldrick's research.

"He's sleeping with a young student. Andrew's girlfriend, as a matter of fact."

"The mythical girl whose name no one knows?" I asked.

He flushed. "I don't know her name, but I can tell you where she lives. In those Granada apartments on the outskirts of Girlville. Here, I wrote it down for you." He handed me a piece of paper with the address. "I think she's home right now. If you hurry, you could find her."

"Stuart, why are you doing this?" I looked at his rigid stance and his angry, earnest face.

"I won't have him corrupting yet another student." He pulled his hand back from mine.

"But I thought research was your concern, not student affairs. Isn't that under Eugene?"

He pulled himself up even stiffer than he was. "Student welfare is everyone's concern on this campus, or it should be. That long-haired idiot is a menace to any student who gets near him. He needs to be terminated."

I raised my eyebrows a little at his fervor. "Hey, Stuart, thanks for this address. I've been wanting to talk to this young woman."

I turned back to Old Central.

"Skeet . . ." Stuart's voice died out on my name.

I turned back around. He stood there staring at me. I gave him a brisk nod and left before he could make some obnoxious comment. I could feel his eyes on me all the way to the front doors of Old Central.

Gil and I headed out to find our nameless girl right away. We pulled into the parking lot of the Granada apartment complex, mostly students with a smattering of retired people and the immigrants who work in the kitchens and back rooms of local restaurants and shops. We knocked at 220-C, and the door was opened by a tall girl with short auburn hair in what my aunts used to call a pixie cut. Her eyes were red and swollen, and she wore a short kimono.

I introduced myself, handing her my card. "We'd like to talk to you about Andrew McAfee and Alec Oldrick."

Starting to cry in loud, hiccupping bursts, she turned and walked to the ratty orange couch, leaving the door open. She threw herself on it and called out between sobs, "Come in."

I glanced at Gil, who looked distinctly uncomfortable, as I walked forward. He closed the door behind him. I sat on the couch beside her and handed her a box of tissues from the table next to me. She took one and wiped her flooding eyes and blew her nose.

"What's your name?" I asked in a sympathetic voice.

"Lissa," she said between hiccups. "Melissa Averill, but everyone calls me Lissa."

Gil wrote it down in his notebook. He would record our conversation, and I would do the questioning.

"Lissa," I said gently. "Tell me what you know about Andrew and Professor Oldrick."

She burst into a new bout of sobs. "I wish I'd never seen either of them! I wish I was dead! I wish they were dead! Both of them!"

"Well, Andrew is dead, and I know you know that because I saw you at his funeral."

She shook her head. "I know. I know. But Alec could just join him in the cemetery. It would serve him right. Only then what would I do? But he's not going to help me so he might as well be dead."

I had a sudden hunch what all the crying was about. "Lissa, are you pregnant?"

A new burst of sobbing was my answer. All she could do was nod her head.

"Who's the father? Do you know?"

"It's Alec's. I'm almost completely certain. I told him it was his. He said it could be Andrew's, and of course, it could be, but I really know it's Alec's. I can feel it's his. He's not married like Andrew so he could marry me but he won't. He says he won't." More sobbing ensued.

I looked at Gil over her bowed head. He was scribbling fast.

I patted her shoulder awkwardly. "Lissa, listen to me. Were you with Professor Oldrick the night Andrew was killed?"

She nodded. "He was so glad Andrew was dead because then he couldn't blackmail him any longer about using university money to pay for that disgusting movie." She stopped crying for a moment and looked up. "His research is very important, and it was the only way he could do it so it's really all right, even though it was kind of an illegal movie with the kids and all." She dabbed her eyes, then looked up at me earnestly. "He has to get tenure, you know. That's the only reason he's saying he won't marry me. He thinks they won't give him tenure, and he'll be out of a job. But his research is really fabulous. They will give him tenure, and then he can marry me. I'll be a professor's wife, and the baby and everything will be all right."

"What time was Alec here with you that night?" I asked as gently as I could. Oldrick was never going to marry this kid, and she would soon be facing tough choices.

Her face was a map of tears. "All night. We ordered a pizza in at seven, and he didn't leave until about four in the morning." She frowned. "He always sneaks out before sunrise. Like I'm something to be ashamed of."

This sent her into another spasm of tears. I wrote down the numbers of the women's center and the counseling center on campus and told her to talk to them. Gil and I walked out of her apartment with a sense of relief.

Gil shook his head as we headed for the car. "Real trouble there."

"Just one more person whose life has been ruined by Andrew McAfee and Alec Oldrick."

Early morning's clouds had pressed in more densely on the town. The lonely sound of the midmorning train whistle and the threatening sight of the lowering clouds sent my gloomy spirits into the gutter. Everyone had a nice, neat way to avoid prosecution. When I had the killer dead to rights, would the chancellor still try to work out a gentleman's agreement?

I amused myself by choosing the expletives I'd use if he did. I didn't have a say in the prosecution of Eugene or Jeremy, but murder was different. If I managed to find evidence that either or both of them were involved in any of the three murders, the noble vice chancellors were going down.

As I dropped Gil back at Old Central, I decided not to let the entire day be a waste. I would drop in at the courthouse and see if I could hurry up the search warrant for Andrew's safe deposit box. Randy Thorsson was the district attorney for Deacon

County. I always preferred to work with one of his two ADAs. I hoped one of them had snared the request for a search warrant. But when I asked at the front desk, I was directed to Randy's office, restraining a groan. Like most DAs, Randy had greater political ambitions and left the bulk of the county's cases to his two assistant district attorneys. Currently, he was considered a shoo-in for the Republican nomination for state senator.

I shuddered at the thought of that prospect. The incumbent state senator was a senile adulterer. This didn't sit well with voters, and Randy actually stood a chance. He had hired an expensive PR firm, and with their help, he was daily becoming a new and scarier man.

Once portly and bald, Randy had remade his image to further his political prospects. Now cadaverously thin and wearing a toupee with enough hair for two men, he remained short and unlikable. But I wasn't sure that was what the electorate would see in the brief TV sound bites. He kept all the high-profile cases for himself—with the help of the ADAs behind the scenes. This triple murder had to have turned into one of the highest-profile cases in Deacon County history.

Once I was in his office, he tried to pass off his latest speech as conversation, strutting and posturing in front of me as if I were a phalanx of television news cameras.

"The people of Deacon County have a right to feel safe in their homes. That is exactly what I intend to bring back to this county. Safety and security. No fear of vicious criminals running loose, waiting to prey on more innocent citizens. And—"

"Randy, that's why I'm here," I interrupted, knowing the speech was nowhere near finished. "Last week, I asked your office for a search warrant for Andrew McAfee's safe deposit box in Kansas City. He was blackmailing people. We believe the contents of that box will lead us directly to the killer."

Randy stood flatfooted in front of me, trying to shift his thoughts from the rest of his speech, so I gave him a helpful nudge: "The sooner we get the proof and arrest the killer, the sooner you can arraign. Of course, that means dealing with all that publicity, so I see why you're dragging your feet, but—"

"We'll have no more of that," he declared with a dramatic gesture of his hands, as if he were on camera. Throwing open the door, he shouted at his secretary, "Maureen, who's handling that search warrant for Skeet? I want it expedited. No more delays, you hear?"

Without even lifting her head, Maureen replied in her own shout, "It's gone to Judge Magda, Randy."

He turned back to me with a smile of satisfaction. "See? I've turned this into a smooth-running operation that truly serves the public's needs."

I edged around him and out of the office, saying, "Yes, you surely have, Randy."

With a self-satisfied smirk, he closed his door. I turned to Maureen. "How long ago did this go to the judge?"

She giggled. "He's been sitting on it for days, but when I saw you go in, I got the clerk to run it down there. Knew he'd be shouting around about how everyone was holding up justice."

I shook my head in frustration. "Thanks. I'll see if I can sweet-talk Judge Magda into approving it fast."

Maureen took a gnawed yellow pencil out of her bottle-black bouffant-wing hairdo and pointed it at me. "Just don't let him try the case once you make the arrest. If you do, no matter how tight you have it tied, he'll lose, and that SOB will walk."

I bit my lip. "Then find some way to cripple him, Maureen.

Because we need this one behind bars before he kills anyone else."

"Been working on that crippling idea for the past year. No such luck yet. I'd love to have Beau Fletcher as acting DA. God, would we see convictions."

I walked out into the hall with Maureen's voice behind me: "Good luck with Judge Magda. She's not her usual self today."

For a second, my body slumped at her words. Another obstacle in a day of obstacles and dead ends. Then, I straightened my shoulders to a military bearing. I refused to let this day defeat me. It was only half over. Things could change drastically if I could get into the safe deposit box.

I took the stairs down to Judge Felissen's chambers two at a time, hoping to catch her during lunch recess. Magda Felissen was a sixty-year-old grandmother with the looks of a model and the sharpest legal mind I had ever seen. I often wondered why she remained in little Deacon County when she could have gone so far in Kansas City. From an urban base, Magda could have taken the federal courts by storm. When I suggested this to her, she shook her beautifully coiffed silver head and said she was where she wanted to be.

I slowed my rapid strides as I reached the judge's chambers. I didn't want to burst in on her breathless and seeming out of control. Standing outside the door, I brought my breathing back to normal and knocked.

Magda cracked the door warily, her face set for a quick refusal of whoever the caller was but warming when she saw me. "Come on in." She held the door fully open. "I need to warn you, though. I've only got enough lunch for me, and I'm not sharing."

I laughed as I entered. "I would never take a hungry judge's lunch."

Magda closed the door after me. "I've been on a diet for the last two weeks, and it's getting to me. Normally, I don't think much about food, unless it's time to eat."

I could believe that. Magda had the figure of a teenager.

She sat back down behind her big desk. "Suddenly, I'm dreaming of corned beef sandwiches and mashed potatoes. Apple pie. Lasagna." She closed her eyes and licked her lips lasciviously.

I laughed. "I can't think of anyone with less need to diet."

Magda blew me a kiss. "When you get older, it gets harder to keep the goodies life handed you. Everything starts to sag or wrinkle. You, too, will learn this one day. Enjoy your looks while you have them." Magda took a bite of her sandwich and grimaced. "Everything on this is low-fat or low-something, and it tastes like it, dammit."

I made an incredulous face at her. "Magda, you haven't a wrinkle on you." I raised my hands in mock despair. "I should look as good at my age as you do at yours."

"Hah. Talk like that only means you want something from me." Magda rummaged in the stack of papers on her desk. After pulling one out, she put on slim reading glasses. "I wonder if it's this search warrant?"

I smiled. "How'd you guess?"

"That damn Randy. He's never talked to me about this. Just pops it up here right before you arrive, as if I'm some dog to do his bidding when he snaps his fingers." Magda read it over with a frown.

"Actually, he'd been sitting on it, afraid to send it to you until I showed up."

"What's wrong with it?" Magda asked sharply.

I made a pacifying gesture with both hands. "Nothing. Randy's just caught up in dreams of state senatorhood right now, and everything looks risky unless you spell out how it can help his campaign."

"The day he becomes state senator we need to wear black and have a wake for common sense." Magda took off her glasses and looked up to the ceiling. "Though, actually, he'd fit right in with some of them."

I grimaced. "I'm afraid you're right there."

After a few seconds of diplomatic silence to consider the low standards of the state senate, I pointed to the requested search warrant. "This is for the safe deposit box of our first murder victim. His wife would have signed a permit to search, but she was killed before the paperwork was done. We have reason to believe this box holds blackmail evidence and will help us solve these murders."

Magda looked up at me and settled the glasses back on her nose. "Were you worried I'd have problems reading it?"

My eyes widened. Dieting was taking a toll on Magda's disposition. "I'm just never sure if Randy has given you the correct arguments. He's not—"

Magda waved an impatient hand as she turned to the document. "Our district attorney is not noted for his accuracy."

I held my breath. Since my arrival six months earlier, I'd had a good working relationship with Judge Magda. I brought her only righteous requests, and she approved them. I'd never known Magda to let anything outside of good legal reasoning affect her decisions.

Removing the reading glasses, she waved them for emphasis. "By rights, I ought to hold this for at least a week. Just to teach that pompous fool a lesson. Did I tell you that mess of a man brought a box of chocolates in here yesterday? Waved them right under my nose. If I weren't a lady, I'd have slugged him."

"Please don't take it out on this warrant. I need to put this killer in jail before he gets someone else."

With lips pursed, Magda looked at me for a long moment. Finally, she set her glasses back on her slim nose, reread the warrant, and signed it. She removed the glasses and inserted one of the earpieces between her teeth as she scrutinized my face. Finally, she pointed her glasses at me.

"You'd better watch yourself, Chief Marquitta Bannion. This felon's already invaded your home and may have been waiting to take you out when he got fat old Wayne Hamlisch." She wagged the glasses at me. "Because you're in a small town, don't make the mistake of thinking the bad guys are any less bad. There aren't as many, but we have our share, and they're just as dangerous."

I stood with a harsh laugh. "I take this guy seriously. Believe me, Magda." I pulled up the bottom of my shirt to display the Kevlar vest I wore underneath.

Magda handed me the search warrant with a sigh. "Find this beast, Skeet. We need this particular bad guy off the streets. His body count is already too high."

I took the warrant and put it in my purse. Magda stood and walked me to the door. "I just don't want your body added to that count."

"Don't worry about me. I was born careful." I smiled.

Magda shook her head and kissed me on the cheek. "Why don't I believe that?"

In the room where the vice president of Kansas City's Mid-Continent Bank brought Andrew's safe deposit box to me, the heat was suffocating. Sweat gathered underneath the straps of my Kevlar vest. One of the reasons I hated wearing them. That and the rubbing raw if they weren't adjusted just right. I'd put up with a lot more, if it would make Karen feel secure.

On my way out of town, I had radioed my office that I had the search warrant and was heading for the bank in KC to execute it. By the time I drove into Kansas City and fought my way through the bank's bureaucracy, it was almost closing. I refused to be put off until the next day, pointing out to the vice president and president that I'd been in their building for several hours before I was finally passed on to them. The president left his vice president to deal with me, leaving with the rest of the staff at five o'clock. Vice president Gardner, looking ill used, finally led me to the room next to the vault where box holders were left alone with their boxes and contents. He did not leave me alone with anything, however.

A short, fragile-looking man with thinning hair atop a schoolboy face, Mr. Gardner was barely thirty. I wondered how he'd climbed so high in such a short time. He set the metal box on the table in front of me and drew out a set of keys. With sparse eyebrows raised, he smiled with excessive politeness, hovering over me.

"You'll give me an inventory of the contents you take?" He managed to make it as much a command as a question.

"I'll list everything taken into custody on your copy of the search warrant and sign it. That's standard procedure." I wanted to order him to unlock the box.

He stared at me, as though doubting my words. Finally, he nodded and sorted among the keys for the correct one. After turning it in the lock, he lifted off the lid of the box with a ceremonial air and placed it on the table.

"Please don't touch anything in the box," I said, pulling gloves and evidence bags out of my briefcase. "We'll need to test them for fingerprints and trace evidence."

Mr. Gardner pulled back the hand he'd extended toward the box. "I'm just to witness?"

"That's right. You'll sign the list on my copy of the search warrant. You may be called to testify in court as to the circumstances under which the box was opened and the items discovered." I drew on the gloves and pulled the box to me.

Peering inside, I saw copies of the accounting documents Gil had been poring over for days. I pulled them from the box and slid them into a large evidence bag. Andrew had made notes directly on them. Perhaps they would help Gil find a way to prove Jeremy's complicity. I wrote down the titles of the documents on both copies of the warrant, reading them aloud to Mr. Gardner.

Underneath these documents sat a four-by-six-inch cardboard folder atop another set of accounting printouts. I'd bet those printouts were the ones for Tom Jamison's little scam. It looked as though Andrew had made notes on these, too.

The cardboard folder pulled at my attention. I wondered if I would finally get a solid clue for the kiddie-porn-blackmail victim. Was it Alec Oldrick or one of the vice chancellors? Or had Andrew blackmailed someone else I didn't know about for some other cause I didn't know?

I gently lifted the folder and opened it to find a photograph that had been slid into it backward. I placed the folder in a small evidence bag, taking out the photo.

A bare-chested man stood behind a bed, smiling down at a young girl about twelve years old. The grinning face belonged to Stuart Morley.

•   •   •

Rush hour ends earliest downtown. Those who still worked downtown hit their cars and fled for the suburbs if they could afford them, for Westport or south Kansas City if they couldn't. By six, the streets began to take on the deserted look that was their habitual night face.

Nights were gradually lengthening, but six o'clock was still twilight, deepened by the blanket of clouds threatening rain at any second. I had parked three blocks away, so I marched up Grand, carrying my shoulder purse and the briefcase that held my new evidence, determined to outpace the contents of the looming clouds.

I shivered in the damp, chill air. Fog curled up from the streets between the buildings, and my feet walked through clouds. Turning the corner into a block of boarded-up windows and long-closed buildings, I walked on alert. The last thing I wanted was to tangle with a stupid purse snatcher this evening. I had too many things to do. Drive back home. Contact Gil and Beau Fletcher. Bring in Stuart for questioning. Test his shoes for a footprint match.

The fog in this side street had built up higher than on the broader, more open boulevard. The clouds seemed to lower themselves to meet it, turning the air to mist. I shook my head at my blindness. How had I missed it? Stuart had an office in Moller and access to the building at night. Stuart had witnessed Tom's threat and hurling of the amethyst. He could have picked up the amethyst with gloves on, leaving Tom's fingerprints on it, then stashed it in plain sight on Tom's deck to frame him.

I came to a sudden stop for a second. He'd asked me out that evening. Had he planned to use me as his alibi somehow?

Shaking my head in the wet air, I resumed my rapid pace. He must have left the library through the underground entrance, gone over to Moller, killed Andrew and stashed the amethyst somewhere, gone back in through the underground entrance, then made a big point of going up the moment they called and chatting with the librarian so she'd remember he was there.

But, if Jeremy had pushed Tom into suicide—and I was certain he had—how did that tie in with Stuart's guilt?

While analyzing the investigation for what I had missed, part of my attention remained on my surroundings, listening for anything with the potential of threat with long-practiced skills from my years on the city's police force.

I hesitated in midstride and looked closely all around me. Something had triggered an alarm inside me. A change in the quiet wind-whipped sounds around me. Visibility was poor in the foggy twilight. I heard nothing further. Chiding myself for jumpiness, I continued down the street.

According to Charlie, the man in the picture, the "Professor," had killed a little girl. Maybe the girl in the photo. I remembered the weird conversation we'd had about hunting and prey. He was a hunter. I could see him killing to keep anyone from finding out about his sexual preferences and the murder he'd already committed. I needed to call Dan about this as soon as I got home. I had told Charlie to call him, but he didn't really have any proof of his story. I could provide some for Dan. We could coordinate our operations.

My eyes scanned shuttered buildings as they loomed through the mist. Only another block until the parking lot.

Suddenly, my back was slammed twice from behind, knocking me down on my face at the same time as the sound of two shots echoed. From the shock of impact, I lost the ability to breathe for a few panicked seconds. Running feet passed my limp body on the wet pavement, and my blood chilled.

When I could bring in air again, I jumped to my feet, digging out my gun from its shoulder holster. On the ground before me lay only my purse. Ahead of me ran a shadow carrying my briefcase.

"Stop! Police!" I cried, only to find my shout breathless and weak. Mist soaking my hair and face, I ran after the thief, sucking in air for another shout. "Stop! Police! You're under arrest!"

The shadow disappeared into a building or between two of them. In the gloom, it was hard to tell. I tried to put on speed to catch him, but the soreness in my midsection and my labored breathing slowed me down.

Out of nowhere, I was struck from the side and knocked down by a larger body on top of my own. A fist smashed against my right wrist as it lay stretched out on the wet pavement, forcing me to release my grip on my Glock.

"Drop it! Police!" bellowed in my ears.

"I can't breathe. Let me up." My voice sounded weak. "I'm a police officer. I was pursuing a perp who shot me twice and stole evidence in three homicides."

The heavy body rolled off me slowly. "Tell it to the judge. I'm going to get off you. Rise slow and easy with your hands on your head."

"Got a female officer on the way," said an older voice.

"You're letting him get away!" I pushed myself up from the ground, only to have my hands kicked from under me.

"Hands on your head, I said."

I rolled over onto my back and glared up at a baby cop in prime physical condition. Some rookie just out of the academy, probably.

"I can't get up without using my hands, because I'm bruised from his shots," I said in my most reasonable voice. "I really am a police officer, and that man you're letting get away shot me knowing that. Call Dan Wheelwright in Homicide. Skeet Bannion's my name. He'll tell you."

The rookie sneered in disbelief, holding my own gun on me. "Right. Just get up with your hands on your head and no fancy moves."

The older, fatter cop had started at the mention of the two names. He came closer, peering down through the murky air to see my face. "Man, she's telling the truth. That's Big Charlie Bannion's girl. Fastest rise through the ranks. Last I heard she was a major at headquarters after her time on Homicide." He pushed the rookie's hand holding the gun away from me. "Ma'am. Sorry about this. Let me help you up."

I took the hand he stretched out to me and rose painfully to my feet. I touched my face, which had met the pavement forcefully twice, and brought my fingertips away bloody. "Thanks. I left KCPD six months ago to be a chief up at Brewster. Came down here serving a search warrant for evidence in three murders when your man found me pursuing . . . probably the murderer, since he only wanted the evidence, and most purse snatchers don't bother to shoot their victims."

The rookie looked angry. "What are you talking about, Bunsford? This was a good bust."

"Here, ma'am," Bunsford said, handing my purse to me.

I pulled out my ID and flashed it in front of the rookie. "Can you read, Officer? Or are they taking illiterates as well as deaf recruits at the academy now?"

The rookie's face flushed. "How was I to know——"

"Perhaps the fact that I was shouting, 'Stop, police,' might have given it away. At least enough to look at my identification." I snatched my gun from his hand and checked it over before holstering it.

I stared into the darkness after my attacker, willing myself to see anything. "He's gotten away now."

"You said you were shot?" the older cop, Bunsford, asked.

I pulled up my shirt to show the vest. "Kevlar. Just bruised like a son of a bitch. You might check for shell casings back that way." I pointed in the direction from which I'd come. "They'll most likely match up with ones we already have from the other killings."

Bunsford started back in the direction I'd indicated. The rookie stood motionless, finally grasping his situation.

"If you saw me running," I said to him, "you must have seen the guy ahead of me. Carrying a briefcase. Did you see where he went?"

He shook his head. "No, I didn't see anyone but a crazy woman waving a gun around." He turned to stare at me. "How was I to know you were a cop? You're not in uniform."

"You've never heard of plainclothes officers?" I asked.

"But they're men." He stopped as he heard himself.

I smiled, icy-sweet. "Not all of us."

My knees burned from smashing into the pavement twice. My face and head throbbed. I tried to hold my body straight and still for fear I would cry out from the pain in my rib cage that moving produced. My wrist cramped with pain where the rookie had hit it. And on top of everything, I'd lost my evidence. The photo was gone.

I forced back tears, tasting bile in my throat. Thank God for the mist. It would explain any moisture in my eyes. I would not cry before this idiot. Who'd just been in the wrong place at the wrong time, I reminded myself. New and nervous and look-ing for a chance to show off his prowess. I'd been there once myself.

"Ma'am, your phone is ringing," he said, bringing my at-tention back to the dreary street where I stood.

I pulled out the phone to find Sam on the line.

"Where are you?" Sam's voice sounded troubled. I could hear voices and machine noises in the background.

I wondered why he thought he had any right to know. But I didn't want a fight right now. More-important things were happening. "Here in the city. Executing a search warrant."

"Sit down, okay?"

I didn't have the patience to deal with his button pushing. "Hell no. I'm on a cold, wet sidewalk and bruised all over. Just tell me. It can't be much worse than what I've just been through."

"It's Charlie." He paused, then rushed back with a ques-tion: "Why are you bruised all over?"

"Is it a stroke? One of those TIAs?"

Sam didn't answer for a few seconds. When he did, his voice had a bitter edge. "Who knows? That'll probably come out of this, but . . ." I heard him take a deep gulp of air. "He's been beat up. Real bad."

"What are you talking about? Charlie?" The idea was ludi-crous. Big Charlie Bannion might be on the beating end, espe-cially if he'd been drinking, but he was big enough and tough enough that he didn't get hurt.

Sam didn't answer for a second. "The guy who was with him is dead."

His words echoed in my head. I shook it to clear my mind. "Where are you?"

"Research Hospital. Emergency room." The sounds behind his voice resolved into those of a hospital waiting room, now that I knew what I was hearing.

"I'm on my way." I clicked off the phone and dug in my purse for a business card, car keys, and a parking lot ticket.

The older cop came up, holding a shell casing. "Here's one of them."

"Good work. Bag it and get it to Dan Wheelwright over at Homicide. He's working this case, too. It may have a tie-in to a child murder here. I've got to go." I hung my purse strap on my shoulder, wincing at the pain.

The rookie gaped at me. "You can't leave. We've got to write this up."

I looked over at him. "My father's in critical condition at Research emergency room. If you want me for your report, you'll find me there, along with Sergeant Sam Musco, Lieutenant Dan Wheelwright, and any number of other officers." I turned to Bunsford, handing him a card. "I should be available at this number if you need further information or want to arrange for me to come in. If not, you'll probably find me at Research."

"Hope old Charlie'll be all right." He nodded good-bye.

I rushed off to my car, hearing their voices behind me.

"We can't just let her go like that."

"Shut up. We can always get whatever we need later. Didn't you hear? Her old man's hurt. Jeez, I sure hope he makes it. He was a hell of a cop once upon a time."

I fought the temptation to snap on the siren and lights as I headed east to catch Bruce Watkins Freeway. But with my luck I'd probably get pulled over by another eager beaver, and that would just slow me down. Still, I topped the speed limits as I raced southward to Research.

I peeled off at the Sixty-third Street exit and drove onto Prospect. I wheeled into the emergency room parking lot, slammed into a parking slot, and sprinted around a nurse wheeling a woman in a wheelchair out to a car. I banged through the first set of doors and then, after a turn through a waiting room, another set. In the tiny room a line of six chairs sat facing a glass window, bulletproof. A set of glass doors showed a larger waiting room opposite the ones I'd just entered, and another set of doors without glass to my right led to the emergency room proper. These would open only when the skinny, red-haired nurse behind the window buzzed me in.

"My father, Charles Bannion, is in here," I told her. "I'm his only living relative."

The nurse stared at me above a tight mouth and the broken nose veins of a drinker. She looked down at some list on her desk and said, "Your husband's already in there."

I let this pass uncorrected. Sam had come to the hospital with Charlie.

The nurse jerked her thumb toward the door. It buzzed and opened, and I ran to pass through before it closed.

Down the hall inside, I heard voices arguing and recognized the loudest. Rushing down to that room, I found Sam and a nurse trying to pull Charlie's bloodstained clothes from his arms as he lay, battered, bandaged, and dressed in a hospital gown, on a gurney.

"I don't need a be in hothpital," he lisped through puffy, blood-spattered lips. "Fix me up. Send me home. Lemme get dress."

His eyes were swollen almost shut, so bloody and bruised that they were turning black. His nose was a misshapen red lump on his torn-up face, his mouth engorged and distorted, his left ear gashed and grossly twisted. The hand clutching the clothes was swollen and immobilized by a splint and an IV.

"Charlie, what are you trying to do? Kill yourself?"

"His daughter," Sam told the nurse. "She's the only one he'll listen to."

"About time," the nurse said with a sniff.

"I got here as soon as I could." I felt an irrational need to justify myself.

"You hurt, Skeeter?" Charlie asked with groggy concern. I could see the bleeding stumps of teeth in his mouth.

"I'll leave you two to talk some sense into him. I'll be back with the doctor." The nurse charged out into the hall.

"What happened, Charlie?" I asked.

"Good. She's gone." He held out his clothes to me. "Here. In hidden pocket. Jacket you gave. Retirement. Got that pishure for you." He chuckled drunkenly, then grimaced in pain. "Fools thought they finish me. But I'm hard to kill. Didn't find the pishure. After all that."

"The EMTs said he kept mumbling about some picture all the way in," Sam said. "They've pumped heavy painkillers into him."

"Oh, Charlie. I told you to take it to Dan. I told you to leave it alone." I fought the simultaneous urges to weep and to throttle him.

Charlie was insistent. "Got it. Right here."

I took the clothes off the splinted arm they hung on, and searched the jacket for the hidden pocket. I'd bought it for him to take while traveling in his retirement, knowing that he'd probably never travel farther than the neighborhood bar. Inside the hidden pocket, I found the edges of a photo and pulled out a duplicate, creased and wrinkled, of the picture I'd found in the safe deposit box.

"Oh, Charlie." I clutched it close. That damn Stuart hadn't won, after all.

"What's this all about, Skeet? Did you have Charlie looking into something for you? Why didn't you come to me, dammit? He's too old and sick." Sam scowled at me.

"I didn't. I told him not to." I moved closer to my father. "Charlie, thank you. I found a copy of this, but the son of a bitch stole it from me. You saved my case."

"Told ya I'm still good cop." He smiled a gruesome smile with his distorted lips and broken teeth, winced with pain, and closed his eyes.

"Maybe he'll go to sleep," Sam said. "They had to give him a lot of pain meds, trying to keep him from going into shock on the way in."

I stared at the wreck of my father's face. "Sam, look at him. Those bastards beat him half to death."

"Broken nose and arm and hand and kneecap, the EMTs are sure." Sam rattled off the litany of injuries as though saying it might keep anything worse from being discovered. "They haven't done X-rays yet. He may have a broken collarbone and some ribs, too. They don't know what else."

"Oh, Charlie," I whispered and stroked his bandaged head. I wished I could heal the way I'd seen Gran do time and again. School had taught me that her herbs and tribal ways were superstition, but deep inside, I knew better. *If Gran could be here, my dad would make it.* But she wasn't. I had to hope the doctors would be enough.

He opened his eyes slightly and tried to smile.

"You know you can't go home, don't you?" I asked, still stroking his head. "You have to stay here where they can take care of you."

"Sure." He tried to wave a hand in his old expansive way, but the pain and splint defeated him. "Hurt like hell. I just didn't want anybody but you mess with jacket. Can't see anything. My head hurts like hell."

He closed his eyes again. Not in sleep, I realized, but in pain beyond anything I could imagine.

The nurse returned with a slight, young African American doctor.

"If we've got him stabilized, let's admit him. The man's not going anywhere, and he can have the X-rays and all the other tests inpatient." His voice was high-pitched but resonant. "Let's get his blood pressure."

The nurse said, "This is the daughter and son-in-law."

The nurse fastened the blood pressure cuff around Charlie's arm and began to pump it. As she let it go and watched the meter, her eyes widened.

"Doctor. Pressure's way over stroke levels."

The young doctor firmly thrust us out of the little room and shut the door on us.

"Oh, God, what now?" I muttered, half to myself.

"The other doctor told him high levels of stress could bring on a major stroke," Sam said. "He could die or be paralyzed, Skeet. Why didn't you ask me if you needed help with this?"

"Because I asked Dan Wheelwright and told Charlie to stay out of it. He pushed his way in anyway. Against my strict orders." I turned my back on him as I watched the door of the room.

The nurse raced from the room to the station at the center of the hall. She opened a cupboard, pulled out vials and syringes, and rushed back into the room.

A different nurse passed us, then turned and said, "Hasn't anyone seen to your injuries yet, hon?"

I shook my head. "Not me. It's my dad that's hurt real bad. They're in there with him now."

"Still, those are some nasty scrapes on your face, and by the looks of your torn pants, your knees are just as bad. They probably hurt a lot." She turned me around, inspecting me, and gasped when she saw my back. "Have you been shot? Those look like bullet holes."

"For God's sake, Skeet, why didn't you say anything?" Sam cried.

"They are bullet holes, but I'm okay. I was wearing a vest." I felt so tired. I wanted the doctor to open the door and come out and tell me that Charlie was okay. Then I would fall down and sleep right on the floor.

The nurse fussed at me and took me to the nurses' station, where she cleaned up the scrapes on my face and knees while we waited. She wanted me to go into a room and remove the Kevlar vest so she could see the impact areas, but I refused.

"Not till after I find out what's going on with my dad," I said.

The first nurse came out of the room in another rush and, noticing us, told the nurse who'd treated my scrapes to take us to the waiting room.

"But the doctor said we could wait in the hall," I protested.

"Your father is having a stroke," the nurse said on her way to the station. "Why don't you go to the waiting room and let us do our best to save him."

She returned with another nurse, pulling a cart loaded with equipment.

"Go on." She pointed down the hall and pushed through the door into the room where Charlie lay.

"I'm sorry, hon," said the second nurse as she led us down the hall to the waiting-room door. "About all you can do for your dad now is wait and pray."

CHAPTER 14

A television blared over my head as I sank into the arms of a brown vinyl chair with its stuffing protruding below the seat. The waiting room held a young Latina with baby and toddler, a beefy white family group, and an older black man. The family group talked back to the television. The young mother tried to keep her children pacified, and the thin, worn old man stared straight ahead at the drab floor tiles.

"I need to call Joe about Brian and explain the situation," I said.

"Is that kid still staying with you?" Sam asked, his tone carefully neutral.

I tried to be brisk and no-nonsense. "Yes. I need to make sure he has a safe place to stay tonight."

"So he's with this guy Joe?" Sam's mouth turned down in a dubious look. "He's some kind of cop, isn't he?"

I ignored him and dialed Joe's number.

Brian answered the phone, "Louzon residence."

"Bri," I said, feeling a rush of relief. "I'm stuck in the emergency room in KC."

"Are you hurt?" he asked, panicked.

I tried to soothe his fears. "Just scrapes and bruises, but my dad's in critical condition."

"Are you going to be okay?" Brian's voice was still tight with worry.

I made my words light and breezy. "I'll be fine, kiddo. I think I'll be spending the night here, so I wanted to make sure you were covered."

"That's okay. Joe said I could stay here until you got back." He sounded matter-of-fact. I didn't detect any sense of his feeling abandoned.

"That's great. Let me talk to him."

The phone grew silent for a second. "You're sure you're all right, Skeet?" He suddenly sounded much younger.

"I promise. Just some scrapes to ugly up my face for a few days." I searched for words to comfort him. "I was wearing my vest the way I promised you and Karen."

He heaved a loud sigh of relief. "Here's Joe."

"Skeet. What's going on?"

"Joe, thanks for keeping Brian. I would have called, but I've run into trouble." It sounded like I was making excuses.

As usual, Joe seemed calm and free of censure. "It sounded like you got hurt."

My breath tightened. "Got shot, but my vest saved me. I'm a little bruised and scraped, but that's not the problem. The perp stole my evidence from the safe deposit box."

Joe grew troubled. "Anyone catch him?"

"No, but Charlie went out and got me a duplicate of the photo I had." I began to rush my words. "The killer's Stuart Morley from the university. At least, we'll want him for questioning and to match his shoe print."

251

"You mean that quiet, stiff guy I met at Andrew's funeral? The one who likes to hunt?" Joe's surprise came across the airwaves clearly.

"Thanks to Charlie we'll get him. The only trouble is . . ." I choked and swallowed audibly. "Charlie was beaten. He's in critical condition. Having a stroke."

"Sorry, Skeet. That's got to be tough. Don't worry about Brian. He's good here tonight. We've already been to your place and fed the animals. I can take him to school tomorrow and pick him up after."

I felt grateful that this man was in my life at this time. I didn't know how I could have handled all this otherwise.

"Joe, you're a lifesaver."

Joe's voice was so calm and confident that, for just a second, I wanted to sink into it. "Don't worry about anything here. Got it covered."

"I owe you big time. I hope I'll be able to get back tomorrow sometime. I'll call one way or the other." I didn't know what I'd do if Charlie's condition worsened.

"Try to get some rest there. Though I know it's hard to do in a hospital. Talk to you tomorrow."

I returned the phone to my purse, feeling relief and shame. I hadn't given Brian a thought after the gunshots until I'd walked into the waiting room. Thankfully, Joe had seen to his needs. Good thing when I was so careless. I had no business with that kid. This just underscored the fact.

Sam inspected my face with a serious look on his own. "I'll bet that hurts like a mother."

I winced at the bright overhead light and TV noise, wished I could have Sam shut it off, but the family group was completely involved with the program. Plus, I didn't want any trouble. I had so much more than I could handle.

"Right now, it's my head and ribs that ache. The medicine she put on numbed the throbbing on the face and knees."

I looked away from him toward the window and door to the outside parking lot. The mist had turned to a downpour sometime while I was inside.

"Shouldn't we have heard by now?" I could hear the whine in my voice and tried to drive it out.

Sam shrugged uncomfortably. "I don't really know, but they told me if he had a massive stroke one day, he could either die or be paralyzed or blind or unable to speak. I guess there are lesser ones that are still bigger than the TIAs he's been having, but I guess they don't have as bad a result as a major one."

Feeling dread, I ran my hands through my hair, wincing as I hit sore spots. "This is really serious, isn't it?"

Sam paced away from me and then back without answering. Finally, he threw himself into the chair next to mine. "Skeet, the beating was bad enough. He was so lucky not to die from it like the guy with him who was apparently the guy he got the photo from. That's why I could bring Dan and Homicide into this. The other guy died."

At the mental picture that conjured, rage poured through my veins. "Did he say who did it? Did he know?"

"He gave me descriptions and told me where he'd seen them before. I told Dan, and he had an APB put out on them."

"Dan was there?"

He nodded and checked his watch. "I called Homicide when I saw the other guy was dead, and when Dan heard about Charlie, he took the case himself."

I felt satisfaction join the fury inside me. I could rely on Dan. "Thank God he already knows about some of this. I'll bet Charlie never called him like I told him to."

Sam stared at me with guarded eyes. "What's this all about, Skeet? You getting shot at. Charlie beat half to death. Dan already involved. Want to clue me in here?"

"It's a long story, Sam."

"It doesn't look like either of us is going anywhere for a while, does it?"

I explained to him the sequence of murders.

"The best I can make out, that stubborn old man decided to do it all himself. So he set up the meet to get the photo and got hit." I ran my hands through my hair, encountering the tender spots again. "If he'd only talked with Dan and given him his informant the way I told him to, he wouldn't be lying in there right now."

As if drawn by the sound of his name, Dan Wheelwright marched through the outer doors, Hoag Masters at his heels. Both men dripped rain. Hoag towered over Dan, who was only slightly taller than I, but anyone watching would have known that the smaller man was the leader. Hoag was Dan's physical opposite: black v. white, tall v. short, muscular v. lean. Despite his height and bulk, though, Hoag moved with a dancer's grace. He had a mind as quick and agile. Some people made the mistake of thinking Dan kept him around for muscle, but no one worked Homicide with Dan who wasn't intelligent and street-smart.

I ran over to greet them. Finding myself enfolded in Dan's arms and then Hoag's, I lost momentary control of the tears I had kept at bay ever since Sam's phone call. For a few seconds, I stood safe in the arms of friends and cried.

Then I pulled back, wiping my cheeks with the backs of my hands and trying to smile. "Sorry, guys."

"Hey, it's not the first time a foxy babe started to cry the

254

minute I showed up." Hoag flashed me a blinding grin. "Only usually I've done something to deserve the crying and throwing stuff."

Dan handed me a handkerchief. "Don't listen to anything that fool has to say. It's a tough time. How's Charlie doing?"

I wiped my eyes and handed the handkerchief back. "I'm not sure. He's having a stroke now, on top of everything." I took a deep breath to keep calm. "It doesn't look good."

Sam stepped forward from behind me. "Any luck picking up the guys who did this, Dan?"

Dan shook his head. "Too early to hope for that. We're staking out that porn outfit. If they come back, we haul them in. We can't do much more without a sketch or an ID from mug shots. I stopped by to see when Charlie would be in shape to work with a sketch artist or go through photo albums."

"I don't know if he ever will." I grabbed at my hair again and caught myself, remembering how it had hurt before.

"Charlie's an old trooper, Skeet. He'll pull through." Dan patted my shoulder tentatively. "Tell me what happened."

"I told you he found a lead in that murder case. He heard there was a photo of someone who'd killed one of the kids they use in their porn operation and paid to have it covered up." I pulled out the photo and showed it to them. "The porn guys got big money to give him false ID and help in leaving the country. They thought he was gone, but he stayed and was blackmailed by my first vic."

Dan looked at the picture and shook his head sadly. "So you've got this guy figured for your murders?"

I nodded, and Hoag's big face turned grim. "So we got this little one's body around somewhere?" he asked.

I bit my lip in frustration. "I told Charlie to take this to you. I told him not to try to handle it himself. And he promised he would."

"But he didn't." Hoag laid his arm across my shoulder. "Charlie's gonna do what Charlie's gonna do. And it's probably not going to be something good for him. This time, it was real bad. Dan's right. Old Charlie's tough as leather. He'll make it. He might even learn from it."

I laughed faintly. "That would certainly be a first." I turned to Dan. "I need a copy of that photo for my investigation. Can you get me one?"

"Sure, I'll send someone by with it first thing in the morning." He stared at me. "Got enough to arrest on?"

"With this, I do. Got a footprint to match up and access to keys. I'll call my office in the morning and have them go to the DA's office for a warrant. But I'll need that copy to get it."

"You'll have it. Think this guy will cooperate with us once he's going down for your murders?"

"Only after he's been convicted. Then, to avoid death row, he probably will."

"Go to it then. I'll get you that copy, and we'll work this murder and attempted from this end." His smile was grave. "Maybe with luck we'll meet in the middle."

"Yeah," Hoag said. "Get that little girl's family some closure."

Without saying anything further, Dan turned around and headed for the exit.

Hoag bent down to whisper to me, "We'll get these suckers, Skeet. For what they did to Charlie and that little girl. We'll get them all."

I kissed him lightly on the cheek. "Thanks, Hoag. I know you will."

Dan waited at the outer door, and when Hoag joined him, they walked out into the rainy night.

The rest of the night passed in a blur of hospital sights and sounds. Joe called and told me he'd sent one of his guys to watch Stuart's house and keep track of him until I could get back with the photo and get a warrant. We couldn't do anything without that, but I let Frank know when I called.

After a further wait, the doctor told us Charlie was being taken to ICU. Sam and I rode the elevator to intensive care, where we were allowed to see Charlie one at a time for ten minutes an hour. At least, the waiting room had new furniture and no television.

Every time I was allowed into Charlie's room, the shock hit me. He lay like a limp doll, with tubes in his nose, heart monitor wires stuck to his neck and chest, and multiple plastic bags, large, medium, and small, hanging from his IV stand. Behind his bed, the video screen for his heart monitor showed the ragged, moving graph of his life and filled the silence with its beeping.

I sat at his bedside and stroked his nonsplinted hand, which lay exposed on top of the blanket. I didn't know what to say.

"Charlie, I know you can beat this," I said during one ten-minute visit. "You've always been so strong. You can come through this. I know you can."

I never asked Sam what he said to Charlie during his timed stints at the bedside of the man who'd been a father to replace the one who abandoned him when he was five. For the forty minutes of each hour that we had to sit in the waiting room, we talked about my murders and about how it must have gone down when Charlie was jumped. We talked about Charlie's strength and replayed old stories of Charlie escapades. We never spoke about what we said when talking to the unconscious body in that glass-walled room. Though each of us could see the other's lips moving while in with him.

"Charlie, I'm real proud of you for getting that photo," I told him in another visit. "He thinks he's sitting pretty. And here you come with another copy. Man, is he going to be in for a surprise. I can't wait to see his face when I tell him my old man got it for me."

I wiped my eyes. "You're still a hell of a cop, Charlie, but stupid." My voice broke into quiet sobs. "Why'd you do it? It was so stupid. You didn't have to get hurt so bad." I pulled myself together and used the same soggy wad of tissues to clean up my wet face. "Still, I'm proud of you, Charlie. Real proud."

It was during the hour after the breakfast carts had come and gone that Charlie regained consciousness for a few minutes. The doctor was on the floor making rounds and checked him out. "It's going to be hard to tell for a while how much of the weakness is from the attack injuries and how much from the stroke. He shows some confusion, but not too much. It could also be an aftereffect of the attack. We'll have the neurologists check him out. All in all, he's doing remarkably well. I think we'll move him out of intensive care this afternoon if he continues to improve."

To the question of how much permanent damage Charlie would have, the doctor answered, "I don't know. We'll just have to wait and see."

Since Charlie had lapsed back into a drugged sleep, I stretched out on a sofa in the waiting room and slept for a couple of hours. When I woke, Sam gave me the copy of the photograph that a uniformed police officer had delivered.

During my next session, I sat in silence for the first five

minutes. Then I spoke. "Charlie, you don't have to worry. I won't abandon you. If you need help at home and we can't get someone in for you, I'll bring you up to Brewster with me. We'll manage somehow. You don't have to worry."

When I came out, I found that somehow Sam had managed to fall asleep with his legs cramped up and his long arms falling off toward the floor. I looked over at his sleeping face.

When I was away from Sam, it seemed unbelievable that we had been married once. But when I was with him the way I had been this long night, it was so easy to fall into the old patterns and habits. After all, he had his good points. Witness the way he tried to watch over Charlie, the way he'd stayed with us both through this whole thing. His loyalty was one of the things I'd always found appealing. It was an old-fashioned virtue and too seldom found today.

When I'd left him, I'd been able to manage it only by focusing on the aspects of Sam's behavior that made the marriage so miserable—jealousy, anger, possessiveness. It would have been too difficult to leave if I'd allowed myself to remember the reasons I'd married him—charm, sense of humor, loyalty.

Since he and Charlie had no intention of separating, I'd have to come to some accommodation with him. Kind of a sister-brother relationship. If he would stop being so possessive and jealous. I had thought that was over. But apparently something about my move to Brewster had thrown him back into the state he'd been in right after the divorce became final.

Standing and stretching again, I sighed as I looked down at him. I was going to have to have one of those miserable talks with Sam to straighten things out. After all this was over.

The morning crept by. Sam woke and left to get us something to eat. Charlie woke again when the hospital lunch carts came around, and Sam and I were allowed in his room together for twenty groggy minutes before he slipped back into sleep.

Joe called me an hour after the lunch carts left.

"He's gone." His voice was frustrated and angry. "He slipped out somehow while Mecklin was distracted by a disturbance up the street that turned into nothing. Probably set that up himself. We think he must be hiding out in the wildlife refuge because we can't find him anywhere else."

"Unless he left for the city and parts elsewhere."

"It was like he knew what we were doing right from the start."

"Like his knowing I was in the city opening that safety deposit box with the photo in it. I just figure he tailed me. Maybe he was already suspicious and made your guy. He's a hunter, an outdoorsman who grew up in the Ozarks. He may well head into the wildlife refuge. If he heads for the city, he'll probably go on down to the Ozarks. We may never get him out of there."

"If he's in town—including the wildlife refuge—we'll find him."

I thanked him and put away my phone, feeling numb. After everything, he might get away. I couldn't think about it.

About an hour later, nurses and orderlies began transferring Charlie to a regular ward. We accompanied him on his trip to a higher floor and a semiprivate room, free of a roommate at the moment. Once he was settled, Sam said good-bye until the evening's visiting hours. And I was left alone with my father.

I moved a chair next to the bed and settled in place, moving stiffly from bruises, scrapes, and trying to sleep on a waiting-room couch.

"Not looking so hot, Skeeter," Charlie said, his voice breathy with strain.

I smiled. "Look who's talking, Charlie. You look kind of like the mummy right now."

"Yeah." He tried to laugh, but it turned into a choking cough, and I hurried to get him some water to sip through a straw.

"Don't try to talk if it hurts, Charlie. I'm just going to sit with you for a while."

Silence settled in the room, interrupted at the doorway by the sounds of quiet nurses' conversations passing by and patients' Help buttons ringing down the hall at the nurses' station. "You know, those charges," Charlie said in a hoarse whisper of a voice. "They're not true. I never . . ."

His voice faded, replaced by another coughing spell. I leaned over him with the glass of ice water and guided the straw into his mouth. "Sshh. Don't try to talk too much."

He gulped water, and once the coughing eased, he pushed my hand with the glass away. "I don't want you thinking your old man was crooked," he said with a little stronger voice. "I wasn't such a great cop, but I was never crooked. I was just scared."

He paused for breath, but shook his head when I offered the water again. I refilled it from the plastic pitcher on the swing table beside his bed. "What were you afraid of, Charlie?"

"The stinking bureaucrats." He tried to lift himself in the bed but failed and slid farther down.

I put my hands under his shoulders to pull him up in the bed. I reached under him and straightened out the waterproof pad that had wadded itself into a mass of wrinkles from his efforts. He fumbled with the bed-control buttons in the side railing, managing to make the head rise slightly before I could come to his rescue.

"Why were you afraid of the bureaucrats, Charlie?" I

asked, amazed that he would admit fear of anyone and that we were having such a conversation at all.

He tried for one of his nonchalant shrugs, but his injuries turned it into a wince. "I was always afraid of them. They could prove anything they wanted against me. And I'd have lost my pension and health benefits. I couldn't stay on the streets much longer. I was a drunk, but I wasn't a crook. But because I was a drunk, they could make it look like I was a crook. So I bailed." A pink-tinged tear ran down the mass of bandages that covered his nose.

"Oh, Charlie. I was one of those bureaucrats. I could have fought them for you." I plucked a tissue from the box on the swing table and dabbed up the tear's path.

"I was afraid they would convince you I'd gone bad." His eyes were slits in dark, swollen flesh, but they stared at my face as if seeking something there. "I couldn't have stood that."

I ran my hand lightly across the top of his shaved head, bandaged in places. "The only thing that could convince me you'd gone bad was your leaving without a fight."

He tried to grin with his misshapen mouth, and it jerked at something deep inside me. "Figured that out later. With Sam's help. Stupid move."

"That's okay, Charlie. None of that matters now."

He reached toward me with his unsplinted hand. " I want you to know your old man's not a crook."

"I think I've figured that out." I took his hand and held it between both of mine. "Now, you just have to concentrate on getting better."

His nod was awkward from the layers of bandage on his head and neck. "I will. You need to get back home. Pick up that damn killer and get yourself some sleep. You look like shit, kid."

I laughed with tears held at bay behind my eyes. "Always with the compliments."

"Serious. Go home. Get him behind bars. Get doctor, sleep. I'm just going . . . sleep here. I can feel it . . . noddin' off."

I stood and looked down at him. He looked asleep already, but he was in the soft sliding away into sleep that pain medication brings.

"I'll be back this evening," I said in a quiet voice. "Just rest and grow stronger."

On a strange impulse, I leaned down to brush the top of his bandaged head with my lips.

"I'll get that killer and lock him up." The whisper faded away in the quiet room as I left.

CHAPTER 15

"Dispatch, this is Bannion. I'm on my way back from Kansas City."

"Hey, Chief. What d'ya need?"

"Tell Frank or Gil to call Beau Fletcher over at the DA's office and have him work up an arrest warrant for Stuart Morley. Three counts, murder one. Tell him I'm bringing photographic proof to back up the warrant. Arrival time about twenty minutes."

"Ten-three, Chief. I'll pass that word on. Over and out." The radio emitted a squawking crackle of static and went silent.

I accelerated, ignoring the landscape along the highway that I usually enjoyed. Today, my entire focus was on convincing Beau to issue the arrest warrant so I could find Stuart and put him behind bars without further delay. I prayed that Beau could manage to keep Randy's nose out of it until . . . well, until we had Stuart convicted and sentenced.

That was never going to happen, but I could hope to delay the DA's meddling until there was less damage he could do. If I could keep the DA and the sheriff from sniffing around until we had all the knots tied, I'd be happy. Beau would have to do all the prep work and research for the trial, writing a kind of script for Randy, and if the slick little fool would just stay with the script, we'd put Stuart Morley away for good.

I was just outside Brewster, still on the highway, when my phone rang.

"Skeet, this is Stuart." His voice had lost its military precision. The hint of an Ozark backwoods accent had moved solidly into his speech. "I've got something you want." He gave a breathless laugh, and I wondered if Stuart was drunk. "And the only way you'll get it is to do exactly what I say."

"What is this thing I want?" I asked.

"Skeet, he took me," Julie cried. "Please come get me away from him, Skeet." Her voice broke off in sobs.

"Julie, where are you?" I yelled.

"Sorry, Skeet," Stuart continued in that strong accent. "She can't talk right now."

He didn't sound like himself at all. If he was high on something, chances of getting Julie back unharmed were going to plummet.

"What do you want?" My jaw locked in a grim line as I pushed the accelerator.

"You got another copy of the picture McAfee had, didn't you?"

I hesitated for a second. *Should I try to stall?*

"Don't bother lying to me, Skeet," he said in a furious tone. "I heard you over the radio."

"Why ask me things you already know?" I had to play for time. Set up a dialogue with him. Calm him down.

"You're not going to take that photo to the DA. You're going to wait until I call you in a little while after I get in position.

Then you'll bring it to the place where I'll be waiting for you with our little sweetheart. There we'll exchange our goodies. And, Skeet, if you bring the cops . . ." his voice grew angry and cold again, "I'll kill your boyfriend's little girl."

Before I could answer, he hung up.

I called Gil Mendez's cell number and said, "Stuart Morley's kidnapped Joe's little girl. He wants to trade her for the evidence against him. He says he'll kill her if I bring in the police, and he probably will. So, none of this can go on the radio because he's listening to a scanner."

"What do you want to do, Skeet?" Gil asked, his voice grave. I heard no sign of the nervous bumbler. This was Gil the investigator, rock solid, just what I'd counted on.

"No radio. Call the office by phone and have them bring officers in with some false calls, innocent things, normal things. Not all right away. I've got a little time before he's going to tell me where to go. The minute I hear, I'll head there and call you. You call and have the others sent after us."

"Sure. We'll bring in everyone we can."

"Next, Gil, you go in person to Joe's office and tell him. No phone call. We've got to keep him under control. He's a good cop, but Julie's his kid. Stay with him. Take him out to the scene with you, or ride with him when we get the word. Let's not have him charging in alone, okay? I'd like to get both the kid and myself out alive."

"You got it, Skeet." He paused slightly. "Listen, shouldn't one of us go in your place?"

"*Et tu,* Gilberto," I said wearily. "I have to go because he's expecting only me. If he sees anyone else, she's dead. I've been a cop years longer than you, Gil. I can handle this."

"I know," he said apologetically.

"Get to the office and have those men drawn in. We're running out of time." I hung up with an angry sigh and tried to decide where I should head when I hit town, which I was about to do. Obviously, I couldn't go to my office or Joe's, in case Stuart was watching.

My phone rang again, and I headed through the town square as I answered.

"Skeet, it's Brian." He was whispering. "This guy kidnapped Julie, and I've been following him on my bike 'cause I couldn't get over in time to stop him."

"What? Brian, this guy is a murderer. He could have killed you."

"Hey, I've kept out of sight behind him. I couldn't call anyone 'cause I had to keep my bike going to keep up with him. But he's stopped now."

"Where are you, Brian? Are you out of sight so he can't see you?"

"Yeah. I peeled off when it looked like he was turning in. I hid my bike and walked up to make sure he parked. He took Julie into this old abandoned house."

"Are you sure?" I asked.

"I saw them. Don't know for sure where his car is parked because the house is blocking my view."

"Where are they?"

"Back of Old Webster on Magee where it runs into the nature preserve. That tumbledown old house. The Eichorn place."

"Got it. I'm on my way, and the rest of the force will be in a minute. Are you sure he can't see you?"

"Yeah. I'm behind a bunch of trees at the end of Magee. He drove into the sanctuary behind the house to park, but if you come up Magee real quiet and park back here, I don't think he'll see you, either."

"Good job. Now, just stay where you are and don't do anything stupid, please. I'm on my way."

I hung up and called Gil again right away. No answer. I called Frank. "I've got a location. Brian saw him take Julie and followed them all the way. They're at the end of Magee where it turns into the wildlife sanctuary out in back of Old Webster. The Eichorn place. Brian's still hiding there. I'm heading out, and I'll contact you when I get there. Start the guys as they come in. Silent alarm. Send as many as you can to secure the perimeter. Contact the sheriff's office. We need a SWAT team. Hostage negotiators."

"Gotcha, Skeet. Gil's on his way to get Joe. I'll phone him with the location. I can head out there, too."

"No, stay there. Somebody needs to deal with Dick Wold and help with logistics."

"We'll start getting bodies out to you. Good luck."

And luck was what I'd need. As I headed through Old Webster, I thought of the other hostage situations I'd experienced. Too damn often, captors killed their hostages before anything could be done. Julie's excited face, big eyes shining and ponytail straggling loose, appeared before me as I drove.

Not this time. This time, I would be there ahead of time, without the bad guy knowing he was watched. I'd find a surveillance spot before he was ready for visitors, and if he started to hurt Julie, I'd shoot the sick son of a bitch.

My Crown Vic crept down the last of Magee. I pulled over and cut my engine when I saw Brian's bike on its side by the road. Directly in front was the row of scrub-oak saplings where Brian hid.

I quietly opened my door and signaled him to the car, at the same time dialing Frank's number. "I'm here," I said softly when he answered. Brian slipped up to my open door.

"Got a big runaround from Dick about his SWAT team being busy, so I've called the Metro Squad and got tactical assistance coming from KCPD," he answered. "It'll be a while before they get here, though. Three of our guys heading your way, plus Gil and Joe. We've got more coming in even as we speak, and I'll send them on."

"Good." I turned to Brian. "Anything new since we talked last?"

He shook his head. "They're still in there. What will you do, Skeet?"

"Don't worry." I smiled at him and returned to my phone conversation. "I'm leaving the kid locked in my car. He'll show any officers who come where Morley has her. I'm going to put myself in position to observe. Just have our guys set up a perimeter. We'll wait till the big guns get here if we can."

"You wouldn't try any hot-dog stunts, would you, Skeet?" Frank sounded worried.

"Don't worry. I'll let the SWAT guys deal with this. I'm just making sure he doesn't hurt Julie before they can get here. By the way, have you checked the status on ambulances? In case."

Frank cursed. "They're tied up on calls. Dispatcher thought he could have one free in maybe twenty to thirty minutes."

First the SWAT team and now the ambulance. Damn Dick Wold. "Let's hope we don't need any, then. At least not for about half an hour. I'm going in now."

I hung up and flicked off the phone's ringer. Instead of putting it back in its cradle in my console, I stuck it in my back pocket.

"I'm coming with you," Brian said.

"No." I glared at him. "Following that car was the bravest and stupidest thing you've ever done. By chance, you didn't get hurt, and it worked out well for us. Now, you'll sit in this car and show the officers where he's holding Julie and where I go."

He started to protest, but I put my hand over his mouth.

"You will not leave this car until our guys get here. This guy is a killer, Brian. Don't go out there and get in my way. Do not give him another hostage."

His eyes had grown huge. He swallowed and nodded slowly. "But what if something happens to you, Skeet? What if you need my help?"

I ruffled his hair. "It's okay. Don't worry. You just stay locked in this car, nice and safe. Help will be here soon."

I turned and headed for the house, using all the stealth I'd learned throughout my career.

CHAPTER 16

Leaving the cover of the scrub oak, I crawled across a short open space to a line of overgrown shrubbery and wormed my way through the bushes, tearing my shirt and pants as I moved along, trying to make as little sound as possible. I stopped at irregular intervals, then began again, remembering what a Vietnam vet on the SWAT team had once told me: "Make only irregular, muffled sounds like animals or the wind might make. Sustained or rhythmic sounds warn your target a human's coming."

The cover of the bushes stopped short of the house itself. Away from the front, glassless windows that faced the street. The side of the house ahead of me was falling in. Trash and broken glass covered the ground around the house.

The back of the house was a night gathering place for underage drinkers, bums passing through along the river, and God knew what else. I didn't relish the idea of trying to crawl across glass and maybe dirty needles.

Eyeing the street-facing front of the house, where Stuart would most likely be keeping watch, I estimated the possible success of a quick run between the bushes and the side of the house. I shook my head.

I might make it without being seen, but I'd be heard. I'd have bet he was listening as sharply as he was watching. This guy was too smart to hole up here and not keep an eye and ear out, even if he still thought no one knew where he was.

I'd have to belly-crawl between the shrubs and the house like the SWAT guy had shown me. I started out from under the bushes. Move, move, stop. Move, stop. Stay stopped. Move, move, move, move, stop. Almost there. Move, stop. Move, move, move, stop.

What was that? I couldn't see with my head down like this and didn't dare lift it.

Too long still. Come on. Move, move, stop. Move, move, move.

I felt the rough wood of the house with my forward hand and breathed a low sigh of relief. Slowly, I pulled my whole body into its shelter. Made it.

I sat back against the splintery boards, just learning to breathe again. My right shin bled through a tear in my slacks, I noticed, and I took a second to pick out a long, thin shard of glass.

Toward the back, I saw in greater detail the deterioration I'd noticed from a distance. Loose boards tilting from the strict horizontal promised the possibility of a view of the inside. The trick would be to get that view without being seen myself.

Carefully, I crept along the base of the house toward the gap in the boards. As I came closer, I heard the murmur of a man's voice.

Just a foot or so more. There.

On the alert for any slight indication that I'd been detected, I peeked slowly and warily through the gaping hole in the side of the house. Someone had kicked or smashed through from the inside to make it. Consequently, I could see into the interior.

The walls inside had taken even greater damage through the years and were a collection of cavities where they still existed. The afternoon sunlight from the front fell in stripes across mounds of rubble and garbage.

I could hear the voice more clearly now. Stuart was speaking to Julie in a singsong voice that clashed with his now-heavy backwoods accent. "You're a pretty little girl, sweetheart. It's too bad you had to get involved in all this."

Julie whimpered once.

I silently shifted my position to see where they were. With my second movement, their silhouettes came into focus against the window's light. Stuart kept glancing out the window toward the road, then back to Julie, whose arm he held tightly. In the other hand, he held a gun.

Very softly I moved myself into a better position, not only to see but to act, if necessary. Fortunately, his attention was focused on the road when it wasn't directed at Julie.

"You know, baby, I could leave old Skeet sweating for a while, and you and I could have a little fun." He let go of her arm and caressed her hair. She stood, petrified. "Wouldn't you just really like that?"

"No," Julie said faintly. "Why don't you let me go?"

Stuart's laugh was high-pitched and eerie. I had no doubts now. He had lost whatever mental stability he'd had. "Oh no, sugar. Can't do that now, but if you're real good to me, I might not kill your daddy's girlfriend when she comes to trade for you. I might even see my way to let you go. But you'd have to be very, very nice to me."

He grabbed her arm again and pulled her toward his face. I silently pulled out my Glock and sighted. I couldn't fire while he held Julie, no matter what he did, but if he let her move any distance from him at all, I'd aim for his gun arm. I hoped the damn SWAT team got here before I had to do that, but I would not let him hurt Julie.

"No," cried Julie as he pulled her to him. She began to struggle, kicking at his legs and beating her free arm against his shoulder. She darted her head forward and bit him on the cheek.

He screamed, jerking her from his face and hitting her with the gun. The blow knocked her over to one of the remaining walls, and she slid bonelessly to the floor.

I aimed at his gun arm, squeezed off a shot, and burst through the wall screaming, "Now! Go, go, go!" I wanted him to think there were others with me.

Blood blossomed on his shoulder, and his gun went flying. He ran for the back wall and dived through a huge hole in it.

I rolled to my feet, but he'd already made it outside. I picked up his gun and stuck it in the front of my pants, keeping a wary eye on the wall through which he'd disappeared. I walked over to where Julie lay, knelt, and checked for a pulse. Strong. She was alive but unconscious. Maybe a fractured skull from that damn gun. Kneeling beside Julie with my eyes scanning the back and side walls, I pulled out my phone and punched Frank's speed dial number.

"I've got her. He's hit, but he got away. Heading into the nature preserve. That'll be a job for the tactical team. Tell them they can use radios and sirens now. He pistol-whipped the kid, and she's unconscious. How are we doing on ambulances? Got one to send me?"

Frank cursed. "Not yet, Skeet."

"Well, shit, Frank. She's hurt, and I'm not anxious to hang around with two vulnerable kids while he rearms and comes back. I'm bringing her in. I've got to get these kids out of the line of fire. He shouldn't get away if we get guys out here to start a search right away."

"Go ahead, Skeet," Frank said. "You ought to hear sirens pretty soon anyway. You'll probably pass them coming in as you leave. I'll relay the situation."

I switched off the phone and stuck it back into my pocket. The entire time I'd talked, my eyes kept flicking around the perimeter, watching for any sign of Stuart's return.

I looked out the hole in the back wall though which he'd disappeared to check for any sign of him. A trail of blood led into the wildlife sanctuary a few feet from the back of the house.

Returning to Julie's still form, I took one last long look around and holstered my gun. I picked up the limp child and moved around the piece of wall against which she'd fallen. I kicked the front door open and stepped through the broken swinging door, carrying Julie's limp body. I looked across the barren yard to the line of scrub oaks that hid my car and Brian for any sign of Stuart, but saw none.

Good. Let him lie in the woods and bleed to death.

I headed for the trees and my car at a steady pace. I didn't dare try to sprint with Julie for fear I'd lose my footing and fall, adding to the head trauma she already had. Still, I tried to walk as quickly as I could.

I was almost to the trees when I saw Brian coming, carrying the Remington 12-gauge shotgun from its holder in my car. Before I could yell at him for leaving the car, he dropped to the ground.

I felt the impact of the bullet before I heard the sound of the shot and Brian's shout of warning together. My leg felt pierced to the bone with a burning pain, and I toppled to the ground. I tried to twist as I fell to protect Julie's head from the impact.

That meant I landed awkwardly and a little stunned. I closed my eyes against the dizziness, forcing myself not to pass out and leave these kids at Stuart's mercy. I forced the pain in my leg away and tried to move to reach my gun, but I carried it on my left to draw with my right, and Stuart's shot had hit my right leg. I couldn't seem to move that side enough to get to my Glock.

Panic flared through me. I knew he was walking up to finish me off, and that would leave both kids in his hands. I twisted my head around until I could see him. He staggered toward me, his right shoulder bloody but his left hand holding a revolver aimed steadily at me.

"You half-breed bitch! You can't beat me. Don't you know that? I've been ahead of you ever since I killed McAfee." He tilted his head slightly and let his left hand holding the gun relax and droop toward his side. "She's a sweet little girl. Thanks to you I'm going to have to kill her now."

I wanted to keep him talking while I tried to think of something, anything, to save us. "You just think you've been ahead of me," I said. "I'm the one that's been ahead of you. Like with Tina. I'd already been there and taken away the papers. You just come dragging behind me, too late all the time." I could move my right hand now slightly, but I couldn't bring it up high enough to reach my holster.

"She should have told me where to go for the papers. Damn fool woman! I'd have gone and searched your house that very afternoon. Instead, I had to follow that fat, self-important bureaucrat, Hamlisch, trying to make like a spy or something. Bet you never knew who'd done the good vice chancellor in." He started to bring up the gun with his left hand.

I pulled my right hand up underneath me in one last, futile attempt to reach my holstered gun. It brushed against something metal at my waist. Stuart's first gun. The one he'd dropped when I shot him.

Yanking it from my waistband, I tugged it up even with my breasts. Sucking in a breath, I gave another giant shout to force back the pain and, I hoped, confuse Stuart, twisting my upper body around, and fired at his chest.

The sound of the shot was a much louder blast than I expected. Head ringing, I watched the spot of blood bloom where my bullet hit Stuart's chest. Heart shot. At the same time, his left arm sprung bloody leaks, and he fell to the ground.

For a moment, in the reverberating silence, I stared in dumb amazement. Then I turned my head back to the place I had last seen Brian diving for the ground. He stood with the shotgun still in both hands, face white with shock, staring at Stuart's body on the ground.

I heard sirens in the distance. Brian dropped the gun and fell to his knees. He started to vomit loudly and violently. In the background, I heard someone moaning in pain and wondered if it was Julie. I should do something about her or go comfort Brian, but I didn't think I could move again right away.

Just as I realized the moans were my own, I lost consciousness.

CHAPTER 17

I woke from a long line of muzzy white dreams. Brian, Jeremy, Charlie, Karen, and Joe had been involved somehow, but I couldn't remember any of the specifics.

My throat hurt. I coughed short and dry, swallowing back a hint of nausea. The cough grounded me from the floaty, medicated state, in which I'd awakened, onto the hospital bed and into a body with an IV in one hand and a throbbing ache in one leg.

"Do you want some water?" Karen spoke slowly, leaning into my field of vision with a plastic glass.

I looked over and saw that she sat at my bedside the way I'd kept vigil next to . . . Charlie's. That was right.

Charlie. God, what had happened to him? I tried to sit upright in a sudden movement, but my head wouldn't allow it.

"What?" My voice was a low croak.

"Have a drink. Your stomach should be okay from the anesthetic now." Karen held the straw to my mouth and pressed her own lips gently against my forehead.

The cold liquid trickling down my throat felt like life returning. I remembered the nurse offering me ice in the recovery room, telling me the surgery on my leg had been successful. I hadn't realized I'd had surgery. I must have slid back under before they moved me into this room.

As Karen set the cup back down, I looked around. My eyes fell on a blanket-covered form on a cot shoved into the corner made by the back two walls of the room.

"Brian," Karen said, watching me carefully. I'd never heard her sound unsure of herself. "He refused to leave you. Sat with Joe and me outside while you were in surgery and wouldn't leave the hospital as long as you're here. He got a little hysterical, but I was able to convince them to let him stay."

"Thanks," I said, my voice steadier from the water. "Poor kid. He's been through so much."

"I think you're his only center of gravity in this world right now." Karen's face wrinkled with concern as she looked over at Brian's sleeping form. "His life's been turned upside down by violence, and you're his stability."

I flashed on the shotgun falling from Brian's hands. "He's one heck of a kid."

"He's going to have hellacious problems dealing with this, you know." Karen's voice speeded up and became more matter-of-fact. She sounded like the old Karen, who knew what was best for everyone. "Just like any recruit who winds up having to shoot someone on his first day on the streets."

"He's strong. He just needs a counselor like you, like those recruits and I did." My voice was becoming stronger by the second, and I felt steadier as it did. Thank heavens, his shot hadn't been the one that killed Stuart. We could help Bri deal with this. We'd dealt with it before.

My mother's people knew that violence changes things. It's

a break in the balance and harmony of the world. After a battle, the elders led the tribe in a ceremony to restore balance and harmony within the warriors who'd taken part in the fighting. Gran always reminded me that women had gone to battle, as well as men, among the Cherokee before so much of the culture was lost in order to fit in with white people and survive.

"You got me through it. You'll get him through it. He's a real stand-up kid." I looked over at Brian again. Karen wasn't kidding about what this would do to him. Still, I'd bet on Brian. He was a survivor.

The first time I'd had to shoot someone (not kill him, thankfully), Karen counseled me through it—and Gran made me come down to Oklahoma for a stomp dance. We've lost the returning-warrior ceremony, but the stomp dance is all about restoring balance and harmony to the world. Karen could counsel Brian, but I didn't know about a stomp dance for him. The People don't like a lot of outsiders at those. They take them very seriously. I'd have to talk to Gran.

"Aren't you going to ask what happened with your leg?" Karen sounded amused.

"I've been afraid to. Do I still have it?" I kept my eyes from the throbbing place under the blankets. I'd heard about "phantom pain," when amputated limbs still hurt.

Karen choked on what could have been a laugh. "Yes. That bullet nicked the femoral artery, though. You were lucky. You won't be running along the river for a while, of course."

"Yeah. Lucky." I swallowed nausea back once more. I could live with however long rehab took, as long as I still had my leg. "How's Julie?"

"Concussion. Joe had an awful time while they checked her out. She'll be okay, though."

Taking a deep breath, I asked the question that had haunted me since I'd opened my eyes: "And Charlie?"

Karen smiled and rose from her chair. "Sam's waiting outside in the hall. I'll let him tell you."

She walked so quietly to the door that she seemed to glide. A minute later, Sam, unshaved, hair disheveled, looking as if he'd slept in his clothes on a waiting-room couch again, ambled in, carrying a purple orchid. He moved as though he owned the hospital, but he walked that way into every place, no matter what it was.

"Don't worry," he said. "It's not from me." He detached the card and read aloud, " 'That's my girl. I knew you could do it, Marquitta. With affection, Jeremy.' " He raised one eyebrow. "Kind of formal for a boyfriend."

I shuddered. "Nothing like that there, Sam. Believe me."

His smile brightened. "Good. Then I'll go ahead and give you my news. I'm studying for the detective's exam. Just like you always wanted me to."

I smiled. "That's great news, but only if it's what you want to do."

He shrugged. "Truth is, I always did. I just didn't want to be compared to you." He set the orchid down and stared at me seriously for a moment before breaking into the golden grin again. "There she is, my sweetness and light. Back to put sunshine into my days."

I had to smile in spite of myself. "You don't look like they've been too sunny lately, bud."

He looked down at himself and laughed. "You and Charlie have kept me running back and forth between hospitals. I think you'd better move back to KC. It'll take a lot of wear and tear off yours truly."

"You look good worn and torn. I probably didn't do enough of that when we were married." I tried to laugh, but it came out harsh and choked. My throat wasn't up to comedy yet.

Sam looked at me for a moment, his eyes serious, then he grinned. "Wearing and tearing? Just my poor old heart, Skeeter."

I cursed myself for touching on any of that, even in jest. Now was not the time for it. In fact, I wasn't sure that any time was the time for it.

"How is he, Sam? How's Charlie?" I asked with a strained voice.

Karen hadn't wanted to talk to me about Charlie. I dreaded hearing that my father had died while I lay unconscious, unable to keep my promise to come back and see him. He'd grown so fragile. If he lived, would he ever be the same? Or would he live as an invalid, needing the kind of constant care I couldn't give him?

"Have some more water," Sam said. "That throat sounds bad."

He held the glass to my lips. I sucked water from the straw while he leaned closer than necessary. He was pressuring me in some way, even though he said nothing. I pulled back from the glass and him. "Enough. Thanks. Charlie?"

Sam set the glass down. "He's doing all right. He'll need rehab. They're transferring him to a place for that in a couple of days." I flinched. Sam noticed and hurried on. "They think he should be able to go back home to live once it's finished. He'll need help at first, but he's going to do all right."

I stared at his smiling face and wondered if I would ever learn to reconcile the different parts of him. Slick, charming seducer. Angry, possessive husband. Loyal, caring family member. "Thank you, Sam. For being there for him."

"He's family. You're family. You know." He laid his big

hand gently on top of mine. "He really wants to try to do things over with you and get them right, Skeet. He's been talking my head off about it."

I looked down at the bed and over at his hand where it lay, completely covering my own. His skin looked golden against my olive tone. I looked back up at him. "We can't do things over, he and I. But we can do new things and try to do them right this time. If he doesn't wind up back in the bars. I can't do much if he does that. He'll kill himself."

"I don't think he will. I think this has been a big wake-up call for him." He looked down at our hands, at the wrists, where they joined, and kept his eyes on them as he spoke. "While you're giving out second chances, I thought you might toss one my way." Looking up, he caught my eyes. "You know, after near-death experience, gorgeous cop decides to go back to the love of her life. That sort of thing."

I felt mesmerized by the hurt and wanting I saw in the eyes he usually kept so cool and controlled. "Sam, I . . . That's different. We—"

The door to the hall pushed open, and Joe peeked in. I gestured him in with relief, snatching at the diversion he offered.

"There she is. Awake and holding court. My hero. And Julie's." Joe looked the same as ever, wholesome, strong, calm. Yet, he had gone through terrors and stress I couldn't begin to imagine, never having been a mother. Maybe that need to be a point of stability for his child was what made him so unchanging and unflappable.

I smiled broadly, happy to be in his presence. I always felt that Sam was demanding things of me, no matter how well he behaved. Joe always seemed to take me just the way I was, no matter how poorly I behaved. Being with him was healing in some way.

"Joe. How's Julie doing? Karen said she's going to be okay physically, but what about emotionally?" I heard a stir and creak behind me and glanced at the cot.

"Yeah. Did that guy do anything to scar her for life or something like that?" Brian asked, sitting up on the edge of the cot. I wondered how long he'd been awake and how much of my conversations with Sam and Karen he'd heard.

"Brian. My other hero. And Julie's." Joe walked over to shake hands and slap Brian on the shoulder. "Feeling a little better now that you know Skeet's out of the woods?"

Brian smiled at him. "Yeah." He cast a shy look at me. "She's my only home. I had to make sure she came through okay."

My eyes went misty on me for a second. "We came through for each other, didn't we? Always will."

Sam laughed the silky laugh that signaled dangerous troublemaking. "One thing you'll learn if you spend enough time around Skeeter is that she always comes through. Maybe a little battered, but she comes out on top. No one can beat her."

Brian shot him a dark look. "She risked her life and almost lost it."

"That she did," said Joe softly. "And we'll never forget that. We shouldn't."

Sam smiled with a defeated twist to his lips. "I'd better head back. I'll tell Charlie you're doing all right."

"Thanks, Sam," I said. "Thanks for everything. We'll talk later about what happens when Charlie goes home. When I find out what happens with me."

"Don't worry, kid." He bent over to kiss me gently on the

forehead. "We'll handle it however it comes. We always do." He gave a brusque nod to Joe and Brian and left.

Joe stepped over to take his place beside the bed, and Brian followed to stand next to him.

"It's good to see you two," I said with a big smile. I reached for Brian's hand to squeeze.

"I won't stay long and tire you out," Joe said. "I just wanted to drop by to say welcome back."

He turned to Brian, his features warped with emotion. "And to say I owe both of you more than my life. Thanks for giving me back my little girl." He threw his arms around Brian for a second, then released him and carefully did the same to me. I could feel his chest shake. "If it hadn't been for the two of you . . . I just can't think about that right now." He wiped his eyes. "You were two of my favorite people before this. Now . . . Anyway, whatever you need during rehab, I'll be around to help with."

Brian nodded. "I'll be there to help her until the leg heals. We should do okay, but if we need something, I'll call."

Joe nodded, his lips pressed together tightly as if to hold back words. "I'll be back during visiting hours. Julie's still here, but she goes home in the morning. If you want me to take you home for some real sleep and a shower, Bri, just let me know. Or I can bring you anything you need."

"Thanks. I'll probably hang around here until we know how long Skeet's in for." Brian flashed a smile that seemed to belong to the days before violence had invaded his life. "I'm glad the midget's getting to go home, though. That's good news."

"You know she's going to be more in love with you than ever now," I said. "You actually became her white knight and rode to her rescue."

Brian looked down, suddenly serious. "Couldn't let that scumbag hurt her. No matter what I had to do." He looked up, haunted eyes in a sick face. "I didn't mean to do that. To shoot him that way. His arm and all."

His whole body was shaking. I reached for his shoulders and pulled him into my arms. He kept shaking in silence, without any sound of a sob. "What you had to do was bad, Bri. But you aren't. You were forced to do it to save Julie and me. It doesn't make you a bad person."

He lifted his head and looked at me, his eyes turned bleak. "But it makes me a killer, doesn't it?"

"My shot killed him, not yours. Yours just kept him from killing me. And he's not the first I've had to kill." I looked at him seriously. "Do you think I'm bad?"

He shook his head. "Of course not. You're great. You're a cop. It's your job."

"It's my job to protect people, yes," I said slowly. "To my mind, all of us are responsible for protecting anyone more vulnerable than we are. Most of us don't do a very good job of it, and that's why we need police." I put my hands to either side of his face and brought it even with my own. "But you did just that, Bri. You acted to protect a helpless child and a wounded police officer from an armed murderer. That's important."

His eyes filled with tears and searched my own. "I thought about Mom. What you said. I couldn't let him kill you guys. I had to be brave like her. No matter what that made me."

"All it made you was a boy who had to grow up too fast and who did a damn fine job of it anyway." Joe said from behind him, his voice choked but firm.

I stared at Brian. "If you want to think you must be some kind of monster, you won't find someone to agree in me or Joe or Julie or any of the people who care about us. Or in the cops who found us."

I closed my eyes for a second, then reopened them to his pleading gaze. "There will be a few people, kids and adults, who will label you 'bad.' But only a few, and they're the stupid ones. Don't let them tell you how to see yourself."

He stared into my eyes for a second, then nodded and pulled away. He shook himself like a dog coming in from the cold or rain and returned to the cot.

Joe gave me a weary smile. "I'll leave you two for now. See you later today."

As he walked out the door, Karen entered, followed by an older woman with rigidly coiffed blond hair. Karen looked troubled. "Skeet, Brian, this is Ms. Carridan. From Family Services."

Brian returned to my bedside and stared.

"Mrs. Carridan, thank you," the woman said with a sniff for Karen. She smiled stiffly at Brian and me. "I'm a social worker, and I'm here to take Brian to a foster home pending the court's decision of where his permanent home should be."

Brian's face froze. I looked instinctively to Karen, who shook her head with a sad look. "Brian is welcome to stay with me, Mrs. Carridan. He's been in my care since his parents died, and he can stay there until the court's final decision. He has no relatives locally."

"Yes," Carridan said with a tone of spite. "And your care led him into a situation where he was forced into violence. Yet another at-risk child. We intend to remedy that."

"Wait a minute, Mrs. Carridan." My voice grew very soft, and Karen's eyes turned wary. "Brian is not violent. Nor is he at risk of anything bad. He's a fine boy, who does well in school and has great musical talent and did a courageous thing to save a little girl's life."

Karen shook her head at me in warning.

"Brian didn't come into danger because of my care. He witnessed a kidnapping and courageously helped to rescue the child taken. Not something for which he should be punished by being put into your miserable system." I was trying desperately to keep from losing my temper. That was what Karen was warning me against. But the sick, frightened look in Brian's eyes tore my control away. "There's no reason he can't stay with me——"

"This is not negotiable. You are an officer of the court, I understand. So you realize that you have no choice but to turn the child over to me." Carridan brandished papers beneath my nose. "Here is the official paperwork."

I looked over the papers and took a deep breath. I looked at Brian. "They're in order. You have to go with her right now, I'm afraid."

His mouth crumpled. I tried to smile at him. "It won't be for long, Bri. I'm getting out of here. I'll talk to your father's attorney. We'll deal with this. Just go with her and remember what I told you about stupid people."

Carridan pulled herself erect in offense, raising her nose and widening her eyes. After taking a few steps toward the woman, Brian threw himself back into my arms. I felt something inside me break as I held him for a few seconds. Finally he pulled free and with a sober face followed Carridan out the door.

At the hall, he turned back to face me, with the woman behind him like an impatient dog pulling at the leash. "I'll remember, Skeet. I'll remember what you told me about my mom, too. I'm like her. You said that."

"That you are."

He wheeled on the Carridan woman and headed down the hall, leaving her to bustle along behind, trying to keep up.

I wiped tears from my face, unsure how they had come to be there when all I felt was anger. "Karen, get the nurse and tell her I have to talk to somebody about the soonest I can get out of here. Hand me the phone first, though. I'm calling Marsh Corgill. If I have to call in every favor I'm owed and spend every cent I've got, I'm not giving that boy up to the damn system."

Karen brought me the phone. Before I dialed, I thought of something else and looked up. "They'll want to inspect my house. Get a cleaning service in there to shovel it out, please. It's a dump, between my being so busy and crime scene leftovers. I've got to make it look like a good home for a kid."

Karen nodded. "You're doing the right thing."

I thought of all that Brian had been through. "I'm not the right person to raise a teenage boy. I've always said that, and it's true. I'm not a nurturing type—we both know that—but at least I care about him and he knows it. At this point, I'm all he's got, and I'm not going to let him down."

I could still see Brian's face as he looked at me right before leaving with that social worker. I could hear him telling Joe earlier that I was his only home. All the secrets of Andrew McAfee and Stuart Morley had snuffed out lives and turned others upside down. Just add mine to the score. I didn't know how all this with Brian and Charlie would finally play out, but my life was never going to be the same again.